"Plea..."

Emma's mouth shaped the words against his fingers.

Cade looked at his dark fingers staining the pallor of her face. "I won't."

He didn't remember putting his hand over her mouth, but he remembered other words pouring forth from her, that delicately shaped mouth with its soft contours firmed in condemnation against him.

Lying awake night after night in prison, trying to make sense of everything, he'd heard again and again her low voice, precise and elegant, reducing his life, *him,* to nothing.

Against his will, his fingers traced that destructive softness. Silky smooth.

She was his enemy, and she had killed everything good in him. Day, night, he'd thought of nothing else but her, her calm eyes, her voice slicing at him. Cade scowled.

She made a sideways movement, and he tightened his grip against her fragile jawline.

Dear Reader,

When two people fall in love, the world is suddenly new and exciting, and it's that same excitement we bring to you in Silhouette Intimate Moments. These are stories with scope and grandeur. The characters lead lives we all dream of, and everything they do reflects the wonder of being in love.

Longer and more sensuous than most romances, Silhouette Intimate Moments novels take you away from everyday life and let you share the magic of love. Adventure, glamour, drama, even suspense— these are the passwords that let you into a world where love has a power beyond the ordinary, where the best authors in the field today create stories of love and commitment that will stay with you always.

In coming months, look for novels by your favorite authors: Heather Graham Pozzessere, Emilie Richards and Kathleen Korbel, to name just a few. And whenever you buy books, look for all the Silhouette Intimate Moments, love stories for today's woman by today's woman.

Leslie J. Wainger
Senior Editor and Editorial Coordinator

LINDSAY LONGFORD

Cade Boudreau's Revenge

SILHOUETTE·INTIMATE·MOMENTS®

Published by Silhouette Books New York

America's Publisher of Contemporary Romance

SILHOUETTE BOOKS
300 East 42nd St., New York, N.Y. 10017

CADE BOUDREAU'S REVENGE

ISBN: 0-373-07390-9

First Silhouette Books printing July 1991

Printed in the U.S.A.

LINDSAY LONGFORD's

biggest writing influence has been, as with so many others, her love of reading. She says she's read toothpaste labels just to have something to read! After studying fiction writing at Northwestern University and writing numerous short stories, she discovered that what she really liked to write was the kind of story she chose to read when she was tired, wanted a lift or just wanted to be swept away for a few hours—romance.

Her husband has been a constant source of encouragement, and with their ten-year-old son, they cross-country ski, hit the cinemas once a week and try not to overload their house with too many books.

To Wes,
for believing my dreams are as important as his.

To the people who work in real shelters like HELP,
because you make a difference.

To the editors at Silhouette,
especially Lucia Macro,
Tara Hughes Gavin
and Leslie Wainger,
for their professionalism, their encouragement and
their magic editorial pencils.

To Jean Fletcher
in the Illinois State's Attorney's office,
and to Nancy
in the Florida Public Defender's Office:
Thanks for the generous time you spent helping me
work out plotting problems. All errors are mine, but
thank you for preventing others.

To Ann Reynolds,
former board member of HOPE, a women's shelter:
What would I do without your help?

Chapter 1

The watercooler at the end of the hallway gurgled.

Emma heard the burp of air rising through the water as if someone were filling a paper cup. Her finger stilled on the third line of the deposition she was studying. She was the only one working late.

Silence. To her straining ears an alive, waiting silence.

Against her green-shaded lamp a moth beat its wings frantically. Gently Emma brushed it away, but it dashed its furry body at the bulb and fell in a pale brown clump on the white papers before her, wings fluttering against black print.

Night quiet smothered her.

Should she call Dooley, the night guard? Her slim fingers, hovering ghosts in the uncertain light, floated over the phone. No, he'd tell everybody of her fears, and she'd never hear the end of it.

The breathing of old bricks and boards alive with memories.

A sigh of wind.

A sudden chill of air and her skin prickling up in goose bumps.

For a long time she listened to the creaks and sighs of the old courthouse. She could have walked its halls blindfolded. Her father's daughter, Southern-born and courthouse-bred, she sometimes felt as though her life had been lived in these red brick walls. Entombed in them.

Still uneasy, she slid her finger the length of the paper, lifted it and carried the moth to the window.

Below her, the street was empty. At the end of the block leading to the bridge, the red stop light flashed rhythmically, its reflection a crimson pulse in the puddles.

Her car, a rain-darkened silver, was the only car in the lot.

A shadow moved near the enormous banyan tree. Holding her breath, her heart suddenly pounding, Emma leaned out to see.

Spring, wet and greening, blew in at her.

Only branches, shadowy, moving in the lift of air.

Sticking her arm into the night, Emma let the skin-warm rain splotch on her upturned arm. Her boss, Charlie, didn't expect her to work as hard as she did. She shouldn't have stayed.

Emma closed the window against the night's frenzied insects. April in Florida and life gone berserk, burgeoning and throbbing in urgent, wonderful excess. Restless, she rubbed her arms. She was itchy tonight, fanciful, wanting something, that was all, not herself. Her skin seemed to bind her as tight as a cocoon. She'd worked too long. She should be looking forward to her upcoming vacation, not hearing bumps in the night.

Edgy, she cocked her head, listening again. It had been such a—a *filled* silence.

When tiredness and imagination joined hand in hand to unnerve her at the burp of the water bottle, it was time to head home.

Emma looked at the bumpy vinyl couch. She could stay in her office overnight. She'd slept here more times than she wanted to count. She could wait until tomorrow to leave for Sanibel Island. But she didn't want to. Her suitcases were packed and she wanted to drive fast in the humid night and let the damp wind wrap around her, stroke her with its wild breath. She shivered.

Scooping up the papers on her desk, Emma shoved them in her briefcase and buckled it. Clicking off the lamp and the overhead lights, she hesitated before opening the door to the hall.

Silly, to be spooked like this. She straightened her shoulders and turned the knob, oddly reluctant to leave her sanctuary.

Ahead of her the hall was its familiar cavernous self, high-ceilinged and dimly lit. The motor of the watercooler hummed companionably as she neared it, her high heels clicking on the confetti-colored terrazzo.

She glanced at the trash can next to the cooler.

Empty. Well, what did she expect? Of course it was empty.

Her wan reflection wavering in the glass of the exit door startled her. Parted lips and eyes huge in the small triangle of her face. Emma frowned. The solitary image glimmered, mirroring her isolation and mocking her power suit and high heels. She pushed against the glass door, erasing the lonely, anxious eyes, and stepped into the night.

She hurried across the shimmering parking lot, sidestepping puddles, heels skittering over the uneven pavement in a nervous rhythm, and was out of breath when she reached her car. "Good Lord," she muttered, inhaling.

She never heard him step in behind her.

He was just suddenly there, a clean soapy scent alerting her too late and then his hand pressing against the small of her back, his voice low and rusty, saying something that made no sense to her in her overwhelming terror.

"No, please!" She turned, opened her mouth to yell for Dooley and felt the hard grip of a hand covering her mouth.

"For God's sake, don't scream." The whisper was knife-edged. "Don't scream," he said again, harshly. "Like I said, I have to talk to you."

"What?" she gasped.

His callused fingers pressed her lips against her teeth, and Emma saw shadows pass over the moon and gather in the darkness of silvered eyes.

In a series of time-slowed movements, exaggerated and important, Cade saw her eyes widen, her mouth open in a soft "oh" of surprise.

In that stretched-out time, he forgot the rain misting around him, didn't hear the far-off car sounds. Every nerve ending tuned to her, tuned to the faint trembling beneath his hands. Darkness all around him and just her wide eyes staring at him and a sweet woman smell heated by her fear rising up to him, sweet, sweet in the silent rain.

Cade shook his head, trying to unscramble his thoughts. He hadn't meant to make her afraid. That hadn't been part of his plan, had it? Facing her, he couldn't remember for a moment just what he'd intended. He'd been waiting out here too long, and he'd had too many doors slammed in his face. Tired. He was so tired, and seeing her fear was unpleasantly satisfying to his soul.

She had to help him. She owed him that.

His hand covered her mouth and two of his fingers curled over a small chin that quivered against them.

He hadn't remembered her as being so slight, hadn't thought of her as soft, defenseless, not ever, not even in his most disturbing dreams, those dark dreams blending and confusing him now with her sweet, rain-drenched fragrance.

She was his enemy. He'd hated her for a long time…forever.

He'd remembered and learned well the lessons the scorn in her eyes had taught him.

"Please, don't hurt me." Her mouth shaped the words against his fingers.

Cade looked at his dark fingers staining the pallor of her face. "I won't. But we have to talk."

He didn't remember putting his hand over her mouth, but he remembered other words pouring forth from her, that delicately shaped mouth with its soft contours firmed in condemnation against him.

Lying awake night after night in prison, trying to make sense of everything, he'd heard again and again her low voice, precise and elegant, reducing his life, *him,* to nothing.

Against his will his fingers traced that destructive softness. Silky smooth.

She was his enemy and she had killed everything good in him with the bright sword of her intelligence and contempt.

When it was all over, he'd gone crazy with anger and bitterness. Day, night, he'd thought of nothing but her, her calm eyes, her voice slicing at him. Thinking about her, her words carving away at his life, numbed him to the hell his life became.

Cade scowled. He couldn't think about everything he'd lost.

She made a small sideways movement and he tightened his grip against her fragile jawline.

The tiny flick of her eyelashes burned his hand. Her whispered ''please'' confused him.

He concentrated. ''I'm not going to hurt you,'' he said, stilling her against him.

''Then let me go,'' she faltered.

Her hip bumped against his groin where sensation collected heavy and thick. Cade took an unsteady breath and moved back slightly. ''Not until you've heard me out.''

As the long days and sleepless nights in prison had slipped mindlessly by, he'd come to hate her. Drop by drop, the acid of his hatred burned away the man he'd been, leaving him empty of everything but corrosive hatred. There were others he should have hated, and he did, oh, he did. Hatred became his closest companion, a demon walking with him every waking moment and striding tauntingly through his dreams, reminding him, always reminding him of what had been ripped from him.

But he hadn't been able to get this woman out of his mind. She was there in the darkness with him, in the night hell of prison. Sometimes, in less desperate moments, he wondered at his obsession, but not often, and not for long.

Now, remembering the flaring heat of her hip against him, he wondered again.

But he knew one thing. Emma Rose O'Riley owed him.

In the shadows and fitful moonlight, looking at her wide, frightened eyes peering over the edge of his palm, feeling her mouth soft against his palm and the tension in her slight body, Cade was baffled by his need to erase that fear, disturbed by the other need stirring in him, a yearning to bury his face in the wispy silk of her hair sifting around her chin, against his fingers, a yearning so strong that he ripped his hands away from her.

"Dooley!" she croaked in a strangled voice and took two staggering steps.

Her sudden movement broke the spell.

"Dooley!" She cried out and veered toward the courthouse.

Woken from a nightmare, Cade shook his head again, trying desperately to think. His plan was spinning out of control.

He wouldn't go back to prison.

Cade grabbed her, his hands silencing her once more. "I don't want to hurt you. Please, don't do anything stupid."

Anger overlaid the shine of fear in her eyes.

That fear had weakened her, but anger strengthened her and made her dangerous to him—and to herself.

If the guard came out and saw them like this... No, that couldn't happen.

"Get in." Cade moved against her, forcing her up against her car. He couldn't botch everything with a wrong move now. He had to get her to the island like he'd planned. There, he'd be able to make her listen.

Off balance and anger-fueled, she slung her heavy briefcase at his knees. It banged on the parking lot as Cade crowded her toward the car.

"Don't touch me! Let me go!"

Wet metal smacked against his hand as he held her facing the car, restraining her frenzied movements.

Think! Cade urged himself. He tried to ignore her tiny gulps, the trembling of her slender body against him and the drifting fragrance of her hair.

Think, you damned fool. Don't make any more mistakes. You knew it was a gamble, but you figured you'd make the cards turn aces up. Get her to the island and sort everything out when she's calmer. Talk to her then. With the toe of his boot, he hooked her briefcase closer so that he could throw it into the car.

Emma swallowed her sobs. Behind her he was close, his breath warm against her neck. Near his outspread palm, her fingers curled against the Honda door. Her cheek was slick with rain, and the front of her thin cotton blouse soaked up the wet of the car. She was so cold, so cold, and the rain so warm.

All around her was the warm smell of the man and the rain rich with earth and spring and life.

Shudders rolled through her, racking her with uncontrollable shaking and chattering teeth.

"Don't make a mistake. Get in the car," the curt voice said, and his hand nudged her forward.

Emma stumbled, her knees giving way. Dooley! Where was Dooley? Drowning in the scent of clean male and earth bursting through the wet night soil, suffocated by fear, she couldn't catch her breath. Unfair to end like this.

Even in her consuming terror, one thought kept soaring back. That quietly harsh voice prodded at her frozen memory. Where had she heard it before?

"Who are you?" Emma moaned against the hard hand once again imprisoning her mouth. Her teeth caught against the tips of his fingers, and she tried to turn around. But he bent her head forward and crowded her into the open car door, his free hand clamping her so closely to him that she felt his muscles coiling against her as he followed her into the car.

He half shoved, half lifted her over the boxy console and dropped her into the bucket seat. "Do I know you?" she insisted as he lifted his hand from her mouth. Her skin buzzed with fear.

"No one ever introduced us," he said flatly. The door snicked quietly shut as he slid behind the steering wheel of her precious car.

Emma heard the rawness in the quiet words coming from the blurred profile. She hadn't been able to see him clearly when he'd thrust her into the car. She wished she could see his face.

In the shocking silence of the car, Emma heard his quiet breathing and her own thready inhalations.

"Give me the keys." He stretched his hand out.

She couldn't loosen her shaking hands gripping her purse. She didn't want to give him her purse. It seemed very important to keep her purse. "No," Emma whispered through dry lips. "I don't think so."

"God save me from stubborn idiots." He sighed and gripped her more tightly as he leaned over her, plucking the purse free.

''You're being reckless, you know.'' His muted voice made the calm observation menacing.

Keys rattled.

His eyes glittered briefly in the darkness as he bent closer. ''Don't do reckless things.''

Terror unleashed her words. ''I'm not going anywhere with you! You can't make me.'' She erupted, fear snapping her control. ''You can't drive and keep me in this car. One way or another, I'm going to get out of this car! I will! So *you* do the smart thing and get out! Take the car. Go ahead, leave!'' Emma frantically twisted the door handle.

A whir of gears and the seat belt clipped tightly around her. The man kept his left hand over the belt release and with his right jammed the key into the ignition slot.

''They'll be looking for me! You can't get away with this!''

''No one's going to miss you, at least not anytime soon.''

''How do you know?'' Emma whispered, terror seizing her.

With the engine vibrating around them, he switched his grip and turned to her once more. ''Your secretary told me.''

''What?'' Emma couldn't comprehend what he was saying. Her mouth was dry.

''I tried to make an appointment to see you. No dice. I called your office.'' Anger spurted in his words. ''Your secretary wouldn't put me through to you. Said you were going on vacation.''

Emma remembered. Desperate to clear her desk before she left and interrupted by the constantly ringing phone, she'd told Julie not to put any more calls through to her, that even if the President of the United States himself called, he'd have to wait until she came back. ''But you can't make me go with you! I'm not—''

''For the time being, you're going where I take you,'' he interrupted, ''and, yes, I *can* make you go with me. I can do that easily. Or you can make it difficult.'' He paused. ''Don't.''

Hostility rushed toward her, and the strength behind the almost whispered words silenced her. She hated her helplessness in the face of sickening fear. This stranger was stripping all her control away, leaving only the terrified child in her.

''Do you understand?'' His toneless words were disinterested.

''I don't understand anything.''

The engine rumbled around her. ''You will. Your travel plans have changed, that's all.''

Emma couldn't swallow. She wouldn't cry. No matter what happened, she wouldn't let him make her cry.

If he knew her, she must know him. What she could see of him teased her with recognition. If she could think this through, she could free herself.

She chose her words carefully, knowing her voice would shake and not wanting him to hear her terror. ''I understand. You're in control here. For the moment.'' She bit off the last syllables.

''You can't stop, can you? Don't you think it would be smarter to keep from ticking me off?'' With one hand, he clipped his seat belt around his wide shoulders and moved the gear shift into first. ''Just keep quiet for now, okay? We'll both be better off if you can do that. Later you can talk all you want.''

Emma stirred uneasily. She didn't like leaving the parking lot. Escape seemed possible with Dooley somewhere in hearing distance. She sat on her trembling hands. ''You were in the courthouse, weren't you?''

He answered, grudgingly, she thought, as he eased her car onto the rain-washed street, bumping over the bricks of the parking lot. ''Yeah.''

''Why?'' Her mouth was dry and she trembled with cold.

''I wanted to see you in your office.''

That silenced her.

Emma watched as he turned left to the bridge that led to the island. Approaching headlights off the bridge winked briefly and disappeared into the darkness behind her.

She had no one she could count on to help her. He was right. No one would miss her until she was due back from vacation. How had she let her life drift into such loneliness?

As they crossed over the darkness of the Intracoastal Waterway where the Gulf of Mexico met Tampa Bay, Emma leaned her hot cheek against the rain-cooled glass. She wouldn't let him get away with whatever he had planned. She'd go along with him as long as she had to and watch for a chance to escape.

She was going to survive this. Then she was going to see him rot in jail.

Again that faint smoke of teasing memory. Emma snapped upright. "Were you in prison?"

He glanced briefly at her. "Clever lady, but I always thought you had the quickest brain around."

Frowning, Emma slipped her feet out of her heels.

There were undertones here she could untangle, facts she could dig up and use to help herself. "You're enjoying this, aren't you?" Her charge vibrated between them.

"*Enjoy* isn't the word I'd have chosen." His fingers curled around the steering wheel as he turned and headed north on the main road that stabbed through the heart of the island.

"That's how it looks to me," she protested.

"Yeah, I reckon I like seeing you squirm." He kept to the posted speed, small concrete block houses appearing, disappearing with each twist of the two-laned road. He looked at her. "Yeah. I like wondering how you feel right now, how you like having your freedom stolen away from you." He lifted his hand from the seat belt release. "Tempting, isn't it? But could you get free faster than I could stop you? And what would happen if you couldn't? Something to think about, isn't it?"

"You were in prison." Knowledge was control. Emma stroked her black skirt with gratification. She'd work her way out of this.

"Putting it all together in a tidy little package, aren't you? You were good at that three years ago."

Emma frowned. She'd only been in the state's attorney's office four years.

She took a deep breath as the car glided to a stop at the north dock. Small, uninhabitable islands clotted the gulf darkness.

Dread slithered over Emma's skin as he threw open the door. The seat belt rolled free, and she tumbled out of the car, not looking back, just running, running, air burning in her lungs.

Pine burs and sandspurs cut into her feet, but the clean salt air of the gulf blew through her hair and she lurched through the needles and burs.

"Don't forget these."

The whispery voice tickled her ear. His heat surrounded her, his wide shoulders touching her. Emma pivoted.

Two narrow shoes dangled from long, hooked fingers, and she glimpsed the man's face in the light of a distant lamppost. Her eyebrows winged upward.

She knew him!

"Don't leave home without 'em." He waggled the shoes at her, but there was no humor in his voice, nor in the face at last clearly revealed to her.

Blue-black hair sleeked back from a face broader, older than she remembered. His voice different, with the sound of a man who hadn't talked in a long time, the sound of a voice ravaged with silent screaming.

The years and something else had grooved heavy lines around his mouth. His face was empty, stripped of emotion. He hadn't looked like this three years ago.

He was thinner than she recalled. Leaner, pared to the bone, but with the same broad, sloping shoulders, the same built-for-speed physique poured into faded jeans jammed into scuffed, run-down boots.

"Long time no see, and all that," he said in his whispery voice.

In court he'd worn a suit, navy with a white shirt and striped tie. Odd she remembered the narrow maroon and gray stripes of his tie. Slate gray like the icy gray of his eyes.

For days she'd looked at his face more than the tie. His expression had never changed, no matter what she said. That blankness had disturbed her then, but now it terrified her.

Cade Boudreau. Oh, yes, she remembered him. She clamped her teeth against her shudders. From way down deep, they came boiling up with the memories of Cade Boudreau on the witness stand.

Cade Boudreau. The last person she'd ever expected to see again.

"So. You remembered." He shrugged. "I thought you might have forgotten."

"I didn't." She could never forget that trial.

Emma jumped as Cade snapped off the heels of her shoes. "Don't!"

He handed them to her. "A pity. Nice shoes, expensive, I reckon, but you can replace them. You don't need any weapons." Satisfaction rode the syllables of his words. He'd liked destroying her shoes.

"You hate me, don't you?" Emma understood.

He hooked his thumbs in his belt loops. "Yes." And then something shifted in his eyes as he watched her. "I thought I did." He sighed and looked out to the gulf.

He waited while she stepped into the ruined shoes. Looking down at her, he frowned. "I thought you were taller."

"You were sitting down." Emma Rose wanted her high heels back. She hated looking up to people; it made her feel like a child. She stood as tall as she could. "I have a tall personality."

A surprised grunt. "That you do. Come on." He motioned to the dock stretching before them.

"I'm not going out there." Through the gaps, dark water rolled to shore and swirled against the sand. Emma hated plank docks. She hated feeling that she would fall through the cracks. "There's no way I'm walking out on that damned dock," she repeated with fear-induced stubbornness, caught between the devil and the deep dark sea.

She looked at the planks again. Yards apart. Opening her eyes wide to keep her tears back, Emma gave him her most intimidating go-to-hell look.

Cade looked at the dock and then at her. "You're going."

"I'm not." Emma dug her feet into the sand.

Grasping the waistband of her linen skirt, his thighs bumping hers, Cade marched her over the gaping boards of the dock. "You're a hardheaded woman."

Emma fought off the need to grab his arm as her feet skimmed over the splintery boards. She wouldn't look down and she wouldn't let him know how frightened she was, but her voice quaked. "You proved your point. Now let go." She twisted against his arm and hoped she wouldn't pitch right into the water where a boat bobbed next to the pier pylons.

"There you are." Cade flung his arms wide. "Free as a bird." A thin smile flashed on his face.

"Sure. Free. With you at my back like some guard." She surveyed the water around her, Cade blocking the way to land.

"You're freer than I've been." Cade lifted his head and inhaled the salt-tanged air. "Every breath I've taken for over a thousand days has smelled like prison and caged men." He turned to her, his voice hard and hostile. "That institutional smell. I didn't think I'd ever get it out of my lungs. A thousand days. I counted them all."

"You're going to kill me, aren't you?" Emma whispered. She looked at the gulf lying smooth like a blanket over some sleeping beast gently breathing.

"Lawyer lady, there've been a lot of things I've dreamed of doing to you, but killing's not one of 'em." His voice was strained. "You're safe. And you'll go home again. Consider this just a small detour in your itinerary, okay?"

Emma rubbed her mouth. Hope sprang up.

For a long time Cade looked at her, his gaze distant and unseeing. "Do you know," he continued in that husky rasp, focusing finally on her mouth, "I can smell the perfume from your skin. Underneath the salt, there's your perfume rising up, the smell of your skin."

He shut his eyes, inhaling deeply. "I haven't smelled perfume in a long time. Clorox. Lysol. No perfume."

Her stomach fluttered as his words rasped out in that ruined voice, and the silence between them filled with something vibrating from Cade Boudreau that made her more uneasy than any physical threat he posed.

"Oh."

"Oh? A nice, noncommittal comment, Ms. O'Riley." He slid his rough hand around her neck, his thumb at the base of her throat. "But just think about it. All those men, night after night. Did you know it's never quiet in prison? All night long, sounds, sounds a nice lady like you couldn't imagine." His thumb moved once against her.

"When were you released?" Emma knew she had to change the mood. He was in some dark place that terrified her. She couldn't escape yet. She wouldn't be able to get past him.

"Yesterday." Cade's face tightened. "In the morning."

"You're going to go back, you know. You know you'll be caught." Emma grasped at straws. She would be lost if she stepped in that leaky boat floating on the swells. "You can't get away with this."

"I think I can. Once you listen to me. Once you understand everything." His eyes narrowed. "That's what I'm gambling on."

"Gamblers sometimes lose their shirts, Mr. Boudreau." Emma didn't understand anything at all.

He smiled recklessly. "So they do. Well, we'll see, won't we?" He gestured to the boat. "Jump."

There was no mercy in his gray eyes. Determination, desperation. No mercy.

The rain had chased stragglers off the pier, and the cones of light shining down were empty spotlights in the shadows.

Looking at the rocking boat then at the unyielding man, Emma saw no option. Frightened by him, afraid of the leap into the dark boat, afraid of so many things, she wanted each precious moment left in her sterile little life. As barren as it was, she wouldn't give it up easily. She'd do what she had to do.

Head down, fists doubled against the shaking of her fingers, fighting back tears, she glanced sideways at him.

Cade saw the hesitant appeal, an appeal he was sure she didn't know she'd made. He didn't want to touch her, not after his unwilling breath of her perfume. It lingered on his skin, his hands, and made him want more, baited him with a hunger he'd never satisfy, not with this woman and not in this life. The shiny lure hid the killing hook. Always.

She hadn't moved. The edge of her skirt moved with the light breeze and the trembling of her thighs. Her rigid back was a dead giveaway to the powerful effort she made to control her fear.

"Go ahead. Jump." Cade watched one small foot inch forward and retreat.

She swayed and a sound escaped her clenched lips. Her narrow shoulders sagged.

He'd pushed her to her limits. Emma Rose O'Riley couldn't make that jump. For whatever reason, she was rooted to the spot and trying not to show it.

She was a gutsy little cat, all right, but her back was to the wall. Tugged by his recognition of that feeling, Cade relented. "Get moving, okay? We don't have all night. I'll lower you into the boat." Impatiently he stretched out his hand.

"No. I'll do it myself."

The soft music of her voice shamed him. He hadn't figured on her having that kind of power over him. He didn't like it.

In that music he heard the echoes of other times she must have called on raw courage to force herself past fear. He could almost admire that kind of grit. "Don't be so hardheaded. Come on. I said I'll help you. I'm not going to dump you off the pier."

The corners of her mouth quivered. "Really? Somehow that surprises me."

"Look, I said I didn't want to hurt you. I'm not going to." Her obstinacy annoyed him. He seized her fists and unknotted them. Her hands were small and cold in his, and as he let her drop into the boat, Cade tried to ignore the shadow of fear that passed over her face. He'd felt the tension in her fists as he'd taken them in his.

He frowned. Her fear wasn't his problem. He didn't owe her anything. She was the one with the debt to pay, not him, not him. The words beat in his tired brain in a monotonous booming. He had to keep focused on them, not on the way she made him feel.

She sank down on the boat seat and covered her face.

The boat rocked as Cade jumped into it. Dropping her hands, she sat up and watched him as he reached for the starter cord.

"Mr. Boudreau," she insisted, "you're being extremely foolish. Kidnapping is a federal offense, and I'm an officer of the court. Don't you understand?" She gripped his hand holding the motor starter. "You're on the surest road back to prison!"

"We'll see." He wouldn't go back, but he couldn't turn her loose. Not yet. Accounts had to be settled, but she was right. The way things were, he'd be sent to prison the minute she was free.

So. He couldn't set her free, and he couldn't turn back. He'd started something that was propelling them both into the unsounded dark. For both of them, this would end where it ended.

He guided the boat into the path of deep water, watching as Emma looked away, her coffee-colored hair blowing around her face. She anchored the wisps with one hand and wrapped the other around her waist, watching him with unblinking hazel eyes.

So much was at stake.

Spray whipped into his face, and he watched the dim shoreline for identifying marks before heading toward a faint outline rising up from the darker sheet of gulf water. It had been a long time since he'd been to the island.

When Cade steered the boat onto the shore that would be sugar-white in daylight, he inhaled with relief. He was safe, at least for the moment. No one would find them.

The wooden boat scraped on the sand.

"What are you going to do?" Emma twisted, hair swinging around her small face, as he jumped into the water.

Cade wished he knew. For the first time he began to wonder if he could escape the snares drifting around him.

He took off his boots then lifted the small motor off the boat and dropped it onto the sand. He reached to lift Emma out. Her waist curved under his hands and his fingers met over the long, narrow line of her spine.

Holding her between the boat and the water, Cade had an instant's glimpse of the irrevocable power of fate to disrupt human existence, a mysterious power that had, unsought, brought the two of them to this moment, to this place under a rain-clouded sky. No matter what happened here, her life, his, would be intertwined forever by this moment on this island.

Her eyes met his, but Cade, shaken by his thoughts, looked away.

Like an unexplored river sliding silently beneath a boat, she slipped between his hands into the chilly gulf. Air-filled, her skirt belled around her and he had a brief glimpse of pale, nylon-sleek thighs. She coughed as a wave splashed into her face. Knowing better, Cade still reached out to lift the wet hair off her face. A glossy helmet, the strands molded themselves to her head and tempted his fingers to move over their smooth, wet heaviness.

He shoved his hands inside his waistband. "Go on up to shore," he said roughly. Quickly he unloaded the cooler and duffel bag. He looked at the waves and held a finger up to the wind, then, nudging the boat directly into the surf, Cade forced it away from the island. The boat whirled in the waves before the tidal current caught it and bore it away.

He exhaled. It was done.

Emma watched the boat drift, bobbing wildly at first, before it disappeared into darkness. Stranded.

The look in his eyes when he lifted her out of the boat had unnerved her. There had been something there that was out of her experience and disturbing. "So. Here we are." She glanced at the pine trees and the sand barely rising out of the gulf. "Now what?"

"Now we talk," Cade said, striding through the water to her. "And we don't leave until things are settled."

Watching him strip off his shirt to dry off the motor, Emma tried to put the pieces together and focus her mind, tried to ignore her fear. Cade Boudreau was a lot of things, but he wasn't stupid. He frightened her, but he wanted something from her and she could use that against him. Wet and cold in the light wind, she shivered.

His skin should have been jail pasty, but it glistened like polished bronze in the fitful light cast by the hide-and-seek of clouds and moon.

The motor dried, Cade shoved his arms into his damp shirt and watched her through narrowed, assessing eyes that told a story whose ending Emma couldn't begin to guess.

Out of her depths, Emma stayed where she was. Even when she was safe in her courtroom, Cade Boudreau had made her uneasy.

When he stepped up to her, his shirttails flapping damply against her arms, Emma backed up. That cold emptiness in his eyes ripped all her pitiful little defenses away, shredded her carefully won self-confidence to ribbons.

She retreated into words, her best offense. "What do you want, Mr. Boudreau? And whatever it is, you're going about getting it the wrong way. Trust me on this." She jammed her hands in the pockets of her sopping wet skirt.

His dry laugh startled her. "What do *I* want? That's rich!" In a swift unwinding of powerful muscles, he was beside her, his lean, austere face filling her view. The heat of his anger blazed around them.

"It's a simple question of fact, not philosophy. You want something. What is it?"

Her skirt dripped onto her ankles as she waited, her stomach churning and churning. She hoped she wouldn't throw up. The drumming of her heartbeat deafened her.

"You're really something, Ms. Emma Rose O'Riley. Butter wouldn't melt in that clever little mouth, would it? All those fancy words and Southern-lady elegance. No wonder you destroyed me."

"*I* did nothing to you. You created your own problems." She pushed him away. He was too close, too close in the dark, and his anger burned against her skin, hot and powerful.

He took a handful of her hair, running the strands through his fingers. "You smashed my life into pieces, and you ask what I want?" The ruined whisper of his voice surrounded her as he leaned over her, his fingers tightening in her hair and his gray eyes glittering with obsession. "Justice, lady lawyer, just some old-fashioned country justice."

Chapter 2

"*Justice?* You had that! A jury gave you justice! They convicted you. I was there, remember?" Emma pulled futilely at the fingers that stiffened against her scalp.

Like fingernails scraping a chalkboard, his voice grated over her. "Remember? I haven't forgotten one damned second. You and your clever words. You were so good you almost convinced *me* I was guilty."

"Twelve people said you were, Mr. Boudreau."

"So they did, thanks to you."

Emma heard the surf hissing against sand, the slow withdrawal of wave to sea. She waited. "You made a terrible mistake, Mr. Boudreau. You were guilty—"

"No." His face was stone.

"Yes," Emma insisted. "But you've paid for it. You have a second chance. Don't destroy every possibility you have for a new life—" She flinched when he stepped closer to her.

"You know, I truly do admire the way you talk. You could make a man think the sky was pea green if you wanted to." He gestured. "Look around you! No judge and jury here, counselor, just you, me, and what happened three and a half years ago. Don't you know talking's not the solution this time?

You're going to have to listen. That may be real hard for you."
His tone edged into mockery.

"Mr. Boudreau." Emma hesitated. Talking was the only solution for her. "I'm trying to cooperate with you. I don't understand why you've dragged me out here, wherever here is, but
I think we can solve this situation if—"

His hands moved to the sides of her head, pressing, fingers
tugging the wet strands. "If I could tear into this clever little
brain right now, I wonder what I'd find?" His thumbs met over
her forehead, his fingers in back, and he pressed, gently. "I
think I'd like that, seeing into that tricky little maze, seeing how
you think, how you figure things out so neatly."

Emma felt the imprint of every single one of his long, hard
fingers tensing against her scalp. His thumbs stroked to the
bridge of her nose and up again. She shut her eyes against the
hoarse fury that came blazing at her.

"I remember everything, lawyer lady!" He bent close to her
face. "Look at me, damn you. You sent me to prison. The least
you can do is look me in the eyes!"

She did, and pain stared at her out of ice-gray eyes, their
bleakness dismaying her. She swallowed. "All right. I'm looking at you. Now what?"

"You took my life away. I want it back." The fury washed
out of his voice, and she heard only exhaustion as he said,
"You're going to get it back for me."

Emma pulled her head away, strands of her hair clinging to
his unresisting hands. "You're not even making sense. I can't
help you."

"No?"

"Even if I could, I wouldn't want to." Emma lifted her chin.

As though unaware of what he was doing, he moved his
rough thumb down her back. A rippling of goose bumps lifted
the hairs on her arms. Or maybe the shivers came from the way
his gray eyes narrowed on her, gray sparking warm and alive in
their desolation. She didn't know, but her breathing went
shallow and she knew she didn't want him touching her, not
while he looked at her like that.

"Take your hands off me, this minute. You've manhandled me enough. I'm tired of it. And, for your information, after what you did, I'd sooner spend a day in hell than help you!"

"That day may come sooner than you expect, counselor." Cade dropped his hands and, holding them palms out to her, smiled mirthlessly. "No deadly weapons," he said in a voice as flat as Florida ranch land. "Relax." He turned away from her.

Emma expelled a long sigh. She sagged with relief. Every muscle in her body had strained against his alarming touch. He'd known what she thought. His sarcastic gesture had let her know.

Letting her head fall back, hoping to loosen the tension-cramped muscles, Emma looked at the cloudy bowl of the sky. Emptiness and her own problems only a mote in the vastness of that time and dark space.

Cade kicked up a burst of sand with his bare foot. Over his shoulder he spoke to her. "You'll help me if you want to get off this godforsaken sand spit."

Staring at his silhouette, Emma answered him in frustration. "I still don't know what you expect or need from me." She wrung water out of her skirt and lifted the edge to dry her face and arms.

Gazing at the overcast sky again, she regretted all the hours she'd let sift through her unheeding hands. Never again. She wished she could believe he wasn't going to kill her. She was having trouble thinking straight.

He strode toward her. "I don't *need* anything from you. You *owe* me."

The emptiness and loneliness of space reflected from his eyes. In her entire life, she'd never seen that kind of loneliness in a man's eyes.

"You keep saying that!" Emma stood her ground. "But I don't—" She held up her hand to stop him, her palm brushing the hard warmth of his chest, and spoke in a rush, pulling her hand away. "All right, for the sake of argument, suppose I, as you say, owe you? What do you expect? A new trial? A pardon? I can't do that!"

His voice was low and drained. "Yeah, I'd like a pardon. I'd like to be able to hold my head up without people looking at me like I'm a monster, but, Ms. O'Riley, what I really give a damn about is my son. I want my son back.''

"What?" Emma was stunned. Her hands dropped to her skirt in bewilderment. His son? She'd had nothing to do with the child. She'd heard he was eight or nine.

"My son. Quint." Under the exhaustion, Cade's voice was somber.

In his husky words Emma heard the wrenching tenderness. "I still don't understand, Mr. Boudreau. I'm sorry for whatever happened to your son, but I don't see how it concerns me."

"You don't, huh? I suppose you wouldn't." He picked up his boots and tucked them under his arm. Sand trickled in a stream down his thighs. "When you took after me in that courtroom like God's own avenging angel, didn't you ever wonder what would happen after the trial was over? Or wasn't that any of your concern either?" Acid etched his words.

"Truthfully, Mr. Boudreau? I didn't think about anything except showing the jury what you had done and showing it so clearly that there wouldn't be a doubt in anyone's mind. I wanted a unanimous verdict. I got it."

Boots thumped on sand as Cade applauded derisively. "Well, bully for you, Ms. Emma Rose." Squatting to pick up his boots, he looked at her, his lips tight. "You got your verdict, all right. Did you ever wonder if maybe I wasn't as guilty as sin?"

"Not for one single solitary instant." Emma looked at him, her anger meeting his. "Why should I?"

"Because I wasn't." His fingers tightened on his boots.

"That's what they all say, Mr. Boudreau. Everyone's innocent," she said tiredly, curiously disappointed to hear the old refrain coming from this man. "You deserved everything you got—and more." Emma looked away from his face.

He rose suddenly but didn't touch her. "Did I deserve to lose my son? To have him taken completely away? Did I deserve that? Innocent or guilty? Did I?"

It was the anguished longing in his voice that reached Emma. "I don't know anything about that," she answered. "I'm sorry for you."

"Sorry's not good enough and not what I'm after. I don't give a hoot in hell what you think about me, but, by God, you're going to help me get my son back, one way or another." He thrust his boots to Emma.

Surprised, she grabbed them and watched as he hefted the cooler to his shoulder.

"Come on. I'm too bushed to argue with you anymore. You've got more turns and twists in your brain than any Brahma bull I ever rode. But we have time to work things out." His tall figure strode past a thicket of sea grapes and disappeared in a clump of pines some distance behind them.

Flinging his boots at him, Emma knew she couldn't trail meekly after him into that darkness.

Cade saw Emma's indecision and didn't give a damn. She could follow or not. He was tired down to his toes, and brain dead. Too tired to think straight, too tired to do much more than haul stuff off the beach and crash.

He bit off the curses rising to his lips, stifling himself as he had for three years. Shutting up and staying dumb and numb. Survival. Not thinking.

Maybe he shouldn't have kidnapped her. It had seemed like an acceptable risk after that amused secretary kept putting him off. She'd figured him for a boyfriend, judging by the laughter in her voice every time he called. Cade rubbed his head. What else could he have done? He wished he hadn't frightened Emma so damned bad, but he'd gone through every channel he could think of and been balked every which way. No. He'd had no other option.

He'd shut down her options, too. No way off the island for her. She'd have to listen to him. In the meantime, she could fend for herself for the rest of the night if she had to.

Cade looked back.

She was wet. Too bad. She didn't have to sit out on the beach where the wind from the open water would blow cold even in spring with a dampness that would seep into her bones before morning. Irritably, he glanced at her again.

Sitting on the sand, staring out at the distant lights on the mainland, she was a small, vulnerable figure. Her hand brushed her feathery hair off her face and she huddled within the circle

of her arms. Watery moonlight washed the coffee-bean color
of her hair with gleaming brown, lingered and vanished behind scudding clouds.

He wouldn't feel sorry for her.

Gazing from the protection of the pines, Cade saw her
shudder, and she curled more tightly into the ball of arms and
knees, tucking her skirt under her feet.

She could get up and get out of the wind. Nobody was stopping her.

Just you and your damned meanness, his brain told him.

Her head drooped onto her knees, the defeated curve of her
ordinarily straight spine stirring him. Cade sighed. Damn it all
to hell and back.

"Hey! Lawyer lady! You'll freeze your a—" Cade knuck-
led his head and started over. "It's going to get cold out there
on the sand."

She didn't look at him, but he thought her knees drew tighter
against her chest as she curled up.

She wouldn't give an inch. Stubborn. He already knew that.

"Tide'll be in around 3:00 a.m. It's already turned." Cade
banged his boots together, shaking out the last of the sand.
"Gonna get real wet then."

"I don't care." Her words wove in and out of the wind,
borne to him on pine scent and salt spray.

Cade breathed deeply. Freedom, clean and real and smell-
ing like life itself. He dragged it deep into his lungs, right down
to his bare toes, feeling clean for the first time since he'd been
in jail. God help him, he couldn't get enough of the smell of
this salt-tanged air. Free. No one watching him, listening to
him, crowding him. Free, by all that was holy, and going to stay
that way, come hell or high water.

Well, he thought, looking past the small figure to the dark
movement of gulf water, he was counting on high water coming for sure by morning or they'd really be stuck, so he might
as well reckon hell wouldn't be far behind, not the way things
had been going for him so far.

There were definite problems.

He wished he could crush out the concern Emma Rose
O'Riley's forlorn shadow aroused in him. Good, old-fashioned

lust there, too. Maybe something else, but concern was tricky enough. Better not think of other, more explosive emotions she stirred up in him.

Volatile, lying under the surface of his consciousness like bombs waiting for an unwary step, those emotions would blow him and his hopes sky-high.

Have to keep his distance, even if he convinced her to make things right.

Couldn't think about those dark prison dreams. Too long without a woman. That was all.

Have to keep away from her, he concluded with fatigue-dulled logic and, stunned, heard his hoarse voice calling to her, "Counselor, don't aid and abet a crime. You're going to catch your death of pneumonia if you stay out there, and I'd just as soon not be accused of murdering as well as kidnapping you, all right?"

With that, she looked at him. "You planned all this? In a day and a half?" She gestured to the cooler and duffel bag, then out to the gulf where the boat had long since vanished from sight.

"Yeah." Cade dragged the cooler off to one side and started scooping out a shallow hole in the sand. Food first. Next, sleep.

Dropping dried pine needles into the depression and topping them with branches and chips, he hunkered down and struck a match to the tepee-shaped triangle. Sitting on his haunches, he watched the needles flare, popping and licking the bigger branches. "Like I said, I tried to talk to you. At your office. I couldn't wait until after your vacation."

She stood stiffly, brushing off her skirt, and Cade watched her, watched the fabric flap in the wind and shape itself to her calves and thighs, watched the wet material cling to the delicate curves of hips and rear end. Then she turned and wind lifted her skirt. Something lace-pale gleamed and disappeared as the skirt flattened against her once more, sketching her woman shape, dipping where thigh met thigh.

His sigh was slow and controlled, but he couldn't subdue the rapid beating of his pulse. He sucked in a deep breath. "Come on over to the fire, counselor. It's going to be a long night."

She hesitated as she glanced toward his supplies. "You're well-prepared. How long are we going to be here?"

"Long as it takes." Cade shoved a twig into the fire and sparks burst skyward. "Reckon I might do some fishing, too."

"Fishing?" She stepped gingerly in his direction.

"Yeah. After we talk." He heard the rustiness of his laugh. "Not many chances to go fishing in prison."

Her feet shushed against the sand and undergrowth. "Why didn't you talk to me in my office when you were there? No one was around."

"Don't know," he lied. He'd been worried about her calling a guard to kick him out before she'd listened to him, for one thing, and seeing her behind that heavy office desk had brought the whole trial, everything before and afterward, closing in on him until he'd had to go outside into the rain. He could never have convinced her of anything in that damned courthouse where the past hung all around him.

The walls, with their smells of books and paper, had squeezed his lungs until he couldn't breathe. If he'd stayed inside those courthouse walls another second, the men in white coats would have carried him out in a straitjacket. "I figured neutral territory might be better."

"I can understand why you decided that," she said, fingering a sea grape leaf. "And you didn't think I'd listen otherwise?"

"That's it in a nutshell, counselor. Got it in one." Cade unhooked the cooler lid and took out a beer and the plastic-wrapped grouper he'd bought earlier. He dropped a blackened grate onto the fire.

"And then I started to scream. You frightened me." Her hands worked back and forth.

"You were going to scream and I reacted."

"Overreacted," she corrected and dropped the mangled leaf onto the sand.

"Looks that way," he agreed, frowning, as a memory of her white terrified face flashed into his mind. "But what's done is done." Cade punctured the top of the canned milk and filled a pie tin. He dipped the fillets in the milk then dropped them into a plastic bag of cornflake crumbs seasoned bayou-style, hot and peppery. He'd missed food with a bite to it. If he lived to be a hundred, he'd never eat macaroni and cheese again.

"You shouldn't have kidnapped me."

Hunkered down, he squinted up at her. "I didn't think I had any other choice." He didn't want to think about that momentary nasty satisfaction as he'd stuffed her into the car and roared off.

He shouldn't have been so rough. Prison had turned him into a bastard. Cade pulled back the tab on a beer.

"People always have choices, Mr. Boudreau."

"You really believe that?" Cade knew better.

"I have to," she said in a low voice. "Or I couldn't do what I do."

Her hair drooped around the edges of her chin, and her skirt and blouse would be good for nothing more than polishing rags once they got off the island. Sadness peeked out of her wide eyes in a paper-pale face. Her lipstick had long ago worn off. No matter where else he looked, the soft curves of her breasts outlined by her damp blouse drew his gaze and kept it returning. Even so, she reminded him of a small child ready for bed and sleep, scrubbed clean and weary.

Her spine was arrow straight again.

Little ruts appeared where her toes, poking through her ripped nylons, wiggled in the sand. Cade looked from her cautious face to her busy feet. Drawn to the elegance of their narrow arches, he wondered if anyone had ever lifted those slim feet and traced their lovely bones with his mouth.

He tipped the beer down his suddenly parched throat. Three years and some were a long time.

He had to be careful.

Lifting the can to his mouth, he gulped again, relishing the yeastiness, and wiped the back of his hand against his mouth. A long time without a lot of things.

"I don't see a way out of this for you," she began conversationally, the silvery sweetness of her voice falling on his ears, "but maybe we can make the best of this disaster." Earnest and persuasive, she continued. "I'll argue diminished capacity. I could do that, at least."

Cade shifted, one knee braced on the ground as he lifted out the cast-iron skillet. "Counselor, I believe you could do any damned thing you put your mind to. Far as I know, you could talk God Himself into switching the poles. So you keep on thinking.''

He checked the pan and wiped it out with a wad of paper before throwing in a handful of shortening. ''I'm convinced you'll figure out a way to save both our hides if I provide you with sufficient motivation.'' He stoked his hostility as protection against the bruised look in her eyes, against the slender fragility of this woman who had held his life in her hands once and on whom his future now depended.

With sudden force, Cade snapped a branch in two and jammed it under the grate before continuing. ''Now I'm going to fry up some fish. If you want some, fine. If not, that's fine, too. But I'm going to enjoy this fish and my beer without remembering how long it's been since I've had either. I'm going to pretend you and I had our chat and Quint's home waiting for me. I'm going to pretend that everything's just hunky-dory, okay?''

Couldn't think about Quint. Cade grabbed the hot skillet and swore. The skillet clanked on the grate.

Emma flinched. ''Okay.''

Glaring at her, he leaned back to grab a piece of ice from the cooler.

Emma watched as his thigh muscles flexed under the faded denim in a long, powerful line that drew her eyes upward to the worn zipper placket.

She looked away.

She'd been lulled into a sense of normalcy as she watched his deft hands flip the fish in and out of pans and plastic, his lean fingers moving swiftly and surely over the thin fillets. Grease hissed as he slid them into the pan, and the smell made her mouth water. She was hungry.

Hungry and no longer paralyzed by fear. In spite of everything Cade Boudreau had done, she finally started to believe he wasn't going to kill her. He had some agenda in mind, and he was angry, frustrated and fatigued, but she no longer felt threatened by him.

Not in the way she used to be, at least. Emma caught the quick up-and-down skim of his eyes on her legs and reminded herself that there were threats, and then there were threats.

Cade Boudreau, with his see-all eyes, was a man who could threaten a woman's peace of mind just by giving her one of his wonder-what-you'd-be-like-in-bed glances. Maybe he checked out every woman like that, maybe his masculinity was responding impersonally to her femininity.

Cade Boudreau's glances seemed highly personal, however, when he looked at her. His glances made her jittery.

The aroma of frying fish sailed up to her, and she sneezed. "I'd like some fish." She leaned forward.

"You'll have to eat it with your fingers."

"Fine." Emma remembered taking sugar bread out to the garden, thick slices of homemade bread lathered with butter and sugar, sugar dribbling down her face and clothes. Nobody had cared.

Just as nobody would really miss her if she never left this island. She reached out her hand to Cade.

Shoving a steaming piece of grouper wrapped in newspaper to catch the grease toward her, his fingers, slippery smooth with grease, slid along hers, and he looked at her for an instant as she drew back.

Emma jiggled the paper to cool the fish.

"Watch it!" His long fingers curled around hers as she almost dropped the hot paper.

Cupping hers, his palms were wide and callused. Working on the road gangs would have toughened them. Once more, his fingers scraped along hers, and a slow heat, molasses thick, jellied in her veins.

She yanked her hands back.

"Hey, easy does it!" he said, grabbing her palms tightly. "If you don't like my cooking, just say so! Don't dump it in the sand."

Their joined hands were close to his warm skin, his sleek chest muscles burnished by firelight. If she extended her forefinger, she would touch the darker skin of a scar that swept down his lean ribs to the jeans riding his narrow hips. Under his ribs, his stomach was concave and ridged with muscle. She wanted to touch that bronzed skin, see if it rang like the shining metal it resembled.

Never taking her eyes off that glistening skin and muscle, Emma saw the gap between belly and waistband widen as he inhaled on a long, indrawn breath.

Somewhere in the gulf, a buoy clanged in the changing wind, warning boaters of shallows and danger, clanging and tolling.

Emma swallowed. In Cade's eyes she saw herself, a tiny figure in firelight, a pinpoint in the darker gray pupils that dilated as she watched, filled with her. She stepped back, dropping the forgotten fish.

Not looking down, Cade caught the wrapped fish before it hit the sand and handed it to her. "Don't ever play five-card draw with a serious poker player, counselor, or you'll lose the rest of your expensive shirt."

"I don't know what you mean," Emma replied, plucking at the tatters of her expensive shirt. She made her gaze steady on his.

"Liar," he said softly, turning away from her and wiping his hands down the length of his chest, just stopping at the snap of his jeans.

Her hands shook with the erratic thumping of her heart. Emma clutched the newspaper package and sank to the sand. What had she been thinking of? Well, she knew what she'd been thinking of, but not why. Her mind didn't run to fantasies like that, at least not before Cade Boudreau had blazed into her life.

He represented everything she found abhorrent in a man, everything she'd fought. So what kind of woman did that make her to be attracted to him? There was a truly frightening thought. Her uneasiness grew.

Yet his grief and longing for his son tugged at her, tempted her to shove aside what she knew about Cade. Danger, danger, chimed the buoy in time with her thoughts.

Across the fire from her, he watched her with half-closed eyes, an unblinking scrutiny that had her nervously picking at the fish. She didn't think she'd be able to eat a bite while he watched her with those knowing gray eyes.

She could. She did. The fish stuck in her throat once when she saw his eyes follow the slow slide of food as she swallowed, but she meticulously finished all the fish before crumpling up the grease-stained paper.

She didn't want to burn the paper in the fire. The fire was too close to the brooding man who watched her with those hooded eyes.

Abruptly Emma stood up. Like a compass arrow magnetized to her movement, Cade's head turned to her. Clearing her throat, Emma sought refuge in speech, refuge from the heavy, enclosing silence and fire heat. "Your son was taken from you?"

Pine needles crackled in the fire as she waited.

"Yes."

"Your wife had filed for divorce before the trial, hadn't she? At least that's what I remember," Emma added hurriedly as Cade stirred and lobbed his paper into the fire.

Paper burned briefly and brightly, its charred bits fireflies in the night. Silence stretched between them, a web of past knowledge and pain.

Emma watched the play of firelight over Cade's harsh face.

"She wanted a divorce. I wanted my son," he said finally, shifting into deeper shadow and leaning against the trunk of a pine.

Emma walked to the fire and pitched in the paper. A flurry of sparks spangled the dark. She hesitated before venturing, "You tried to get sole custody?"

"Yeah." His voice was low and fatigue-slurred. "I was worried about Quint. Francine wasn't happy. She was angry with me. I was afraid she'd never let me see him if she had custody. He was all I wanted out of that marriage. She could have had everything else." After a long time, he continued, "And everything's what she got."

Prodding at him for a reason she couldn't explain even to herself, Emma asked, "Why didn't you file for joint custody originally or fight for it later?" She rubbed her arms and moved closer to the fire. The air was damp.

"You lawyers always have an angle, so what's on your mind now?" Cade muttered.

"No angle, Mr. Boudreau. Just common sense."

"Yeah? For a man facing a three-year maximum prison sentence, all the rules switch. Judges prefer a mother's custody, especially when good ol' daddy's in jail. She got Quint and I got prison. Want to talk some more about common sense, counselor? I'm all ears and ready to listen." Cade linked his hands and pulled them over his head, twisting and turning, working out the kinks.

A sudden flare of fire highlighted the bleakness in his tightened lips, shone against lean muscles sculpted long and taut.

Emma wished he'd button his shirt.

As she stared at his gleaming skin, the heat of an unfamiliar tension looped and slithered down her throat, her arms, down, down. Shivering from heat or cold, she couldn't tell, she gripped her elbows in her hands and moved closer to the fire. "Because you were convicted, you were denied any kind of custody? Are you trying to convince me that she perjured herself to get custody?"

"Gosh, you're too smart for me, lawyer lady. I confess. You hit it smack dab on the nailhead again. No wonder you're such a crackerjack lawyer." Sarcasm overlay the exhaustion in his voice. "Yeah, I think that's one of the reasons she lied. And to get even with me."

Emma frowned. "I find that hard to believe, Mr. Boudreau. I heard the evidence, saw the pictures. I think the truth came out in court."

"I don't think you'd know the truth if it reared up and bit you on your fine little fanny, counselor."

"My prosecution was a good one!"

"Guess what else, bright eyes?" Pulled bonelessly up, Cade rose and stepped out of the shadows into full firelight. An old anger pinched his nostrils and blazed behind the smoke of his eyes.

"Yes?" Emma sunk her heels firmly in sand. She'd backed up for the last time where Cade Boudreau was concerned. She pleated her skirt as she looked him straight in the eyes and lifted her chin.

"I'm not allowed to see him. Not allowed to visit him. Not *permitted!* My son, and I can't even talk to him." He drove his fist against the tree trunk. Head bowed against the tree, he struck his fist again and again against the bark.

The pulpy smack of flesh against wood sickened her. Tears welled in her eyes. So much pain.

Even knowing he'd brought it all upon himself, Emma couldn't watch his self-inflicted punishment. She scrubbed the stinging tears from her eyes.

Emma drew a shaky breath when Cade dropped his hands uselessly to his sides. His broad shoulders shuddered as he leaned forward into the support of the tree.

Cade saw Emma wiping away her tears. Stepping around the fire, he stamped down a spark that had exploded onto the sand near her feet. Grimacing, he looked at her as he bent his fingers back and forth. "I'm a damned fool, that's all." Glancing at her, he scowled. "You're cold."

Emma saw the deep scrape along his knuckles, the red ridges in his forehead, and then the slow withdrawal of his arms from his shirtsleeves held her motionless. Wide sloping shoulders tapered to a narrow waist where the ruched scar interrupted the polished flow of his skin. He shrugged out of his shirt and handed it to her. "Here. Put it on."

It was warm, warm from fire heat and skin. "All right," Emma said doubtfully. She closed her fingers around the soft cotton then slipped his shirt on. Enclosing her, it smelled of firewood and smoke and Cade. "You'll be cold," she murmured.

Her voice chimed in Cade's ears, mingled with the sigh of water on sand, the whisper of wind in pines.

He was so tired, and the sight of her in his shirt caught him off guard, ambushed him. She was so small, the shirt hanging off her shoulders, down to her knees.

"No." He reached out and slowly buttoned the shirt, starting at the bottom. His knuckles grazed her stomach, and he felt the sudden quiver and stopped, looking down at her bent head before moving up in a careful fitting of button into buttonhole, one after the other, his fingertip brushing once against her breast, surprising a faint, hushed sound from her.

That unguarded sound was straight out of his prison dreams. His fist clenched on the shirt as heat rose up and burned, burned, and his heart was thudding against his ribs.

Emma said, "I can finish."

Cade bent his head to the final three buttons, concentrating. She was enveloped in the folds of his shirt, delicate under his hands. "No, let me," he said, his fingers skimming under her chin, against the slender column of her throat. Creamy smooth, he thought, bemused by the feel of her as he pushed the final button into its slot.

Her hair was caught under the shirt. Carefully freeing each strand, Cade flipped the collar up and let his hands slide through the drying strands of hair, their silkiness catching on his fingers, her flushed skin burning under his touch.

Snared by the softness and fragility of her, drained by weariness past endurance, he hovered in a limbo of desire and memory.

"Do you know," he added, trying somehow to make clear to her why he'd acted the way he had, knowing his words were unraveling threads of dreams and hurt woven during unending nights, "when I was in prison, I'd think about you, night after night."

Her eyelids closed, shutting him out, but that was okay, she could still hear him, and it was important for her to understand, but he couldn't quite hold on to what he wanted to tell her. Something.

"Mr. Boudreau—"

He scarcely heard her. "I couldn't think about Quint or I'd have killed myself, and thinking about you blanked out the sounds of the men around me, all those desperate, lonely men."

"I don't want to hear this," she said.

"No?" Cade lifted her hair, let it fall against his hands. The edge of desperation in her voice penetrated the black hole he'd fallen into. "I liked thinking about you, hating you. Hating felt so good. It kept me alive."

He remembered the energy that hate had generated. He'd clung to hate like a lifesaver.

"Made the days easier to get through. But late at night, hate kept getting mixed up with other things. I'd lie there, looking at the ceiling, and I'd remember Quint, and I'd start blaming you for the way he was taken from me, and then all night long, your face would be there, floating in front of me in the dark."

His memories were moving over him now like water in the bayou, dark and treacherous.

"Please stop," Emma said.

Muddled, wanting to escape the headlong sweep of memory, a fast-moving current over unseen dangers, Cade made the mistake of looking down into the clear depths of her eyes and drowned there, tangled in the weeds of dreams.

He wove his hands through her hair, down her arms to her wrists where he circled the thin bones with his thumb and forefinger. Her bones were delicate. "You walked over to me the day I was on the stand, looking right at me the whole time with that contemptuous tilt of your chin, and then you leaned over to question me."

Cade smoothed his fingers languidly up her arms, past her elbows, then he continued, that day replaying itself on the screen of his mind.

"The sun shone through those dusty courthouse windows right onto your hair, your face, and there was this light all around you." She'd been swallowed up by the light, blinding him, like the angels on church windows. Cade swung her wrists. "You had on a yellow blouse, and when you leaned forward, there was a little bitty gap between the buttons, just big enough to see this piece of lace and just above it, a tiny mole. Right there."

Lost in memory, he touched the spot over her left breast, his thumb lingering and unmoving over the rapid thrumming of her heart. And then she spoke, breaking the spell.

"Mr. Boudreau. Cade," she said indistinctly, "you're tired. You don't want to think about things like this—"

"Wanting? Oh yes, I did a lot of wanting during those three years," he went on, his syllables slurring in spite of his best efforts. There was something else he had to tell her. "But you want to hear truth? How about this? I want you, Emma Rose O'Riley. I want to take you down on this warm sand and see firelight in your eyes and all over your skin, all that pale skin shining in firelight so I can forget how you looked in my dreams. Darkness and not sleeping with all the noise around me, hating you, wanting you."

"Cade." She lifted his hands. "You need to go to sleep now. You'll be able to sleep."

"Can't sleep," he said, hearing his words fade into incoherency. "Too much noise."

She led him around the fire to the pine tree. "Go to sleep," she said, pushing the duffel bag behind him as a pillow. "I promise, it will be quiet here."

"Stay." He wrapped his hand around her ankle. Her face had always stayed until early morning's dim light crept in, that faint light letting him drop like a stone into sleep.

"No."

"Yes."

His fingers were warm and tight on her leg, one finger stroking the curve of her calf. Her hair fluttered against her cheek, and her wary, soft eyes locked on his.

A sudden spurt and flurry of sparks surrounded them like a current touching two islands in the gulf, then dying out in the darkness, leaving them alone, her skin cool satin under his hand, memories washing over him.

Chapter 3

Emma saw the strength in those tensile fingers clamped around her ankle, felt their roughness, knew it was the force of her will against whatever stirred in his eyes.

He destroyed her pitiable defenses with one low, forced whisper that drifted in the wind.

"Please." And then, keeping her ankle within his grasp, he loosened the warm bracelet of fingers holding her captive.

Lifetimes of loss and grief in that one syllable, and she not mean enough to leave. Knowing it wasn't in her best interests, Emma stayed.

Wondering at her actions, disturbed by them, she still stayed and watched Cade Boudreau through the long night.

His chest moved with his breathing, a slow in-and-out like waves rolling in to shore. After a while, she found her own breathing synchronizing with his, and so, curiously linked by breath and touch, she stayed.

He never took his eyes from her. As far as she could tell, he never even blinked. Impossible, of course, she knew that, but the strangeness of this night suspended disbelief, lent an otherworldly quality to everything in the watery light of the moon.

Bound by that spell of moon and gray eyes, Emma hunched motionless on the sand with the fire at her back. Once the horn of a passing fishing boat and laughter carried over the water, and she turned to look.

Against the dark gulf, light tinged the mainland with a soft gray, a just-there light colored with the promise of dawn. A flock of sandpipers ran rapidly along the shore and took off, wheeling and turning in the lightening sky, their clear whistle marking their passing. The world turning and life going on.

Unexpected peace crept into her, and she curled up on the fire-warmed sand. Just before her eyelids drifted shut, she saw Cade shudder, then she slept.

She stirred once as she felt the light brush of something cover her and, cushioning her cheeks against her fists, drawing her knees up to her chest, she turned into deeper sleep.

Cade never knew when he fell asleep. One moment he was caught in the past, the next he woke to a sky rinsed by rain into a brilliant blue. He stood and stretched with bone-cracking energy in the bright sunlight. Reborn into this blessed radiance streaming around him.

He'd missed all this.

He shook his head, clearing out the spidery webs of memory from the night: strange, disconnected fragments that seemed unreal in the heat and white light of a spring sun.

He'd never liked being indoors. That had been the worst part of prison, the part that had made him desperate enough to waltz Emma Rose O'Riley into the night and drag her here. Everything was clear in this dazzling light and, renewed by the deepest sleep he'd had in a long time, he saw how his determination to regain his son had overridden caution and sense.

Cade stretched again and looked at Emma snuggled under the light tarp he'd thrown over her after she fell asleep. His heels sinking in the loose sand, he approached her.

Her long dark eyelashes lay against her parchment-pale skin. She looked as if she were the one who'd spent time in jail, not him. Her thin fists were tucked under her pointy chin, and he could see the light blue veins of one slim wrist and the shadowy line of her throat. Purple shadows lay like bruises under spiky eyelashes.

Well, poor lawyer lady had a right to be tuckered out after what he'd put her through.

His anger and resentment of her lingered like a sore tooth, throbbing but bearable. He'd lived with those feelings for years, feeding them and watching them grow into plants with a poisonous beauty. This other feeling, though, the one that had held him captive by firelight, was the one he didn't know how to handle. It hinted of hurt, whispered of pain, sang a song of whirlpools dragging him deep and never letting go.

He couldn't afford to let her get under his skin. He couldn't afford the cost of scratching that itch.

He *needed* his anger.

Or Quint would be lost to him forever.

Yet, crouched beside her, safe from the power of her clear eyes shining with intelligence and unexpected loneliness, he watched her for a while, watched the drift of her eyes under the translucent lids, the barely perceptible move of the tarp over the comma of her small figure. Like confectioner's sugar, a streak of sand powdered her cheek. He yielded to the urge to brush away the grains.

Against his finger, her eyelashes lifted, light as a butterfly's wing. Her eyes opened.

Cade knew the instant she came fully awake. Her eyes lost that dazed, lost-in-sleep softness, and her pupils went dark and big as she saw him.

"Oh!" she said, tears coming to her eyes and her nose wrinkling as she fought a cheek-splitting yawn.

She was warm and sleep-rumpled. One strand of hair zigzagged both ways like a crooked-tail cat he'd seen once. A dull red sleep handprint creased one pale cheek.

Cade watched the flow of pink tint her cheeks. "Mornin', beauty," he said, hunkering on his heels, reckoning his actions had sure enough made him Beast to her Beauty, but liking the look of her all rumpled and sleepy.

Shutters snapped shut in misty hazel eyes. She touched the tarp and glanced at him. "You covered me up," she accused.

"Shame on me." He grabbed the edge of the tarp. Trust her to go on the offensive. The M of her upper lip pursed over the tender lower curve. Cade reached out to touch that fullness, then snatched his hand back. Instead of silky smooth skin, his fingertips scraped the bristles of his morning beard.

Safer. No way was he going to touch her again. He didn't like—now there was a lie, he thought—he *liked,* a lot, touching her. That was one of the problems. He cleared his throat. "Ms. O'Riley, look." He scratched his chin, not sure how to go on, but knowing that every word was crucial if he wanted to see his son. "I apologize for last night."

"Apologize!" She sat upright, her mouth gaping. Her words were sleep-husky. "After what you did—"

"Wait a minute, okay?" Sandpapery scratching as he rubbed his chin again. She'd believe the earth was flat sooner than she'd believe he wasn't lower than a snake's belly.

"Yes, Mr. Boudreau?" she said in that snooty little tone that made his blood curdle, the tone saying clearer than spring water that he wasn't much better than what went out with her trash.

So why should he care?

He didn't. Why should he? He could live with his share of guilt. Let her think what she wanted if she could get Francine to let him see Quint. Of course it would help if Emma Rose didn't swear out a warrant for kidnapping as soon as they got off the island. "Hang on a damned minute, will you?"

"I'm not going anyplace." She dragged the tarpaulin around her determined little chin, her whole posture aggressively waiting.

Cade pulled his ear. It was going to be real hard to get past all that distrustful stubbornness. All he could do at this point was plow ahead. He frowned. "Yeah, I owe you an apology." He held his hand palm up. "I know I acted like a damn idiot, but I had a reason."

"I can't imagine what," she interrupted, sitting up arrow-straight.

"I can make you understand what happened if—"

She was paying attention. Leaning forward, she frowned, her eyebrows delicate in her pallor. "I know *what* happened, and *why* doesn't change anything, Mr. Boudreau!"

"It should." He stood up, thinking hard, scuffing the sand. "Look, I'm not trying to change your mind about me. Nothing I can say would do that. I don't care. But will you let me explain? Aren't you lawyers trained to see both sides of a situation—at the very least? Didn't you wonder why I dragged you off?" Cade stooped, looking right into her questioning eyes, betting on her intelligence to trap her interest. "Aren't you a little curious?"

She wrinkled the tarp under her chin and nodded. "Last night you explained why you were so rough in the parking lot. I can almost understand your behavior. But you never explained what you wanted to talk about." She cocked her head, thinking. "Yes, I think I want to know why you came looking for me one day after your release from prison."

She paused and continued, her fingers drumming lightly against her knees underneath the tarp. "I'll listen. But I warn you, don't expect anything from me." She added vehemently, "You're in deep trouble."

"Last night you said I'd paid my debt. I'm supposedly—uh, rehabilitated, right?" He hated that word. "Isn't that the purpose of prison?"

"Some people think the purpose of jail is to keep troublemakers off the street," Emma added tartly.

He grimaced. "Yeah, that, too." She was going to make him fight for every inch. "I put in my time. Don't I get a chance now to put my life back together?"

"You didn't go about it very sensibly. Kidnapping me was only a little less irrational than holding up a bank."

Cade squashed irritation and kept his voice calm. "I'm not arguing with you. We've been over that. I know I've been dumber than a doorknob. All I want you to understand is *why* I did it, that's all. I know, I know—" he waved his hand as she started to interrupt "—it's not going to change anything, you made that clear, but there were—"

"What? Extenuating circumstances?" Emma scoffed.

"You're the lawyer. Suppose there were extenuating circumstances?"

She looked at her fingers. "I doubt it, but go ahead."

Cade drew a deep breath and plunged in. "Okay. The trial's over. Suppose what you believe is wrong?" Springing up, he released some of his tension.

She rose with him, the tarp dropping to the sand.

Cade pressed on. "Believe, at least, that I'm sorry I frightened you. If we could have talked, none of this—" he indicated the island "—would have happened. That's first. Second." He ticked off the point on his index finger, hesitating. "I didn't want a divorce from my wife. In my way, I cared about Francine. I would have stayed married. Because of Quint. He had a right to two parents."

Emma was touched by the depth of feeling in his voice. She remained silent. She listened and tried to separate her own feelings from what he was saying. "But, Mr. Boudreau, your divorce doesn't have anything to do with me or the trial. I don't understand why you're going into this. Your divorce isn't an issue."

"Yes!" He wheeled around to face her. "It is. Francine wanted the divorce. I wanted Quint. I told you I believe Francine used the conviction to get sole custody. And then got an injunction so that I couldn't have any contact with my son. She thought she had to." His bitter words spewed out. "I know what she was thinking."

"That's fairly obvious," Emma interjected. "But why come to me?"

He paused. "I didn't know who else to go to." He held her gaze.

Emma recognized an evasion. She knew enough about him now to tell he was leaving out something.

He hooked his thumbs in his belt loops. "Yesterday, when I went to your office, all I wanted you to do was ask Francine to let me see Quint. Just to *see* him." His voice scratched out the last words.

"Mr. Boudreau." Emma wasn't quite sure how she wanted to bring up the next point, but she had to. "Your wife—"

"Ex," Cade ground out.

"Your ex-wife," Emma continued, "had good reason to keep you away from her. You attacked her. She said it wasn't the first time."

"I know what she said. I haven't forgotten."

"You almost killed her."

He folded his arms over his chest. "Did I?" His eyes were narrowed, and in the glare of sun she couldn't see his expression.

"Throwing her down a flight of stairs sent you to prison for three years!"

He walked slowly away from her, then reached down to hook a shell with two fingers. Cupping it in his hand, he stood with his back to her, facing the blue-green gulf.

Emma made herself remember the pictures she'd used to prosecute the case and get the conviction of aggravated battery. "Why would she let you anywhere near her or her son again?"

He whirled. "My son, too," he said harshly, "and I want to see him, not her."

"Nothing you've said has changed my mind. I can't, I *won't* help you." Even though the words were blunt and uncompromising, she didn't regret them. "I have no sympathy for men who abuse women. None. Ever."

He turned the shell over and over in his fingers, looking at it. A white scar sliced the blackness of one thick eyebrow.

Her heart beat faster. She tasted the coppery bite of fear, but she'd had no choice. She had to tell him the truth. Anything less, and he would have heard the lie. Her feelings on this subject ran too deep.

His face was remote and closed. "That's that, then." He bounced the shell up and down, faster and faster in the blinding sunlight. One long, high toss with the shell vanishing in the white glare of sun and sand, and then he caught it easily with a quick twist of his wrist. "We're at a standoff."

Emma slumped in relief. She hadn't known what to expect. She saw the control he exerted and speculated about what could have snapped that iron rein on that afternoon long ago. Even in the grip of what had driven him last night, he had been careful not to hurt her. Her instincts urged her to believe him, but her common sense told her she'd be a fool if she did.

"An impasse." She nodded. It had been easier than she'd expected. "That's that, then. Now, how do we get back to the mainland?"

Cade tossed the shell to her. "See this?"

Emma caught the rounded pearly shell with colors coiling in muted lavenders, blues and cream to form an eye at the center. Confused by the change of subject, she looked at Cade. Pity moved through her at the bleakness on his face. "It's beautiful, but I don't understand," she said. "What is it?"

"Shark's eye." His wide shoulders angled with the lift of his arm and, looking at the mainland, he shaded his eyes. "Quint used to be afraid of swimming in the gulf when he was, oh, about four, I guess. Whenever we found these, I'd tell him it was safe to go in the water because the sharks couldn't see him without their eyes. He'd giggle. Sometimes he'd go swimming. Usually not. Unless I let him ride on my shoulders." Cade exhaled heavily.

"How old is he?" Emma asked, stroking the mingled colors of the shell. Cade Boudreau had comforted his son with such tenderness. It was difficult for her to reconcile that kind of father with what he'd done. Her own father had never— Cade's voice snagged her wandering thoughts and brought them back to the moment.

"Eleven." Cade walked over to the cooler. "He was almost eight when everything fell apart." As he bent down, the lean line of his spine curved forward.

"Mr. Boudreau." Emma followed him, despite the easy-to-read message of that wall of ridged muscles. "Here," she said, laying the shell on the cooler lid. She looked down and began unbuttoning his shirt, which she'd slept in. "You'll need this now that we're leaving." She had undone the bottom button before he spoke in that gritty voice that disturbed her with its echoes of dark, long-endured pain.

"What makes you think we're going?" He coiled his finger around the shell, touching it gently, and then with a curse flung it under the pine tree near the cooler.

"But there's no point in staying! I *told* you I can't help you! There's nothing more to be done. I want to go home." Frustration whipped her voice high.

Working furiously at the buttonholes, she damned herself for being every kind of fool. She should have lied and told him anything he wanted to hear. That's what she'd planned to do.

So why hadn't she? He'd seemed so reasonable in the light of day, that's why. Because she'd been an idiot, that's why.

She ripped the final buttons out of their holes and flung the shirt at him. "I'm going home!"

"Really? Take off." His scornful smile didn't reach his eyes. "But *I'm* not leaving until I'm good and ready. I'm not ready now, and I won't be until you decide to talk to Francine. Oh, you don't have to wait for me, counselor. Go on ahead. One problem you might want to think about, though. I don't see a boat, do you?" Cade waggled his lean fingers shoreward.

Emma looked around wildly, appalled as she remembered the rickety boat floating into darkness. What had she expected? That sometime during the night he'd swum out and retrieved it? She hadn't understood how important seeing his son was to him. She'd handled the situation badly.

She whirled to peer at the empty gulf.

There was no boat. She could see that. No boat.

"Lots of luck, counselor. I figure you'll have a mighty long swim. Tides are peculiar around here. They'll slow you down some. Oh, there's the riptide just off shore. Well, damn, I forgot all about that. It'll be a problem."

"I can't swim that far!" Emma was angry now.

"Too bad," Cade said. "And me thinking you could do just about anything. Can't walk on water, either, I'll bet?" He mocked.

Emma blinked as a thought slapped her in the face. There had to be a way off the island. Cade Boudreau had planned this and, in spite of everything that had happened, she didn't think he'd taken complete leave of his senses. He had a way off the island. If he did, she did.

How dare he think he could bluff her!

No boat. Not one that she could see, anyhow. "Mr. Boudreau—"

Cade lifted the lid of the cooler. "Tell you what, Emma Rose. Why don't you call me Cade? Make it easier on both of us. No sense being so formal." Emma's stop-and-go sputters filled the air. Emma Rose speechless? A treat to behold. Miracles were still possible.

"But just in case you decide to stay on for lunch," he said, enjoying the way irritation puckered up her soft lips, "there's only canned milk, cool beer—for a while—and cornflake crumbs. If you're reasonably pleasant, I could be talked into sharing." He dangled the bag of crumbs her way and relished the angry red sweeping up her throat to her cheeks.

"You have to be the most, the most—" She was gasping with the force of her fury, spitting mad.

Sheer devilry tempted Cade to tell her she was beautiful when she was angry, but good sense squelched his fleeting impulse to push her button with the chauvinist line.

Amusement rose in him at her indignant expression, a feeling so long-forgotten that it was almost new. Cade sat on his heels, savoring the lightness swelling up from the dark place in his soul while he watched Emma wind down.

"*Mr.* Boudreau," she emphasized finally in tones so cold and measured that they would have silenced a courtroom, "I have to see a man about a dog." With a majestic tip of her chin, she sailed away from him, down the curve of the shore, moving faster than he'd expected.

"See you later, Emma Rose," Cade said, letting his gaze linger on the twitch of her fanny as she hopped up and down over pine needles and shells in her bare feet. She'd shed the shredded nylons during the night. She needed privacy now. There was no way she could get off the island, not without his help. He'd made sure of that.

Let her stew in her own juices for a while, and she'd be back. Hot, tired and thirsty, she'd agree to almost anything.

Oh, she'd figure out a plan to trick him and probably think he was fool enough to fall for it. He'd seen the glitter in her eyes. That would be okay, too. He had a trick or two up his sleeve.

Her determination to work her way out of the situation appealed to something he thought destroyed by his time in prison. He'd expected her to lie, but she hadn't. Her steadfast refusal to give in to him while still not lying intrigued him.

Cade reached for the discarded shirt. Buttons lay scattered on the sand around him. He pushed his finger through the rips around the top buttonholes. Good thing it wasn't his only one.

Shrugging it on, he smelled the elusive fragrance that seemed to cling to her. Underneath the piny smokiness, he breathed in the wildflower scent of Emma Rose and was swept with such hunger for unnameable things that his hand shook with the force that thundered in his blood and left him dry-mouthed and hurting.

With the sun directly overhead, the sand burned against the soles of Emma's feet as she picked her way carefully through shells and driftwood. Anger still rushed under her skin, and perspiration popped out on her forehead. She blotted it with the hem of her skirt. Dried sand showered her. "Phaugh," she muttered, wiping off the grains sticking to her skin.

She had woken to the light brush of Cade Boudreau's fingers wiping sand off her cheek and looked into his gray eyes. With his shoulders shading her from the sun and snared in the tangles of dreams, she'd recognized what flashed in those cool gray depths. Her heart had leaped once, hard, bringing her wide awake with a rush of adrenaline. Bang-banging against her ribs and in her veins, her pulse rocketed through her in a dizzying, headlong sprint that left her breathless.

But not with fear.

It wasn't fear she felt looking into his gray eyes. No, what terrified her was her yearning to warm herself in the fire she saw there, to dash herself into those flames glowing far down in Cade Boudreau's lonely eyes.

Trying to forget that moment of weakness, Emma walked faster. She followed the curving path of firm sand left by the outgoing tide.

With every step away from the camp fire and Cade, her certainty grew stronger. There would be a bridge, a causeway long-abandoned revealed by the withdrawing tide. There would be something to take her off this island.

Her lips were cracking. She should have drunk some of the milk before she stormed off. Or even the beer, she thought regretfully, touching her bottom lip.

Ahead of her the shimmering white sand narrowed before diving into a thicket of mangroves and undergrowth. Emma stopped. She didn't see a way through the heavy growth. Should she go back? Try the other side of the island?

Stooping for a low-angle view of the thicket, she spotted a brown, horizontal slash that seemed out of place. She stepped closer, bending down for a clearer look and trying to avoid the jagged upthrust of roots and the sharp edges of shells carpeting the narrow strip of sand.

A wooden boat harbored snugly at the high-tide mark between two sturdy mangroves. The same rickety boat Cade had shoved ruthlessly into the night.

She didn't believe for a second that the boat had magically appeared just because she'd believed one would. No, she thought testily, Cade had planned for the boat to be there. Well, she'd concluded he hadn't stranded them, so why should she be surprised?

Behind her, Emma heard the slap-slap of feet pounding on wet sand. Whirling, she turned to see Cade eating up the distance between them with each hammering stride of muscled thighs.

He'd seen her!

He sped up, and her heart roared with the pounding of his feet against the sand.

Seeing his grim expression, Emma turned and ran carelessly toward the boat, not planning what she'd do if she reached it, not even thinking, just driven blindly by the primitive urge to flee before the sound of those relentlessly pursuing feet.

With her breath coming hard and raspy and her steps slowed by sand, Emma forgot everything in her flight. The stabbing pain against her naked foot was sudden and horrible and sent her stumbling just as Cade tackled her in a blinding spurt of speed.

"Oomph," Emma gasped as his arms wrapped around her waist and sent them both in a dizzying, twisting fall to the ground, her skirt ballooning up. She saw sand, sky, whirling above her and then Cade's face underneath as she sprawled across his solid length, his arms wrapped around her.

The thick placket of his jeans scratched her inner thigh. Emma heard the beat of her heart in her ears and felt the shuddering thrum of his under her breasts. The curl of a wave, cool in the heat enveloping her, splashed against her injured foot, and the throb of pain in her foot echoed the beating of her heart.

There was one of those moments of utter silence that her grandmother used to say marked the passing of an angel. Dark in the noon sun, Cade's eyes were the only focal point in the world and invited her, urged her to enter their darkness. His left arm tightened in the indentation of her waist while the right slid over the curve of her hip, his knuckles grazing the damp skin of her thigh.

A gull squawked, and in a poetry of music and sinew, Cade sat up, facing her and holding her tight. "I saw the stingray." He pointed to a ripple of sand where the ray had been hidden.

Cade's hand glided down, lingering over the curve of her calf with a brush of callused fingers, and then curled around her thigh as he pulled her toward him. "Let me see your foot."

Worn denim slid under her skin and Cade grimaced as he touched the bright ooze of blood in the arch of her foot. "It hurts." The sharp pain went up her leg.

"Yeah." He frowned and watched her as he gently pressed the skin around the embedded tip of the ray's tail. "Bet it hurts like hell."

Emma looked at the barbs and the thin line of blood. She shut her eyes and then opened them to find Cade looking at her in concern.

"You okay?" Cade cursed himself silently for not being faster, for not yelling when he saw the stirring of sand just before she stepped there.

"Fine," she said, and her voice came from very far away. "Fine, thank you."

"Polite to the end, aren't you, counselor?"

"I'm fine. It's not too bad, really." Her pain-squinched face put the lie to her words.

"You won't die, not from this, anyway." Cade probed the tender skin of her foot. Her wince brought his eyes to her face and he stopped. His gaze dropped to her hands.

Her fists were doubled in her skirt.

"Doesn't hurt, huh? Would you swear to that in court?"

Her smile was shaky. "Probably not." She licked away a tear.

"All right, then, hang on, and let me get this damned thing out. Here." He placed her fist on his thigh. "Every time it hurts, pinch me, okay? You'll feel better."

"Why?" Her voice had that low huskiness that feathered his skin.

"I dunno, but it's all I could think of to get your mind off this." Blood spurted as he worked out the last of the barbed tip.

"Oh!" Her hands clutched his thigh and Cade felt that clutch right up into his groin.

"Worst is over, beauty." Cade rubbed his thumb over the wound on the bottom of her foot. He closed his hand around the high arch as he stroked against the sole, following the slash of red up to her narrow toes with their pink polish. As he pressed against the wound to stanch the flow of blood, he supported her foot high on his leg. Her heel was a light weight against his zipper as he kneaded the puffiness out of the cut.

Her head dropped back and her eyes closed. As shock passed, color seeped into her pinched face. The long curve of her throat gleamed in the sun. From the loop of her skirt over her thighs to the arch of the foot he held, she was all gentle curves and vulnerability. She had been hurt because of him.

His thumb stroked the ball of her foot.

He hadn't meant to touch her again.

Cade lifted her foot and placed his lips against the swollen skin. He couldn't remember ever feeling skin this delicate and silky.

Her eyelashes fluttered at the touch of his mouth.

"I want to get some of the poison out until you can soak your foot. You'll heal faster," Cade said through the thickness in his throat. His blood flowed slow through him, and the weight of the sun's heat and his long wanting drained him. He could no more have left that spot than he could have flown to the moon.

"Go ahead," Emma murmured, and felt Cade's lips press against her foot and pull at the swollen cut. His mouth angled into the arch, his eyes holding hers, and she knew the dull flush on his cheekbones didn't come from the sun, felt the pull of his mouth and tasted the rush of honey in her blood.

"Emma, I didn't hurt my wife."

Each pull and suckle of his lips against her foot pulled at something deep, deep inside her, sent hot-and-cold shivers skimming over her skin and had her moving restlessly against the steady pressure of his hot mouth against her foot.

Heat moving through her and a rising tide of aching like nothing she'd ever known and Cade Boudreau watching with those gray eyes that burned her like summer lightning streaking through an electric sky.

God help her. *She believed him.*

Emma knew at that moment when everything turned to honeyed heat inside her that Cade was more dangerous than she'd imagined.

Not because his love for his son touched something in her. It did. Not because his anger and strength frightened her. They didn't.

He was dangerous, infinitely so, because he turned her senses against her. With a touch and a look, he made her her own enemy. He made her want the stroke of his callused fingers, crave the touch of his mouth and yearn for something she couldn't name.

"Enough. Please, that's enough," she whispered, pulling her foot free and trying to stand up. She winced as she rested her weight on her foot.

Holding her foot captive, Cade rose to a kneeling position. "Wait." Starting at the ripped buttonhole of his shirt, he tore off a wide strip. "Put your foot on my leg." His muscles, solid and sturdy, bunched under her sole as he balanced and steadied her foot on his thigh. He wrapped the cloth carefully around her foot, doubling it over the throbbing cut.

Every touch of his hand against her skin was heat drawing her closer into the flames of destruction.

Even as he tucked the flap of cloth under the binding, his palm resting on the finished bandage and still burning her through the layers of material, Emma knew she couldn't stay another night on the island with him.

Inside her, something had pushed its wings free and spread them out to dry in the heat of his touch. Even knowing what she knew about herself, she hadn't been able to prevent the cocoon bursting open.

Because he had slipped past her defenses into the kingdom of her self-doubts, Cade was terrifyingly dangerous.

"Mr. Boudreau," she said, forcing steadiness even as she hid her fists to contain her trembling, "get us off this island. I'll talk to your ex-wife."

As she spoke, he slid his palm up the calf of her leg past her knee and stopped, his finger resting on the pulse at the back of her knee. "Surrender, beauty? I'm surprised," he said in his ruined voice, and he rose, coming right into her space, filling the blue sky above her with his skeptical gray eyes. "And you know something? I don't trust you a tinker's dam right this minute. See this?" He twined his fingers together. "Me and you. I'm sticking to you like glue, counselor, so forget whatever trick you've planned."

Springing from nowhere, his sudden aggressiveness had Emma stepping back into ankle deep water before she realized what she was doing. Behind her a wave boomed and hissed onto the shore with the swelling tide.

Chapter 4

"What do you mean?" Water foamed around Emma's feet, shifting the sand underneath her.

"Simple. I'm not letting you out of my sight." Cade stepped forward. "I may be a crude ex-jock who parlayed catching a football into a college education, but I'm not dumb enough to fall for your quick hoist of the white flag. Ergo—"

Emma blinked in surprise.

He paused. "Yes, counselor, even with a two-bit education, I learned one or two five-dollar words. Ergo," he repeated with a sour smile, "I can't believe that I've miraculously convinced you of my sterling character and innocence in one day." His smile twisted. "Have I?"

The note of regret in his raspy voice stroked over her, and Emma rubbed her arms, smoothing down the goose bumps rising in the wake of that low-pitched harshness. She didn't see why he needed to use her to see his ex-wife. He could have gotten another lawyer. Most of all, she didn't understand her response to his touch.

But she did understand her need to deal honestly with him, and so she replied as she had to. "I shouldn't believe you, but I do. Still, I have questions about what happened."

"So why should I trust you out of my sight? How do I know you won't call the cops as soon as we're on shore and have me arrested for kidnapping? See the difficulty?" Cade lifted one shoulder, and the lean muscles along his ribs lengthened and glinted in the noon sun.

Emma thought about her answer. He didn't trust her. Sand swirled as she lifted her feet. "I told you I would talk to your ex-wife. You have my word on that."

Cade studied her. "Yeah, I think you'd keep your word."

"There's no problem, then."

"Oh, there's a problem. See, I don't know what you've left out, what loopholes you can dance though and leave me, as the saying goes, 'twisting in the wind.'" Cade rubbed the back of his neck. "One scenario keeps running through my mind. You calling the legal beagles, me being hauled off to the pokey, and you going to talk to Francine. Everything back to square one. Except *I'd* be back in prison. You'd have kept your word, some satisfaction to your honest little heart, I guess, but no satisfaction for me. You see where I still have a problem?"

His frustration troubled Emma. She knew what he wanted from her. She just didn't know what to do about it. Finally, she raised her still-shaking hand and ticked off her points. "Mr. Boudreau, I believe you love your son. That alone made me consider your request very seriously." Emma sailed over the fact that Cade Boudreau hadn't *requested* anything. He'd *demanded*, right from the beginning. She folded down a second finger. "I also believe I acted correctly—as well as legally—in my prosecution. I believed at the time you were guilty." She took a deep breath, waiting for his angry interruption.

Cade didn't even blink.

"Now you've introduced new elements, made me doubt my actions three years ago. You've made me doubt myself. I'm a *good* lawyer. I work hard. If you were innocent, then—" Emma paused, sick at heart "—then I have to rethink a lot of things I took for granted." She folded down the third finger. "If, going on instinct and what you've presented to me now, I accept your innocence, I can't ignore the possibility that I might be wrong again. I'm caught, you see. Either I erred badly then, or I'm making a dreadful mistake now." She bowed her head then looked at him. "But I also believe in the power of the human heart to change. I accept that you didn't assault your wife."

Tension tightened Cade's lean muscles.

She sighed. "Maybe what happened was an accident. I don't know, but *something* happened, and I'm going to find out what. I'm trying to understand why you kidnapped me. Let's call it an unusual meeting arrangement and put that issue aside." Emma closed all her fingers into a shaking fist and shoved it into her skirt pocket. "I'm not trying to trick you. I have no hidden agenda."

She rubbed her fingers against the grains of sand in her pocket seams as though they were magic charms. What she wished for, she didn't know. "Anyway, I'm being as straight with you as I can be."

"Maybe yes, maybe no." Cade reached out and grasped her by the arm. "I've gambled once on you, so I reckon I might as well play out the whole hand." His fingers slid up and curled under her armpit before sliding down to her closed fingers. "In the meantime, come up on shore before you drown."

Emma looked at the surf, which had risen around her. A minnow nibbled her calf and darted off. The hem of her skirt danced once, then hung heavily as Cade pulled her out of the water and toward him. Even with Cade's shirt as a bandage, salt water stung her foot. She still felt the shape of his mouth over the wound. Unsettled, Emma stumbled on the sand. He'd been so tender. Not what she expected.

Cade's grip steadied her as she bent down and tucked the loosened end of the bandage under a crease of fabric. He'd been so careful with her. Had anybody else ever treated her with so much tenderness? Bending over, she said, "It's settled, then?" Her face was pink.

"On one condition." Frowning, Cade shook his head and then held his hand with its coupled fingers in front of her once again. He leaned toward her. "Like I said, you and me, beauty, for as long as it takes."

Looking at the entwined fingers, Emma flushed from head to toe as pictures flickered in her mind, a shining bronze flash of Cade's naked skin sticking to hers, his coarse blue-black hair sliding under her trembling fingers and his hard muscles damp against her. Emma's stomach twisted.

Disturbing images moved across her closed eyelids.

"Impossible," she said through lips that tingled with each beat of her heart.

When she opened her eyes, he was still there in sand-dusted jeans and morning stubble, all intent male and focused on her. Emma knew the moment he picked up on her thoughts.

As his eyes narrowed to slits, the pupils darkened and the angles and planes of his face sharpened. His nostrils widened once as though he'd caught her scent. Still twined together, his fingers moved down the side of her face, down her throat, sliding so slowly it was torture, down between her breasts in a sideways nudge that slid the first two buttons free. She remembered the look on his face when he'd buttoned his shirt over her, remembered the skim of his finger against her breast, felt the breeze now on her bare skin and the stroke of his fingers back and forth.

"Closer than your skin I'm going to be, beauty. It has to be that way." His fingers stilled as the third button worked loose. "And such beautiful skin." His breath exhaled against her cheek and the knuckle of his index finger eased under the lacy edge of her chemise, nudging it down the curve of her breast. Slippery silk trembled with her heartbeat at the peak of her tightening nipple. "Like pink pearl," Cade murmured, and gently, a feather drift against the puckered skin, he brushed the peak free of the soft lace. His fingers lifted the lace up, dragging it over her breast and down, the lace moving against her nipple in a slide of silk over skin.

The scrape of lace on her skin was pleasure-pain. Blood rushed to the center of the tightening bud and she ached, ached while the bright sun beat down on her, filling her with aching heat.

And then Cade touched the tip of her breast with his finger. Once. Emma's spine arched sharply like a bow curved to launch an arrow. "Ah!" The small fierce sound that escaped her should have embarrassed her, would have, but couldn't in the touch of Cade's hard finger on her.

Shuddering heat coiled in her tighter and tighter, and she lifted to him, wanting more, wanting an end to the aching, needing something that only Cade Boudreau held the power to give. In that mindless instant when the rhythm of her body moved to his touch, Emma sensed a need in herself she'd never imagined.

Her knees buckled. Her fingers slid against the smooth warmth of Cade's chest, not bronze, not metal, but warm man-flesh flexing to the glide of her fingertips, warm skin over the hard, pounding male heart that raced to her touch, rocketed with her pulse.

His mouth moved over the slope of her breast, up her throat, tracing the burning path of his fingers. His mouth moved over the soft underskin of her chin to her lips. Hard and fast with a hunger and wildness she couldn't comprehend, he took her mouth.

"Open for me, Emma Rose." His mouth coaxed, persuaded, took and took. "I want more." His teeth nipped her bottom lip, not gently, urgently.

She moaned and his tongue took possession of her mouth as his hand cupped the small softness of her breast.

His voice, harsh and rough, guttural with passion, surrounded her, urged her to share that dark hunger driving him. "Wildflowers and honey. Like nothing I've ever tasted." His thigh, hard with muscle and need, moved between hers, and he surged against her in the pagan rhythm of his tongue, moved into her softness and held her there, captive to his hunger. He held her palm flat against his chest, moved it on his warm, bare skin to the ridges of his stomach. "Open for me, Emma, touch me—"

He should never have spoken. Absorbed, Emma wanted to ignore the voice that reminded her of who she was, who he was. She had never been *wanted* like this, never felt that her touch was so *necessary* to another human being. For the first time in her life, she understood obsession. This hunger, this craving, was what people sold their souls for.

And, for a fleeting moment, she was almost willing to pay the price.

She might have, too, if Cade hadn't spoken. Foolishly thinking herself safe, she might have fallen into the trap. Long ago she'd decided that nothing could be worth abandoning herself to this kind of craving. But how had she not known its power? How had she so underestimated this force?

"Emma, touch me." He took her hand.

And how could she be both grateful and angry that Cade's voice ripped away the hazy spell?

"No." Emma pushed against Cade's strength, never doubting that he would yield. She knew, despite all his strength and hunger, Cade would stop. "I don't want this."

Cade's breath mingled with hers. His palm slid down to cup her derriere, and he gripped her tightly to him, pressing her so hard against him that the pulse of his arousal beat against her, beat in rhythm with her own pulse. The tiny shudders rippling over his skin as he inhaled heavily were her own.

Finally he lifted his head and spoke to her in a voice still thick with longing. "Are you sure? This is a hell of a time to yank the reins, beauty." He stepped back, releasing her.

Heaven. Hell. Emma shivered with loneliness.

Cade's lips, the mouth that had shaped itself to hers and urged her to cross boundaries she'd never dreamed existed, were thinned with control.

Red slashed his taut cheekbones. "I reckon we have a bigger problem than either of us expected, counselor. Unless you want to pretend you weren't kissing me back just now?"

Emma's hands flopped in the air.

"No? Good." Cade's chest moved heavily. "I was pretty damned sure there were two of us involved in this little scene."

He'd folded his arms over his chest, a barrier against her. Her fingers still trembled with the memory of that brown skin under them, and the heavy pounding of his heart.

"It wasn't your fault." Emma jumped at Cade's laugh.

"Thanks a lot." Looking at the sand, he rubbed his neck. When he lifted his gaze to her, his eyes glittered with amusement. His mouth twitched as he said, "Can't tell you what a relief it is to know I was just a pitiful victim of your mad passion."

Emma felt the lash of embarrassment. She'd almost—no, *had*—invited Cade's kiss. She couldn't blame him. She knew what he'd seen in her eyes. She understood why he'd kissed her. What horrified her was why she'd kissed him. She lifted her hands once more and again dropped them. There really was nothing she could say.

"Mighty quiet, counselor." The corner of his mouth twitched again.

He was definitely amused. And at her expense.

"I'm thinking, that's all."

Like some lean, satisfied cat who'd lapped up all the supper cream, he was standing there watching her, letting that gray gaze wander over her. "Not much to think about, just a little old kiss. No big deal," he drawled, laughter sneaking around the lazy syllables.

"You're absolutely correct." Emma glared at him. "And I was thinking about business."

"Honey, that kind of business is carried out on street corners, not deserted islands."

"Mr. Boudreau, what occurred was the result of shock." Emma couldn't help the prissiness in her voice.

"Yeah, sure was shocking, all right."

"I meant—the stingray." Emma was light-headed.

Cade grinned at her. The megawatt power of that teasing, mischievous grin, a grin that erased the harshness of his face and overwhelmed her with its sure, masculine enjoyment had her stepping back.

"Careful!" Cade steadied her with his wide hands linked around her hips, his thumbs joining just above her thighs.

Emma jerked as heat speared up from his light touch. Shock. It *had* to be shock. "I can stand," she said, and wondered how anybody could stand on legs like melting butter. "Please, thank you." The polite phrases tumbled nonsensically from her mouth.

Straightening, Cade lost his grin as he smoothed her hair. "Look, what happened wasn't your fault." He tucked a strand neatly behind her ear.

"But—"

The teasing had disappeared, but his eyes were guarded as he spoke. "I'm a big boy, counselor, not some teenage stud muffin who has to check out anything and everything on display. Yeah, you stir up something in me, something I'm not used to, and sooner or later I'd have checked it out. And maybe you had a little curiosity, too, in spite of your buttoned-up style."

Emma knew what curiosity had done to the cat and felt the scald of Cade's mouth against hers all over again. She shivered with heat and pain.

Cade shot her a concerned look and wiped his hands down his sandy jeans. "Hell, we don't even like each other, but there's been something smoldering between us. Now we both know. And we're adults, so we go on. It's over." He paused, and a light flickered briefly in his eyes. "But, lawyer lady, let me tell you, you've got a kiss that packs a wallop." His eyes lingered on her lips.

Where Cade's eyes skimmed, Emma burned. Embarrassment washed in wave after wave over her, and she shivered with burning cold.

Watching her carefully, he frowned as he placed the back of his hand to her forehead. His fingertips touched her temples. "You're clammy."

Emma wanted to laugh. Cold? With the sun burning her up inside?

"Counselor, I think you need some shade and water. You didn't have anything to drink this morning, did you?" Cade's voice was abrupt.

"No, no, I didn't." Reassurance flooded her. A little water, and she'd be herself again. Looking at Cade's frowning face dark in the bright sun, she smiled. "Something to drink. Of course." Emma held Cade's arm as he led her up the beach, pain slicing into her with each step. All these tingles and hums would disappear as soon as she had something to drink. And some shade. She wasn't used to being out in the hot sun. So simple.

Sitting under the pine tree, rubbing her forehead with ice chips and sipping melted ice, Emma knew it hadn't been shock, hadn't been too much sun and too little water, and that it wasn't simple. Even parked on a log five feet away from her, Cade

Boudreau could still make her skin hum with one of his looks that turned her inside out. No, not simple at all. Very complicated and frightening.

"Okay now?" Cade stretched his legs in her direction as he shifted on the log.

"Wonderful," Emma said, her voice hollow. Ice melted into her hair.

"So." His voice was low and careful, as if he were walking a tightrope. "What are we going to do?"

Emma chose to think he was returning to his insistence on staying with her once they were off the island. She would ignore the upsetting sizzle between them, pretend it didn't exist, and sooner or later, it wouldn't. She could handle the situation. "Mr. Boudreau, I live with my mother and her housekeeper. I can't show up with you in tow." She reached into the cooler for more ice and rubbed it across her dry lips.

"Yeah, I understand that." He stood up. Coming to her, he ripped off another strip of his shirt, doused it in the melting ice of the cooler and wrapped chunks of ice in it before draping it around her neck. "You need to cool off faster." He plunged her wrists into the chilly water.

"Better?" He stared at her, his strong fingers moving water over her wrists and elbows where the blood flowed close to the surface of her skin.

"Oh, yes," Emma answered, trying to slide her wrists free of his grasp. She should feel cooler.

"You still live with your folks?" Restlessly he stood up.

Emma sighed as coolness seeped through her. "My mother."

"Somehow I figured you in some high-priced beach condo," Cade said.

Emma closed her fingers around a piece of ice and lifted it to her eyelids. "No, an old house, on the river."

"Should be big enough then to find room for me," Cade declared.

Emma opened her eyes and sat upright. "Impossible," she said and went beet red as she remembered saying the same word earlier and what had followed. "Lucy and Mama won't be expecting me. It'll be hard to explain," she said uneasily. "And, besides, I've given you my word!" She flung the cloth at her neck into the cooler and stood up. The pain in her foot stabbed her.

"You have. And, like I said, I truly believe you'd honor it. But Quint's too important to me to leave anything to chance, so it has to be like this." All unyielding, determined male.

"All right! I give up!" Emma's legs were spaghetti. She wanted to go home. If she had to drag Cade Boudreau with her, so be it. "Tag along if it makes you feel better! But don't interfere with me when I talk with your wife!"

"Ex," Cade reminded.

"Just leave me alone to do what I've said I will! If you don't, so help me, I'll get the handcuffs myself!"

He nodded and raised a hand to stop the flow of words. "Fair enough. You're giving me a chance. That's all I wanted."

"Believe me, it's a lot! I may even be involved in a conflict of interest. I don't know. You don't comprehend how complicated this is, ethically as well as legally. You storm in and think I can solve a situation that's three years old. A situation that may be entirely out of my power to do anything about."

"If anybody can, you can, counselor." Cade's smile wasn't friendly.

"Fine, now pack up and take me home." Emma whirled away from him. In a frenzy, she seized rags, bags and cans, hurling them into the cooler.

Like the second skin he'd promised to be, Cade moved behind her sorting out and packing up. When they'd finished, his tattered shirt and her blouse were soaked with perspiration. Emma tugged at the cooler, moving it shoreward, but Cade, giving her a look that froze her on the spot, lifted it to his shoulder and hiked to the edge of the water where he dropped the chest with a thud that should have been heard on the other side of the world. When he returned for the duffel bag Emma was reaching for, his glance dared her, *dared* her to touch it.

Emma didn't.

"Wait on the shore with the stuff. I'll get the boat and circle back."

"How nice. Solitude." Emma couldn't believe the nastiness in her tone.

"Right. Enjoy it, beauty, while it lasts. But I'll be back." Cade's smile was as nasty as her tone.

Emma shut her mouth to keep from sticking her tongue out at Cade's broad back as he strode out of sight. She hadn't been that childish when she was eight. She was seldom angry. She never raised her voice. Where had all this anger and bitchiness come from?

She wanted to go home and be herself again, not that confused, angry woman who longed for the touch of Cade Boudreau.

The putt-putt of the motor scattered her chaotic thoughts. Cade guided the tiller easily, and as he turned the boat, his tattered shirt ribboned around his sleek skin. With beard stubble shadowing his jaw, he looked tired, disreputable and dangerously sexy—like a hardworking pirate home from plundering and pillaging.

Emma tugged at the bandage on her foot. She'd always had a secret yen for pirates. From her shore-bound safety, she envied their recklessness.

Cade dragged the boat in close to shore and anchored it. The glass-clear water parted in an inverted vee at his thighs as he lugged the cooler and gear to the bobbing boat. The chug of the engine emphasized the silence. He wiped his face, slick with sweat, on his forearm and then splashed water over his face and chest. Drops glistened on his skin. As they dried, white salt spots dotted his smooth muscles.

"That's it." He stood with his hands braced on his lean hips and waited for her. "Anything left?"

"I'll check." She limped to the hollowed-out fire circle. They'd left no litter, no pop tops to trap wildlife. They'd left no trace of what had passed in those dark hours. But something important had happened. Emma looked around. A gleam of light caught her eye. She went to it, sifted the pine needles and lifted out the shell Cade had flung away. The shell that had freed his memory of his son.

Emma rubbed its pearly colors. He had eased his son's fear. She tucked the shell into her pocket where it lay shade cool against her fingers. "Nothing. All clean," she called out and hurried to the boat.

She noticed that in the last few moments Cade had changed into a faded blue T-shirt. Around his wide shoulders and biceps, his muscles ironed out the wrinkles, but the light cotton fell in loose folds around his narrow hips. His boots poked out of the top of the duffel. He'd tied a bandanna around his forehead, pushing back his thick black hair.

It wasn't fair, Emma thought resentfully as she looked at her sand-encrusted skirt, her wrinkled-beyond-redemption blouse and bandaged foot, that men could transform grubbiness into rakishness so easily. God was clearly male.

"C'mon, I'll lift you in." Cade's hands encased her waist and swung her into the boat.

"Thanks," she said through tight lips. She avoided looking into his gray eyes, afraid he could see her thoughts. She scooted onto a seat and faced forward. She would take Cade Boudreau home with her. She would do what she'd promised. Her fingers slipped into her pocket and stroked the satiny shell. She wouldn't turn him in to the police.

"Hang on." Turning the boat, Cade watched her hair stream from her face. She was all sandy and pink from the sun, like a sugar-sprinkled strawberry and just as tempting. He'd never, in all his prison dreams of her, dreamed the kind of response that had arced from her slight body to his. It had sandbagged him into forgetting all his warnings about touching her. The curving, slender feel of her in his arms as the tender bud of her breast unfurled under his mouth had swept him past caution.

Maybe he had convinced her of his innocence. She said she believed him. He could trust her.

Maybe not.

But he would be with her, watching every second.

The tremor in his hand on the tiller translated into a sideways sweep of the boat through the water. What he knew was that he couldn't trust himself. Her soft, big-eyed gaze made him forget all his reasons for not touching her. Well, he'd touched her. He'd satisfied his curiosity about her.

Sure he had.

Water sprayed around him as he opened the ancient engine full throttle. Sure, not a bit of curiosity about what her long legs would feel like locked around him, trembling with the same force that had bowed her narrow spine under his palm.

Nope, none at all. Cade scowled into the spray.

On shore with the boat emptied and the gear piled on the long dock cluttered with openly curious people, Cade was afraid that Emma would take off like a deer, but she didn't. She dug the keys out of her pocketbook, glared at him and insisted on driving barefoot, fast but in control down the island's main road.

As they reached the bridge off the island, her foot started bleeding again. Slamming on the brakes, she whipped the car to the side of the shell road.

"It's all yours, Mr. Boudreau," she said in her low, sweet voice. Her face was frosty with hostility and pain. Her delicate chin tilted skyward, and she wouldn't look at him.

"I won't say, 'I told you so,'" Cade muttered as he adjusted the seat for his longer legs. She was probably ticked off because she'd kissed him. Well, he was still revved up from that kiss and feeling a little hostile himself.

If he'd been in this mood when he was younger, he'd have stormed into the first bar he saw and picked a fight with the biggest, baddest jerk in the place. Wouldn't matter who got thumped the worst, either.

That was what he'd always liked about football. Knocking heads and running over people. A great outlet for built-up tension. Roping calves. That worked, too. And hot, wild sex, sex that left you wrung out like a dishrag in musky, tumbled sheets.

He made the mistake of glancing at Emma out of the corner of his eye. She was unwinding the bandage from her foot, which was propped on the dash. From the folds of her skirt, a scallop of lace dangled between her legs.

Cade stopped listing stress relievers.

"Turn right." Emma chewed the edge of her thumb.

A long row of royal palms lined the road that wound east and west along the river. Cade knew this road. He'd raced it a hundred times in his jazzed-up Mustang before he lost his driver's license and wised up. He and his black-jacketed buddies had christened the twisting road with jug wine one crazy night. Forever after, River Road was Rich Bitch Boulevard.

Houses spread farther and farther apart, separated by hedges and enormous swoops of green that provided privacy from passersby. Yards were lawns here. He'd mowed enough of them for extra cash. Of course Emma would live in one of these shiny, white-columned mansions. Old money. Lawyers, doctors, rich folks.

Not hard-scrabble folks like his.

Beside him, Emma moved restlessly on the seat.

"Nervous, counselor? Wondering how you're going to explain me?" Cade didn't like recalling how he'd had to go to the back doors of these houses to collect his yard money. "Don't worry. I'll try to remember not to spit on the floor or scratch in public."

"Such a cheerful guest. Do you always carry a chip on your shoulder the size of a two-by-four?" She was high-strung. "Or do I just bring out your nicer side?"

"It's all this." Cade gestured to the ornamental iron gates and heavy growth hiding the huge old houses from view. The kind of wealth these mansions represented still made him uncomfortable.

Emma twisted on her seat away from him. She looked out the window at the wide river flowing beside them. "I won't apologize for the way I live." That edginess still tightened her voice as she said, "Turn in here."

Her terse command cranked Cade's aggression up one notch higher. The closer Emma got to home, the more she settled into a real princess mode. "Yes, ma'am." He flipped two fingers to his forehead. "At your service, your ladyship."

Her silky eyebrows drew together in perplexity, but then comprehension sparked the green flecks of her hazel eyes with a little aggression of her own and she lowered her chin regally. "Very nicely done. Have you considered chauffeuring full time?" She lowered her slim legs and placed her folded hands in her lap.

"I may have to yet," Cade growled. "Although people around here are probably leery of hiring ex-cons." Hanging his arm out the open car window, he drummed irritably on the door while he guided the car with the fingertips of the other hand resting lightly on the steering wheel.

"I hadn't thought about that." Emma's fingers tightened and twisted together in her skirt.

"Not many civilians do." Cade kept his gaze on her betraying fingers. He wondered what she was thinking. "I'll find a job. I have to." He could swear a glint of concern moved over her face.

"What about your ranch?" Sitting straight up like a proper young debutante on her way home from a date at the country club, she still coiled her hands together.

"Yeah. Well, that's something I'll have to talk to Francine about. I guess she sold it. Let it go for taxes." He slapped his open palm against the car door.

"Cattle ranching's expensive."

Cade snorted. "Damn right. Scrubland's been running somewhere around twenty-five hundred an acre, and you used to need ten to twelve acres to support a cow and calf. Most ranchers try and work it at two acres per, at least that's where things were headed before I got detoured on my path to fame and fortune. There's winter feeding, hay, molasses—" Cade's voice died out. He'd worked so hard on that ranch. He'd intended to hand it down to Quint. A dynasty.

"If it's been sold, can you buy it back?"

Cade turned briefly to her and looked out at passing hedges and oak trees. Her hands were still and her whole attention on him. He liked the look of concern glimmering in her soft eyes. "Don't you know how ranching goes in south Florida?"

"It's a lot of work." Emma worked a comb through the tangles of her hair. Her slim arm was a sun-pink curve against her coffee-brown hair.

"Lot of work. Lot of money." He glanced Emma's way again. Cade gripped the steering wheel. He wanted to brush her soft pink cheeks with his hand and see that dazed look in her eyes again. He was smart enough not to, and spoke instead. "The saying is, you gotta marry land or inherit it."

"You didn't."

"No." Cade wanted to laugh at the dreams he'd had. Couldn't weep and wail, might as well laugh. "I bought the cheapest scrub I could and worked night and day to run cattle on it." He'd paid for his ranch with dawn-to-dawn hours more times than he could remember, and he'd almost turned the ranch into a paying proposition.

"So can you get your ranch back?"

He did laugh. "Counselor, there's a pipe dream for you. That land was probably sucked up by the first cattleman with cash or financing. I have whatever clothes are in my duffel bag and a thousand dollars in a savings account. That's it." Cade slapped the car door again. "Not much to show for thirty-six years."

"Then how do you plan to support Quint if you're given joint custody?" Her voice was fire smoke drifting around him and just as impossible to keep out.

"I'll manage. I always have." He'd take any work available in order to have Quint. "There'll be something. I can work fishing charters out of Cortez. Anything."

"We're almost there." Emma interrupted his morose thoughts. "Half a mile around the next bend and up the driveway." She bit the edge of her thumb again.

They sat in silence as Cade negotiated the bends under the trees overhanging the narrow drive. Suddenly, the house loomed in front of them.

"What the hell?" Whatever Cade had expected, it wasn't this.

Paint flaked off tall, once-white columns on a veranda that circled the huge house. A thicket of rhododendron bushes formed a tunnel as he drove up the last few yards. Vines climbed over the cracked, peeling sides of the house, and straggly hedges of hibiscus exploded with red and yellow.

Stunned, Cade turned to Emma and her ceaselessly twisting fingers. All the sweet sass was gone. Her wide eyes were wary, and she looked like a little kid forgotten at the park.

"My home," she said with a smile that quivered at the corner of her mouth. "All this." Imitating his earlier gesture, she indicated the wild, uncared-for grounds, the Queen Anne's lace tall in the overgrown lawn.

Chapter 5

"Lord love a duck, sugar, what happened to you?" Lucy shook her head as she looked at Emma's foot and her sandy clothes. Cropped short, Lucy's dusty red hair curled tightly away from a square, freckled face crinkled with good humor. "Your mama's not expecting you until next weekend. Whatever are you doing back before your vacation got off the ground? You're dribbling sand all over the floor, sugar."

Lucy's marmalade-over-toast voice left Cade breathless. He glanced around the hall. Pictures, faded curtains—called draperies, probably, on this side of the river. Tall ceilings with slowly rotating fans, dark cherrywood furniture in what he could see of the dining room. Nothing to account for Emma's rising agitation. Not his business, anyway.

He didn't realize he'd taken a step closer to her until the red-haired honeybee grinned at him with so much friendly nosiness plastered all over her puss that he found himself grinning back in companionship.

"Where's Mama?" Emma's voice rose.

"Out in the garden enjoying the afternoon air, sugar, same as always."

Lowering her voice, Emma added, but Cade heard the quiet question, "How was the weekend? Will she be upset that I came back early?"

"I doubt she'll notice. She's had a good day, though."

"Oh, wonderful." Exhaling with relief, Emma craned her neck and looked down the hall to the old clock. "I lost track of the time."

Before turning to Emma, Lucy raised a sly eyebrow as she took in Cade's muscles in the T-shirt and the fit of his jeans. "Don't blame you, sugar. Fifteen years ago, I'd o' lost track, too." She grinned even wider at Cade. "Maybe even five years ago."

Red streaked up Emma's neck. "Lucy, this is Cade Boudreau, a—client of mine."

"Oh? I should have known. Too bad, sugar." She shrugged, but didn't make clear for whom she felt sympathy, Cade, Emma or herself.

Cade had hoped to get cleaned up before running into anyone but, obviously alerted by the squeaky turning of the brass key in the rusty lock, Lucy had come loping out of the kitchen and down the hall. He and Emma hadn't had time to decide how they'd explain her early homecoming. Since he'd insisted on sticking with her, Cade reckoned she was going to let him sink or swim.

He had to admire Emma's slickness. A telltale flush, but she hadn't stuttered over the introduction even though her eyes daggered warnings as she turned to him. "Mr. Boudreau, Lucy Hampton, my mother's second cousin once removed."

"How do you do, Ms. Hampton?" Cade made his raspy voice smoothly formal and slightly teasing.

Emma turned to him as though seeing him for the first time. He liked the wide-eyed astonishment that flitted across her face. Five-dollar words weren't the only thing he'd picked up in college.

"Sorry we've messed up your afternoon, but Emma insisted on coming home and taking care of this matter." Cade couldn't remember the last time he'd teased anyone. He and Francine hadn't joked around much. He hadn't realized he'd missed that part of his rowdy childhood.

Lucy twinkled at him. Left to her tender mercies, Cade figured he'd be lounging on a yacht sipping bourbon and branch water with his whole history laid out if the smile spreading across her face meant anything. He let his grin regret that fifteen years she'd admitted to and the five he knew she hadn't.

She was like the earthy, easygoing stock he came from. He felt at home with her.

Emma forgot her anxiety as she watched Cade and Lucy. He wasn't the least bit ill at ease. Lucy didn't fluster him. Nobody was uncomfortable except herself.

His faded blue T-shirt and worn jeans might as well have been a tuxedo. His blue-black hair should have looked as sticky as hers felt, but instead looked rakish. He rocked on his heels and his jeans, worn to white across the zipper placket, tightened. Lucy's smile went on high beam, Cade's lopsided grin lifted the side of his mouth, and Emma felt deserted.

It was as though they knew a secret she didn't.

She'd never been any good at teasing. As a kid, she'd never been sure she got the joke. There always seemed to be something that everybody else caught, and she missed. Cade seemed more at home in her house than she did.

"Lucy, could you show Mr. Boudreau up to a bathroom and the guest room? I'm going to change my clothes, then I'll go on out and see Mama." Emma took a deep breath. "Oh, Mr. Boudreau will be staying for dinner. Is that a problem?"

"None at all, sugar, that old chicken's like rubber. It'll stretch." Lucy ran her light blue eyes over Cade's lean body. "'Course, Mr. Boudreau looks like a man with a mighty appetite, so—"

Emma's ears burned white hot. Cade's mouth had taken hers like a man starving. "Whatever, Lucy. I'll help you as soon as I can."

"Take your time, sugar." Lucy tucked her arm inside Cade's elbow. "Now, Mr. Boudreau, I knew some Louisiana Boudreaux. Any kin of yours?" She called over her shoulder as she led Cade up the curving stairway, "I'll take good care of Mr. Boudreau, Emma. Don't worry now, hear?"

Hurrying down the staircase fifteen minutes later after a rushed wash-up and clothes change, Emma frowned as she wrapped a scarf around her waist. Lucy and Cade's verbal sparring had sent a small pang of unexpected and unwelcome loneliness through her.

She'd never been bothered before by Lucy's clear relish of the difference between men and women. So why now? She swung open the heavy French doors leading to the garden. Maybe because Lucy was so casual with Cade? Maybe because Lucy's teasing warmed the chilly gray of Cade's eyes and softened the carved lines of his face?

She jumped when Cade's palm curved around her waist. "What?"

"I told Lucy to point out the way, and I'd catch up with her later." Cade studied her. "What's the matter?"

If it was anybody but Cade Boudreau, she'd think it was concern lowering those arched eyebrows over his thin, high-bridged nose. "Nothing." Emma edged away from the warmth of his fingers spread wide on her hip. "Everything! I need some peace and quiet. And privacy!" Cade at her heels, she stalked out to the garden.

"Hey, Mama." Emma leaned over and kissed her mother's powdery cheek.

"Oh, darlin', aren't you ever going to quit talkin' like that?" Agitated, thin fingers fluttered over her mauve and blue voile dress that draped onto the weeds and grass beside the chaise longue.

"I know, Mama. I forgot. Forgive me." Emma leaned over again and kissed her mother's smooth forehead.

"Of course, darlin', but you're forgettin' your manners." Rebecca O'Riley waved languorously to Cade.

Emma introduced her mother and her kidnapper, the man she'd sent to prison, the man who'd sworn to be her second skin. Without looking at Cade, she knew what his expression must be.

All her life she'd watched men—and women—react to her mother's magnolia beauty. Tall, slim and deep-bosomed, Becca O'Riley with her red hair flaming like the sun was mesmerizingly beautiful. Her leaf-green eyes were like deep pools in the creamy skin of her oval face, and her long, elegant neck was as firm as Emma's.

Her fifty-one years had scarcely left a trace. Lucy, six years older, and Becca were opposite sides of the coin. One earthy, the other aristocratic. Different, but both fascinating and irresistible.

Especially to a quiet, bookish girl who lived in the shade cast by the adult, fiery-haired cousins who wielded charm like a feminine weapon. Chubby, dark-haired and pale, Emma had been misplaced in a family of women who attracted and effortlessly held the attention of men. Casually ignored by both women and clinging like a limpet to her father's tall strength, she'd trailed silent and adoring in the wake of her three adults, loving them with all her small, lonely heart.

Later, she'd learned about the masks women sometimes wore in a grown-up world.

Adoration fled, though love, altered and stunted, remained. Anger and fear had rooted in her soul.

Her mother's smile tilted engagingly at Cade, but confusion swirled in her leafy eyes. "How nice of you to visit, Mr. Boudreau. I don't believe we've met before?" Uncertainty drifted in the delicately blurred syllables as she gracefully extended her hand to Cade.

"Not to my knowledge." Cade nodded, his expression guarded.

Emma was surprised and uneasy. Everything would have been much easier had Cade been, like everyone else, bowled over by her mother's charm and beauty.

With a languid movement of her arm, the elbow-length sleeve of her dress floating gently, Becca sketched an invitation for Cade to sit down on a white, wrought-iron bench. "Emma, darlin', did your daddy come home with you?"

"No, Mama." Emma heard the rasp of denim as Cade crossed one booted foot over his knee.

Becca looked around. "I'll have to ask Lucy. Perhaps he came home earlier?" Becca looked worriedly at Emma.

"No, Mama. I'm sure he didn't." Emma couldn't look at Cade, but she saw his foot go still. Like a touch, she could feel the absolute focus of his attention on her.

"He must be seeing a client late, then." Her mother settled against the cushions of the chaise longue. "Mr. Boudreau, I hope you'll stay for dinner. I'm sure Emma's daddy would want to meet you."

Cade's drawl was as smooth as her mother's. "Yes, ma'am, I reckon I'll still be around at dinnertime. Thanks for the invitation." He leaned slightly in Becca's direction. "I'd like to meet Emma's father."

Emma pressed her fingers to her eyes. "Mama, Cade and I have some papers to go over before dinner. Why don't we let you rest, and we'll see you later?"

"Of course, darlin', but call your daddy at the office and ask him not to be too late, will you? So nice to meet you, Mr. Boudreau." Her mother sipped from the frosted glass that had been on the small table beside her. Her attention strayed to the bright yellow blossoms growing on a vine. "Emma, we have to get somebody out here to trim the vine before it takes over the whole wall in that part of the garden. Remind me to tell your daddy, will you?" She sipped again and carefully set the glass on the table and wiped her fingers on a paper napkin. "Everything's going so wild," she murmured regretfully to Cade. "I don't know what's happened. I used to have the *prettiest* garden." She closed her eyes and leaned her cheek against the cushion. "Y'all go on in. I'll just wait out here a little longer for Andrew."

"See you later, Mrs. O'Riley." Cade's shadow fell across Emma, and his hard palm spread against the small of her back.

The pressure of Cade's hand on her unsettled Emma, and she took a longer step. "We'll go up the back stairs."

"Whatever you say." His clipped tones told her he understood more than she wanted him to.

Leading him around the five-foot-tall clumps of Spanish bayonet lining the brick walkway, Emma pushed aside the spiny tips of the yucca, expecting Cade to drop behind her. Instead, he crowded close, using his longer arm to clear a way for both of them.

"This is a big yard."

"Mama likes to garden."

"Not recently." His voice was flat.

"Not for a while. She—she doesn't always feel up to gardening." She wouldn't let him criticize her mother. He didn't know anything about their family.

"Yeah, I noticed." Cade swatted aside the feathery leaves and lavender blossoms of a low-hanging jacaranda tree at the back door. "So you do it? What gets done, anyway?"

Emma wrapped her fingers around the doorknob, which jiggled loosely, and took a deep breath before replying. "Mr. Boudreau, we're here to figure out a solution to your problem, not to talk about my house, my mother or the state of my yard. It's not your concern, so back off. Please," she added as she opened the door and finally felt that warm hand drop away.

Cade raised both arms and jammed them against the door frame. "Fine, beauty, I'll do that. You keep your little secrets to yourself and we'll work on mine. But I've been last-named to death, and if you call me 'Mr. Boudreau' one more time, I swear by all that's holy, I'll start spitting nails." He loomed over her, a threat that had nothing to do with spitting nails implicit in the angle of his shoulders, the tension in his fingers on the doorjamb.

Cade's aggression jarred Emma to her heels. Cade was wound up and looking for an argument. He could have been expected to act like this after she'd called a halt to their kiss, but he hadn't. He'd been distant, but not hostile, all the way to her house, then he and Lucy had established a teasing camaraderie. Everything, in fact, had been going along terrifically. Until she'd gone out to the garden. His belligerence made no sense.

Emma beat a strategic retreat. "You're absolutely right, Mis—" She swallowed the last syllable. "*Cade.*"

"Right." He didn't move. If anything, he seemed to use up more of her space. "*Emma.*" His forearm slid down the warping wood of the doorway, stopped close to her shoulder. "Emma Rose." His voice was low. "Emma Rose who lives in her big old house with her mama and her mama's second cousin."

"Once-removed," Emma whispered, not knowing why.

His left arm, like his right, coasted to a halt near her other shoulder. Cade wasn't touching her, just standing in her doorway, looking at her, but he surrounded her.

"Your garden hasn't been hoed." His raspy voice curled around her like morning fog. "Or pruned or fertilized in years, Emma Rose." The muscles of his neck were tight cords, and the vein along his neck throbbed.

Emma stared past him at the tangled growth of trees, bushes and flowers in the yard and wondered if they were talking about the same thing. "I know." This was how she'd felt looking out her office window while the spring rain came steadily down.

"Green things need taking care of."

She nodded and saw the long red stamens of the bottlebrush shrub stir in the late-afternoon breeze.

"Who takes care of you, Emma Rose? Your mama who 'takes the afternoon air'? Your daddy who isn't here?" Cade's face was pulled tight with an emotion Emma couldn't read. "Where is your daddy, Emma Rose?"

"None of your business, Cade Boudreau." Emma shoved her hands into her pockets, rubbing and rubbing the shell's smoothness.

"Such a simple question, beauty, why not answer it?"

Cade didn't touch her, but Emma felt as though he'd run his palm up against the light hairs of her neck.

"Why do you want to know? It's not important."

"I think it is. It's such a harmless thing to tell a guest, isn't it, Emma, especially if it's unimportant? You should know, being a lawyer, the more people pretend that something's not important, the more it makes everybody else sure something's being covered up. And that that *something* is real important." His fingers gripped the doorjamb as he continued. "So where is your daddy, beauty?"

"It doesn't concern you!" Emma turned abruptly away, but Cade stopped her with hands on her shoulders, her back to him as she replied, "There's no mystery."

"No? Even though your mama keeps expecting him to walk through these broad doors any old minute now?" he jeered.

"I don't want to talk about this." Like a child, Emma closed her hands over her ears.

"All right." Cade gently pried her hands away. "Secrets are funny, though, Emma Rose." He turned her to face him. "Sooner or later, and you can count on it, they pop out, and at the damnedest time.'' He smiled that smile that wasn't a smile and closed the door behind them, shutting out the view of the wild garden.

He was much too close.

In a walk that was first cousin to a run, Emma flew through the kitchen, his words trailing after her.

Cade followed, his steps echoing the hurrying sound of hers.

Breathless, Emma halted at the bottom of the stairs that led from the back of the house to the upstairs bedrooms and porches. ''Leave me alone!'' She heard her desperation and couldn't do anything about it, not with Cade watching her with his too-knowing eyes.

He let his knuckles hover over her cheek, tracing its contours in air. ''Go on up and take a real bath, Emma.''

''Please, go away.'' Emma stilled the tremble of her mouth. She couldn't hold on much longer. Inside she was flying apart. She didn't want Cade Boudreau anywhere near her. Trying with all her strength not to plead, she said, ''We can work everything out at my office.''

''I don't think so.'' His face was expressionless. ''Not any longer, I'm afraid. I'll see you at supper—'' One eyebrow lifted. ''Excuse me, dinner.''

From his lounging pose against the washed-out, cream-and-green-striped wallpaper, Cade stared at her with something in the shifting gray of his eyes that sent Emma to her bedroom in a nonstop dead run up the old stairs.

His voice carried up the steep stairwell. ''That's a mighty lonely looking garden out there, Emma Rose.''

Shuddering, Emma leaned against her door and tried to block out Cade's softly taunting voice. She couldn't.

Even more impossible than she'd imagined to have him in her home. Cade watching her, watching her mother. Emma rubbed her eyes frantically, free for the moment from Cade's alert gaze. How was she going to stand it?

One shaking hand flat against her bedroom door, Emma locked it. The click was like a gunshot in the stillness of her room.

She heard Lucy calling Cade.

A few moments after, as the hot steam of the shower rose around Emma, the water gurgled down the drain taking with it the grit from her injured foot. She let memories, new and old, wash away with the sand. Emma didn't realize tears were sliding down her face until she turned off the water.

Later, while she sliced tomatoes and drizzled balsamic vinaigrette over the red circles on their bed of lettuce, Emma stayed as far away from Cade as she could. His quick hands deboned the chicken breasts in deft, sure movements, but his gaze followed her.

She rinsed her hands under the faucet, then bumped into him as he turned to hand the plate of chicken to her.

"Sorry," Emma muttered, pulling free and grabbing for the roll of paper towels across from him.

"Here." He handed her a square of paper.

"Thank you," she said stiffly.

Cade banged the plate on the counter and two plump chicken breasts fell off. "Relax, counselor. I'm not going to jump your bones or put you through the water torture until you confess. At least not here in the middle of beans and squash." He shoved a handful of yellow summer squash at her. "You're safe. Besides—" he gestured with his head "—Lucy hasn't let me out of her sight long enough to get into mischief. If you're worried I've been out talking with your mama, you can turn off your busy brain."

"I didn't—" Emma turned off the faucet while her brain whirled merrily away.

"Of course you did." He backed her against the sink. "You're so damned afraid of what your mama's going to say to me, or what I'm going to ask her, that you're jumping out of your skin."

"I'm not—" Emma's words were cut off again.

"Yeah, you are. But I don't really give a red-hot damn what's happened in this house. Sure, I admit to being curious, but your business is yours. Not mine. And my business is why I'm here. So throttle down. I can keep my hormones and curiosity under control." He plopped the chicken onto the plate and thrust it at her. "Here. Do whatever you want to with these. I'll chop squash."

He did. Under the flashing knife, the pile of squash fell like yellow coins through Cade's swiftly moving hands before Emma had sprinkled lemon and oregano over the chicken.

"Done. Now I'll go clean up." The knife clattered on the counter. "Don't worry, Emma Rose. I won't bedevil your mama even though I wonder why you're the one shouldering the burdens around here." He slid his finger down her bare shoulder to her wrist. "Such frail shoulders for the weight—" he glanced around the huge kitchen and out the window at the garden "—of all this."

Emma's arm tingled for a long time after Cade disappeared.

"Hey, sugar." Lucy swung open the door from the dining room with her hip and poked her head around. "You and tall, dark and mysterious cooking up anything interesting out here? Y'all doing all right?"

"Fine," Emma said through clenched teeth as she slammed the oven door. "The chicken'll be ready in forty-five minutes."

"Hey, sugar, you getting tired of the teasin'?" Lucy cocked her head. Her cheek rested on the edge of the door as she examined Emma.

"If you want the unvarnished truth, Lucy, I am." Emma sank down in the kitchen chair and put her head down. She wished she could lay her head on Lucy's shoulder and bawl. She couldn't do that to Lucy, though. She never had. There were things she'd never told Lucy, and it was too late to dig up buried skeletons now.

"There's more than business going on between you and Cade Boudreau, Emma. I'm not blind, and that man's carrying around more charge in his little finger than most men carry in their jeans. If you want me to think that you can be around that man and think about nothing but business, well, more power to you, sugar, but don't expect me to believe you." She chuckled.

Emma's voice wobbled up and down the register. "Lucy, I'm helping him with a custody case. It's complicated. Cut the teasing, okay?"

"Shoot, you know I don't mean anything. God just gave me a big mouth and not enough sense to know when to shut it."

Emma managed a smile. "Don't worry. You know I love you in spite of that big old mouth. I'm just tired and I'm taking everything too seriously."

"Nothing new there. You always were a solemn little owl trailing around with all those books clutched in your arms. Got to learn not to take life so earnestly, sugar. It's kinda like a play. Somethin' new's forever waiting in the wings. Keeps you on your toes."

Emma laughed. If Lucy only knew! "That's the secret, is it? Looking at life like an adventure?"

"Unvarnished truth again?" Lucy's cheerful round face was surprisingly pensive. "Sugar, I learned a long time ago that pretending to be happy had more going for it than wallowing in misery did."

"So you go around pretending to be happy all the time?"

"Let's put it this way. I choose to be happy. Ignore the bad times and keep busy. Keep 'em laughing and don't let anybody see you cry. Works for me."

"You don't ever let anybody see you when you're sad, do you? I never noticed. Didn't you think we'd care, Lucy?" Sadness swept Emma at the thought that Lucy, dear and special, saw her role in life as the clown who had to entertain everybody.

"Emma, life's hard even for beautiful women like your mama. For someone like me who came into this world poor and with no prospects except working my rear end off, life doesn't offer many choices. Nobody's got the time of day for a plain country girl. I learned early that honey catches more flies than vinegar—'course I wondered what was so great about catching flies—but anyway, everybody loves a kidder, and every king needs a court jester."

"I'm all for cheerfulness, Lucy, but pretending the way you're talking about strikes me as living a lie." Emma traced the line of wood grain in the kitchen table. Who was she to judge Lucy's choices? Lucy wasn't the only one pretending.

Lucy's light blue eyes were shrewd. "Maybe so, sugar, but that's how I get through. Not taking anything too seriously. Each day I wake up bright-eyed and bushy-tailed, wondering what's going to walk through that old door out there." She wiggled her shoulders at the front hall. "And today has been a blue-ribbon day, what with Mr. Cade Boudreau sauntering in here." Her grin folded her face into its familiar lines. "Lord, that man moves like a well-oiled piston."

Emma wrinkled her nose, not wanting to think or talk about the way Cade moved. "I don't get it, Lucy. For someone who sees life like a cereal box with a prize stuck in it, why did you stay here with Mama and me? And Daddy. Why didn't you leave? Go off somewhere exciting? You were my age, right? Twenty-eight when you came to live with us? You could have done anything." The table was smooth under Emma's fingers, worn satiny by decades of O'Rileys who'd gathered around it.

For several sweeps of the clock hand around the white clock hanging over the sink, Lucy didn't answer. When she did, her words had Keep Out signs hanging all over them. "Honey, I was thirty-five, not twenty-eight, my husband had died, and Becca and Andrew said they needed me here."

"But I don't understand why you stayed all these years."

"There were reasons enough."

"You were still too young to sacrifice your life like that."

"I did what I wanted."

"Really?"

"Yes." Lucy's answer was uncharacteristically curt.

Emma was silent. The gas oven hissed as the temperature gauge adjusted the heat. She'd never guessed what lay behind Lucy's cheerful face. One more person wearing a mask. What had it cost Lucy to play the role of clown? Whatever it was, the price would have been high. "Didn't you ever—"

Lucy broke in. "Since this chitchat has gotten way too serious for someone of my shallow nature, color me gone." She winked and spanked the swinging door shut with her rear end as she left.

Slumping in her chair, Emma chewed the edge of her thumb. Even Lucy, who seemed so straightforward, wasn't what she seemed. How could you ever trust anyone? How could you be sure of your intuition and judgment? Her intuition had made her believe Cade, but could she be sure she wasn't making a mistake about him? She'd hovered on the edge of the precipice once with him. And wanted to leap into the void.

Maybe it hadn't been her intuition guiding her.

She dropped her head into her hands.

Cade's footsteps announced him. Emma raised her head warily. His hair was wet and black, shiny and smooth as onyx. A different pair of jeans, equally old and faded, flowed over his well-defined thighs and cupped his buttocks. Lucy was right. He did move like well-oiled machinery, solid and powerful. X-rated, Emma thought, as she watched his thighs bunch and flex with each stride.

Emma looked away from the sight of Cade cleaned up and slicked down, looked away from his gray eyes staring at her as if he could see right down to her soul.

When Emma lowered her eyes, her face going pink, Cade clamped down on the surge of aggression that made him want to take Emma's pointed chin and make her look at him until—until what? He squelched that thought, too.

"No dinner bell, Emma Rose?" He laced sarcasm into his question.

"Quit badgering me." Her chin came up.

"Can't afford to." Cade knew the truth of that statement. Dragging a chair to him with his booted toe, he straddled it, folding his arms over the back. He drummed a rhythm on the sides with his thumbs. "Did your mama or Lucy give you the third degree about coming home earlier than they expected?"

"No." Giving him an irritated glance, she stood up.

Cade nodded. "I didn't think they would."

"They don't stay up with the porch light on. They have no reason to worry about me."

He'd figured Emma was odd man out in this family. Sure, they loved her, he guessed, but, like the garden, nobody paid attention to her. The lawyer lady thought she was so tough, but she was vulnerable and sassy, and she'd been left to fend for herself for much of her life as far as he could tell.

"Do your own thing, do you? Stay out all night long if you want to, huh?" Cade knew what the tightening in his muscles meant, he just didn't know why the idea of Emma staying out all night with some yuppie lawyer should make him feel like putting a fist through the wall.

"I live my own life. I'm grown up." She was letting him know she understood what he was getting at.

"Sure you are. Grew real well, too, until—" Cade looked her small shape up and down leisurely "—what—fifth grade?"

She rolled her eyes, but a tiny smile tugged her lips. "Sixth. I was always the tallest kid in my class until then, so I'm still used to thinking of myself as tall, you see." Her smile moved into her eyes. "It doesn't make sense to anyone but me."

"Not a bit, counselor." Cade watched her dress float around her. She looked like sherbet in her peach and green dress. The late-afternoon sun was shining through the light material every time she moved. He wasn't noble enough to look away from the slender shadow of her thighs, from the darker shadow where they joined. Cade tightened his hands around the slats of the chair.

Bending over, Emma opened the oven door. Her skirt swung forward. The backs of her knees were pale dimples, infinitely fragile. Cade drew a deep breath. Oregano wafted toward him.

Thankful for an excuse to move, he unwound from the chair and adjusted jeans that had suddenly shrunk. "I'll take that." He wrapped a dish towel around his hand and lifted the heavy metal roaster with the bubbling chicken.

He'd said he could control his hormones. He still thought he could. It was his sneaky desire to protect her that kept blindsiding him. He'd been okay until she looked at him when they opened the front door. She'd looked the same out on the dock when he'd told her to jump and he could see she couldn't but was damned if she'd admit it or ask for help. She'd straightened her shoulders then, too, with that same stubborn will and that same look of appeal in her eyes.

Cade settled the roaster on the counter. He was in trouble. What he sure as hell ought to do was hightail it out of Emma Rose's house, head out to the bayous and find the first woman who got his juices stirring. The fact that that plan held absolutely no appeal whatever really hacked him off. His palm slipped onto the roaster. "Damn it to hell!" He sucked the reddening skin.

Jerking open the freezer door, Emma grabbed an ice cube and reached for his hand. Just what he needed. Emma Rose up close and worried about him.

"I thought it was once burned, twice shy?" She smiled. "Better be careful."

Her just-washed hair tickled his nose. All around him rose the clean sweet smell of Emma's skin. What he wanted to do more than anything else in the world at that moment was grab her around her small hips and slide his hands up under that peach and green dress and see if she was as soft all over as she looked. Slide his hands right up to that shadowy juncture that had appeared and disappeared through the peach and green dress with her movements in and out of the sun, pull her up on top of him and take her, take her right there in her kitchen filled with the scent of oregano and her.

"Give me the damned ice and let's have our damned supper and get business over with. Okay?" He growled. There was no other word for the harsh sound rising out of him, shocking him.

Not even in his wildest nights of sweat-soaked sex had that sound ever slipped out of him, but he recognized the ancient blood-deep sound.

He'd put his stud to a mare once and, as the stallion covered the thrashing mare, he'd heard the same primitive note in the wild whinnying trumpeting to the skies, and he'd gone away aroused and hurting.

"Cade? What's wrong?"

"Nothing, damn it." Every blood cell in his body was making its urgent way to the one part of his body that had seized control of him.

"Let me get another ice cube."

"I'm fine. Let me handle it, will you?"

"Certainly." Emma walked over to a cabinet and reached for a large platter.

Her soft lips were pursed in annoyance. He wanted to move his thumb across them, smooth them. As she stretched, peach and green fabric followed the uplift of her arms, her breasts.

Cade grabbed another ice cube and turned his back to Emma. Pressing against the counter, he stayed there, rubbing the melting ice over his palm until the haze left his eyes. He wiped his damp hands on his shirt and hoped Emma didn't notice their tremor.

Too close.

He'd forgotten where they were, what he had to do, forgotten everything in the heat that had kicked him faster than desire had ever roweled him with sharp spurs.

Forgotten everything except Emma Rose in her sherbet-colored dress.

Chapter 6

Cade watched Emma all during dinner. The candles in the branched Waterford candelabra cast illusory light over their faces. Moving in and out of the flickering candlelight, Emma's pale face wavered before him, while her mother's face grew even more beautiful in the kind light. The candles reflected in the older woman's green eyes, and the light turned them into jewels gleaming in the warm evening.

Lucy worked diligently to make them laugh, but amusement had fled from Cade during that moment in the kitchen with Emma. He'd been shaken to the core. It had scared the hell out of him, but he still couldn't keep from watching her as she faded into the wallpaper.

Becca's voice became more agitated as they ate. "Lucy, are you sure Andrew didn't call?"

"Don't worry, I'm sure everything's fine." Calm and matter-of-fact, Lucy cut up her chicken. "Have some squash, Becca. Emma and Mr. Boudreau could open a restaurant."

"I don't want anything to eat, Lucy! *Why* hasn't Andrew come home? His dinner's going to be ice cold!" Becca rose suddenly. "Emma, did he call you?"

Emma's fork clattered to her plate. Even in the wavering light, Cade saw her face stiffen. "No, Mama. Please, sit down and finish dinner. Daddy would want you to."

Cade leaned forward. Emma was upset.

Becca smiled at Cade. "It's just that I wanted him to meet you, Mr. Boudreau."

"Don't worry, Mrs. O'Riley. There'll be time," he reassured her, knowing he did so only to erase the miserable look from Emma's small face. Wanting to change the subject, since it disturbed Emma, he looked outside to the dark garden. "Since Emma's helping me with my case, I wonder if you'd let me repay you in a small way, Mrs. O'Riley? You mentioned some yard work?" Cade leaned toward Emma's mother. "I could clip and mulch, do a little digging if you like."

"Why, how kind of you to offer." Becca sat down and sipped her iced tea. She touched her mouth with her napkin. Her green eyes sparkled.

Charm must have been bred in her bones along with the breathtaking beauty, Cade decided.

"Not kind at all," he said. "What do you think, Emma?" At last he turned directly to her. "About me raking and hoeing for your mother?"

She leaned back from the table into the shadows. "If you want to. That would be fine." Her voice was so wooden he scarcely recognized it.

Despite everything he'd put her through, she'd never been spiritless. Cade wanted to take her narrow shoulders and shake some life into her, infuriate her until color came surging to her face and she came spitting and clawing at him. Not that he could quite picture Emma Rose spitting and clawing. He didn't care what was going on with Lucy and Becca, but he didn't like the way Emma was fading into the shadows, as if she'd vanish if he blinked.

"But maybe you'll be needing me around all the time?" Cade needled, goaded by her apathetic expression. "Who knows what might come up?" Lifting his glass to his mouth, he challenged her.

"Do whatever you want. I don't care." Even her spine was drooping.

"Really? I reckon I'll just hang around you, then, while you're working. I don't want you to have to come looking for me. Wouldn't want to cause you any extra work," he drawled, leaning back in his chair and stretching his legs. "Don't you agree, Lucy? We should make Emma's work easier?"

"Sure. Speaking for myself, I'd find it mighty hard to concentrate with you in the same room, Cade Boudreau." Lucy came close to fluttering her eyelashes. "You'd be a dangerous man to have around."

Cade laughed and raised his hands in surrender. "Not me, Lucy! Just plunk me in any old corner and forget me. I can keep quiet."

"Not likely! You'd not be a man to forget even if all you did was breathe."

Emma's chair scraped loudly on the wood floor as she stood up. "Mama, Lucy, if you'll both excuse me, Cade and I need to get started. It's late."

Swinging forward, the bell of Emma's hair hid her from his eyes as she gathered plates and cutlery. Slowly Cade stood up. Well, he'd gotten a reaction from her. He just couldn't figure out what it was.

"Of course, darlin'." Becca turned anxiously to Lucy. "You'll let me know when Andrew comes in, won't you?"

Cade wondered why Lucy glanced quickly at him before nodding.

If he hadn't promised Emma that he'd mind his own business, he'd like to get Miss Lucy alone for ten minutes of conversation. He was mighty curious about what was going on behind the curtain of Emma Rose's smooth brown hair.

Brushing crumbs and blowing out candles, she looked everywhere but at him. As she cupped the flame, her little cat face shone momentarily, sad and lonely, then she pursed her lips and disappeared into darkness.

"Down this hall." Flipping on a light switch, she motioned to a passageway leading off the dining room. In a strained voice, she said, "Lucy, I'll get the dishes later. Don't worry about them. You and mama go on ahead, all right?"

"Sure, sugar, y'all get started." Lucy measured Cade with twinkling eyes, but it was the shrewdness peeking out that charmed him. "Mr. Boudreau, I, for one, would be real grateful for any paths you cut through that overgrown jungle. Emma, what about you?"

"Yes, of course. I thought I made that clear." Emma stumbled over her words. He still couldn't see her face.

"It's settled then." Cade wanted to hustle Emma out of the suffocating atmosphere of the room. He urged her to the passageway with his hand on her neck, not caring what anyone thought.

She quivered when he spread his fingers.

Cade kept his hand there and waited for her to look at him, or tell him to turn her loose, or swat his hand off. Something. Anything. Just not this withdrawn shell cool under his palm. He wanted Emma back.

Once, just enough to move the floating ends of her hair, he jiggled her neck.

She swatted his hand off and sent him a vexed look as she walked down the hall. Drawing a deep breath, Cade followed her past the open door of a large room where floor-to-ceiling bookshelves interspersed with tall windows draped in heavy maroon material.

"Not in here?" He touched her shoulder. The sherbet dress was cool, like her skin.

"That's Daddy's office." She kept walking.

Cade noticed the pipe caddy and a pipe in an empty, thick ashtray. Stacks of law books filled the floor around an enormous dark green leather chair. An open newspaper tented the Oriental rug next to a couch.

He must have been wrong. He'd decided the mysterious Andrew didn't live here anymore, but the room looked as though he'd recently left it.

"Nice."

Emma ignored him until they reached a small octagonal room that had probably been a sun porch but was now enclosed with jalousies and wallpapered in yellow and white. "In here."

"Can we cut to the bottom line, counselor? I can ignore that interesting dinner if you can." He stepped one foot closer to her and watched with more satisfaction than he should the flow of pink up her neck.

"I can certainly concentrate with you in the corner, and I'm sorry you didn't care for dinner." Politely snippy.

His Emma was back.

His? Cade frowned. Retreating, he slicked both hands over his hair. "Great. So what happens now? What do you still need to know?" He strode to the far side of the room and looked out. The gleam of the river caught his eye where the yard ended. Place had to be worth a small fortune. He touched the opaque glass of a jalousie. He should leave. While he could.

"Sit down."

"I think better walking around." Energy was surging through him with no outlet. Why had he thought of her as *his?*

"Please, I—I'd rather you sat down while we talk."

He circled the teak desk where she'd settled. "Am I making you nervous?"

She pulled out a deep file drawer of the desk, blocking him. "Not at all." She flipped through folders until she stopped at one.

Reading it upside down, Cade saw his name. "I would have thought you'd have to keep all your official records in your office."

"These are my personal notes. I keep a trial notebook from the day I first learn about a case to the day the offender is convicted or released. I like to record my observations as they occur. Impressions blur as a case drags on and goes to trial."

Black type on a white label, his name on a folder in Emma Rose's huge house. Bureaucratic, official, reminding him of all he'd lost. Yet it hadn't been black and white. Nothing had been clear-cut, maybe for Emma, but not for him. "What was your first impression of my case? No," he said and took her hands with his, closing the folder, "not from notes. From memory. What did you think? Tell me." He shoved the drawer shut with the heel of his boot.

"You don't want to know." Her fingers moved under his.

"I want to know."

Her eyes dimmed. "When I first looked at the pictures, I thought you had to be a monster."

"You don't pull your punches."

"You asked." She tried to withdraw her hands.

Cade tightened his hands around hers, locking her gaze on him. "And?"

"And I wanted to put you away for as long as I could." She met his gaze uncompromisingly.

"What did you think when you first saw me? Did I look like a monster?"

"Monsters wear masks." She looked away. "But, no, I didn't see the mark of a monster on your face."

"What do you see now?" He had to make sure that she saw him in the present, not with the eyes of the past. Before she went through her notes, she had to remember whatever had convinced her on the island.

She tugged against his hands. "Does it matter so much?"

Cade hunched on the edge of the desk. "It matters to me."

She stilled. Her hair caught the light and fringed around her chin. If he brushed it back, his fingers would slip through its squeaky-clean strands. He pressed his hands on the sharp edges of the desk. Exhaustion and stress had made shadows under her eyes. She was going to fall in a heap at his feet if he didn't shut up and let her do whatever she needed to and get to bed.

"Tell me."

"I see a man who's at the end of his rope."

"What else?"

Her sigh was a light sound that broke the silence. "A man who loves his son. A man who's on the outside looking in."

Cade looked away. She inserted one finger slowly between the covers of the thick manila file. As her finger slid down, opening the folder to reveal the crisp white pages with her tiny, cramped handwriting, he reached over to shut it again. The past lay cradled in her hands, and now, when push came to shove, he wasn't sure he wanted to face the ugliness and questions again. He'd survived by remembering and hating and wanting revenge. He'd nursed on the bitter acid of hatred for three years.

Give up that bitterness and face the past? Like being naked on the main street at high noon.

She turned the first page. Cade stood up and surrendered to his ghosts. They were all around him—his younger self, working and coming home only to crash into bed, the woman waiting irritably for him and the son he'd taken everywhere. He'd sowed the ground, but he still didn't know what had happened.

While Emma read silently, methodically turning pages, Cade paced the room, unable to sit still. He picked up the inch-tall brass monkey on her desk, flicked the weight scales clutched in its paw, put it down, picked it up again. He didn't disturb Emma's concentration.

She ruffled her hair up the slim column of her neck, ran her fingers through it. Sighed. Sighed again and pretzeled in her chair. Where her hair parted, a line of tiny, fine hairs dusted her silky skin.

She looked at one paper a long time, eventually leaning back in her chair and propping her legs on the desk, her ankles crossed.

In the dimpled glass of the jalousies in front of him, Cade saw the shimmering reflection of thighs and the edge of her pale peach panties. Emma Rose liked pretty underwear. He liked Emma Rose's pretty peach underwear himself.

He rubbed his forehead on the glass.

"All right." She slapped the folder against the desk.

"What did you find?" Cade felt like the monkey balancing the scales as he waited for her answer.

"Nothing." She tapped her pen against her teeth. "All of my notes support everything I acted on. I don't see anything that doesn't fit. I—"

"What? You've changed your mind now?" Cade doubled his fists on the desk and leaned over her. "You can't. You said you believe me."

Emma waved her pen at him. "Stop pushing me. I'll tell you frankly that anyone reading my notes would find no problem convicting you."

"But Francine lied." Cade fought the nightmare lurking in his mind.

"According to you. Nevertheless, something happened to her. Even in my notes, I've jotted down my reactions to her injuries. They were typical of spousal assault. Injuries to her face.'' Emma looked down as though she couldn't look him in the eyes. ''She had a broken nose. Injuries to her ribs—'' She carefully lined her pen up with the edge of the folder. ''Bruises on her breasts.''

Cade's breathing was harsh. He'd seen the pictures. He'd had feelings for Francine in spite of everything. Now Emma's words brought back the rage that had churned his stomach as he'd looked at the vividly colored photos of Francine's injuries.

''I don't know what happened.'' Cade spaced the words out through clenched teeth.

''Something did. The neighbor who came in saw you with the baseball bat in your hand, standing over her.''

''That was how I found her! I picked up Quint's bat because he'd left it on the stairs!'' Cade still remembered the shock.

Emma continued as though he hadn't spoken. ''If, however, you weren't responsible for—''

Cade slammed his open hands flat on the desk. The brass monkey bounced and fell over. Emma didn't move. ''I would never, never have done that to her. Beat up a woman? She was my wife, the mother of my son!''

''That doesn't stop a lot of men.'' Emma's voice carried no expression. ''Some doctors and hospital workers don't even react to injuries like hers, even though these are so typical they could've come straight out of a textbook on spouse battery.''

''What are you saying? There's nothing I can do? Nothing you can do?'' Cade gripped the desk hard. It was happening all over again.

''No, I'm not saying that. One person knows for sure what happened.''

A nightmare. He was never going to see Quint again.

''Francine,'' she continued. Rubbing her hands over the folder, Emma went on in that same dispassionate voice. ''And I won't hound her.''

''Is that how you see it? Hounding her?''

''I do. If she lied—''

Cade took her chin in his hand, making her look at him. ''Why do you keep saying *if, if?*''

She tried to twist away, but he wouldn't let her. Either she believed him or she didn't. He couldn't understand the way she was talking about the case.

"Why? Because something certainly happened to that woman!" Emma jerked to her feet. "And even if she lied, someone broke her nose and ribs! Someone beat her around the face and breasts! Maybe she lied to protect herself. I don't know! But I'll tell you as clearly as I know how that I don't want her hurt again. *I* won't be the catalyst that causes her more pain."

"That's it? You're backing off?"

"I already told you I'm not, but I want you to understand that whatever I do, I will do very, very carefully, and that I don't see Francine as the enemy. If *you* see her that way, you and I can't work together. You'll be second-guessing everything I say and do. I can't function if you're analyzing my every move and breathing down my neck."

"Counselor, when I start breathing down your neck, believe me, it'll be for a whole different reason, and breathing's not all I'll be doing."

Emma's hand flew to the back of her neck and stayed there. Her eyes were suddenly very green. "Don't do this," she whispered. "You're not helping the situation."

"No, I'm not." He frowned. He had to stay as businesslike as Emma was, or he was going to start something he couldn't finish. Start something that would only end in disaster. He knew it.

"Stop, then." Her hand still hovered over her neck.

"I'm just so damned frustrated and hemmed in I want to beat my head against the wall." He knew why he was having trouble. Wanting Emma had taken over like a fever in his blood, spiking out of control and testing him. "I don't know what I think about Francine any more, but she's still Quint's mother, regardless of what happened. I'll stay out of your way. I'll let you work without interference."

"You have to, or we'll both be in trouble."

"Yeah." Cade knew she meant legal trouble, but there were several kinds of trouble they'd be neck deep in if he let what was in his jeans overpower his good sense. "Just tell me what you plan in advance, fair enough?"

Hesitating, Emma played with her pen. "It may seem fair, but I can't promise that. I'll tell you whatever I believe you need to know."

"Do you always keep such a tight bridle?"

The pen dangled between her fingers. "What do you mean?"

Cade plopped the pen down between them. "You like to control things."

"Of course." She nodded to the pen. "You don't?" She rolled the pen across the desk as she said thoughtfully, "It's the only way I can guarantee results I want."

"Well, counselor, I'll give you a little free advice. Most of what happens in life can't be controlled, but if you want to pretend it can be, go right ahead." He righted the monkey and jiggled its scales with a faint clinking of brass. "One day, you're going to look up from your books and something's going to be staring you in the face you're not ready for. You won't have your files and lists to help you. What'll you do then?"

"You think I don't know that?" Annoyance curled the edges of Emma's words.

She took the monkey out of his hand and placed it carefully in its spot at the corner of the desk blotter. The skim of her fingers against his was as light as air and as bone-deep unsettling as an earthquake. Cade stuffed his fists in his pockets. Safest place for them.

She turned the monkey a degree or two. "That's why I have to plan and make my lists. I don't want to be surprised. The better prepared I am, the less chance I'll be, as you say, staring something in the face. I don't handle surprises very well. I need to know what's around the corner before I turn it." Her smile was a little off center and she picked up the pen again, holding it at eye level, a barrier between them. "I'll act in your best interests as long as I don't harm your ex-wife or son."

Digging deep into his pocket, Cade pulled out a dollar bill. He smoothed it and anchored it under the monkey. "You're my lawyer now. For the time being, that's a retainer."

Sliding the bill out, Emma folded it in half, creasing and recreasing it before doubling it again. She laid it on one of the brass circles of the scale. The disk pinged as it dropped to the desk. For a moment Emma sat there, her head bowed. Finally she lifted her head, tucked the strands of hair behind her ears and, looking straight at him, pulled down the empty disk until she'd balanced the two circles. "Justice, then."

She laid the dollar on top of the papers in the file folder before closing it. "First, I'll call Francine's lawyer, see if he'll get permission for me to talk with her, maybe clear it with her, not likely but possible, for you to see Quint under my supervision. That's first on the *list* for tomorrow."

"And if Francine won't agree to any of this?"

"I'll be surprised if she does, but who's to say?" Emma took off her glasses and hunched her shoulders before she dropped her head wearily against the back of the chair.

Cade told himself it wasn't really borrowing trouble as he rubbed his knuckle against the bridge of her nose where her eyebrows had drawn together. "I know, trust my lawyer and shut up."

"I couldn't have said it better myself, especially the last part." A tired grin curved her mouth. Her eyelids drooped. "Go to bed, Cade, we'll straighten out anything else tomorrow."

"Whatever you want, counselor," Cade said, stroking the silk of her eyebrows as he pressed his knuckle gently against the knot of pain between her eyes. "See you in the morning." He turned and walked away from the small figure curled up in the leather chair. He wanted to stay, to stroke her forehead smooth of pain. He knew he had to leave.

Walking down the hall, hearing the low murmurs of Lucy and Becca, Cade wondered how many more times he could make himself walk away from Emma. His body clamored with wanting her. Carefully, very carefully, he straightened a photograph hanging on the wall.

The man in the photo had Emma's eyes, but his roguish grin was all his own. In shorts and with his shirt tied around his waist, he stood bent-kneed at the front of a sailboat whose sail filled with wind and shone against the sunrise. Even in the fading tints of the twenty-some-years-old picture, Cade sensed the power and charm behind the grin of the man smiling straight at the camera.

In gold and blue, the name of the boat swept across the side. *Beautiful Becca's.* Cade looked more closely at the picture. In the lower corner, just barely there, a small girl looked at the golden man, her little cat face sun-struck, blazing with love.

Cade sucked in air. As he looked at the expression on the child's face, a lump grew in his throat.

Emma Rose.

And her mysteriously absent father.

Who held the camera steady on the man, not noticing the child tucked in the corner? In a way he couldn't put into words, Cade knew it was a passionate, sexual picture taken by someone absorbed completely by that lazy smile.

A disturbing picture.

He didn't like it.

Making sure Lucy and Becca didn't hear him, he walked to his room. He had no desire to talk to either of them at that moment.

For a long time, Cade lay stretched out in his jeans and shirt on the large bed in the large room of Emma's very large house and thought about the picture.

He couldn't sleep.

Prison hovered in the faraway corners of the room and floated in his mind between quick cuts of the picture of Emma and her father.

Sighing, Cade surrendered to wakefulness and picked up his boots. Big as it was, the bedroom closed around him. He couldn't stay inside.

Slipping down the back stairs, he eased open the kitchen door and walked around to the garden. Gulping in air, he calmed the panic chewing at him. He hadn't expected prison panic to stay with him. Even his shirt choked him. Jerking it out of the waist of his jeans, he couldn't unbutton it fast enough and furiously ripped it over his head and off.

Squatting, Cade placed his palms flat on the ground. The earth was damp and real, not concrete. Only night sounds filled his ears, not the grunting of men in prison. He stayed there letting the earth and its life fill him with peace. He might have stayed there all night, but a flutter of white captured his attention.

Rising silently and staying in shadows, he moved to the far corner of the garden.

He shouldn't have been surprised.

Invisible from the house, Emma sat hunched on the brick wall in the wild clusters of flowers and vines. Her legs were drawn up and her folded arms pillowed her head. Bare toes peeked from under the edge of her white nightgown.

He almost picked one of the flowers to hand to her. If he'd been a different kind of man, more like the men she'd grown up knowing, he would have.

Instead, he stripped a handful of blossoms and pitched them at her. "Can't sleep either, beauty?"

Petals showered around her and clung to the tendrils of her hair, her shoulders, her cobwebby gown. "No." Unsmiling, she remained hunched up.

She'd huddled in that same defensive posture on the island.

"Bad dreams?" Cade neared her, a handful of creamy white gardenia petals perfuming his fingers with their heavy scent. His touch would turn the thick petals brown.

"No," she repeated, looking toward the house.

Cade heard the distant music throbbing in the darkness. One rose petal lay in an upturned curl of hair near Emma's ear. He brushed it away and its fragile scent came lightly to him. She sat stone still, a statue in someone's fantasy, her nightgown falling in graceful folds around her covered knees, blossoms scattered around her, their color night-bleached wax. Their flower scents eddied around him like morning mist. "What's out here in your fairy-tale garden, beauty? Magic?"

Emma murmured something Cade couldn't hear. He looked where her gaze was fixed. Through the opened windows of her father's office, the sweet, piercing notes of a violin came to her, tender and melancholy.

Behind the drapes, shadows moved. Emma's father must have come home after all.

As Cade watched, he saw that Becca dipped and swayed to the strains of the waltz in a solitary dance, her arms upraised to an invisible partner.

Puzzled, Cade looked again at Emma. Her cheeks were
damp where tears slid in a steady, silent flow. "Aw, beauty,
don't cry," he muttered, opening his hand and cupping her
thin, cool neck. Gardenia petals fluttered around her, down the
childlike square neck of her nightgown. He wiped her cheeks
with the tail of his shirt. "Please, don't cry. If there's one thing
I can't stand, it's that. Goes right through me like nails. Don't
do this to yourself."

"I'm not crying," she said while sticky tears dripped around
his shirt onto his hand.

Cade sighed. "Of course you're not. Reckon I was wrong.
Must be the River Jordan overflowing, huh?"

Quint had cried once in great, belly-booming sobs, swearing
all the time that he wasn't, rubbing his eyes with grubby fists
and trying his absolute eight-year-old damnedest to be brave.

It was the last time he'd seen his son.

"Aw, Emma Rose, come on, it can't be this bad," Cade
murmured, smoothing away the unending trickle of tears,
helpless in the face of her silent, wide-eyed weeping. "Can it?"

"No." Her voice was clogged with tears.

The violins stopped.

In the lighted window, Lucy held the raised arm of the
turntable. Becca circled once more. Her dress swung and settled around her long legs. Looking around, she asked Lucy
something Cade couldn't hear. Lucy shook her head, and Becca
walked out of the room, her fingers trailing across the desk.

Behind her, Lucy straightened scattered papers. Stooping,
she picked up the newspaper lying on the floor then left, turning off the light.

Emma looked at him with tears seeping from the corners of
her hazel eyes. Cade could see the face of the child in the photo.
Over the ghostly woman's face floated the child's joyful, love-
filled smile.

"Tell me what's wrong, Emma Rose. I'll fix it. Unless it's
one of those woman times, and you just want a good cry,"
Cade teased, running his palm up and down her neck. He
hoped she'd smile, at least. When she didn't, he knew whatever was wrong wasn't fixable. One tear hung at the corner of

her tucked-in mouth. He blotted the small spot with the back of his hand.

His touch must have been the last straw for her. Her shoulders collapsed, and soundless sobs shook her while his hand grew wet with her tears.

Her silent weeping unnerved him. Only the shaking of her shoulders betrayed her.

"Hey, c'mere," Cade said, wrapping her in his arms, thinking only to comfort the child he saw, forgetting for the moment the woman he was taking close to his bare chest, forgetting all the reasons he had for staying away from the woman who'd filled his sleepless nights. "Easy does it," he said, smoothing her wet face. "Shh, everything'll be fine. Don't cry anymore, okay?" Where had the child in the picture gone?

Emma rubbed her face against his wadded-up shirt, against his chest, and Cade remembered too late that he wasn't comforting a child huddled lost and forlorn in a nighttime garden filled with the incense of gardenias and roses.

He shuddered.

His arm clamped around her waist.

She nuzzled closer, and her warm tears slipped down his belly. Clutching him like a lifesaver, her doubled-up fists suddenly met in the small of his back.

"Emma," Cade said, reaching around to loosen her grip, "you have to tell me what's wrong." He'd meant only comfort.

Her wet cheeks brushed his belly.

His groin filled, heavy, and it happened so fast he wasn't prepared. He'd thought he was in control, that he could stay away from her, but urgency was sweeping in a tidal rush, hurting and hard and hammering his blood through him in a painful aching, and he couldn't, not this time, stay away from Emma Rose.

Not with pleasure cramping his tight muscles seeking release, not with this rushing turbulence shutting down his brain, no, not this time.

Taking her hips, he pulled her hard to him, rubbing his open hands over the curves of her back, letting his hands slide between her and the brick wall. Her bottom was supple and soft, and Emma Rose wasn't wearing any of her pretty underwear this time. His fingers clenched on her hips.

"Cade," she murmured incoherently, rubbing her face back and forth against him. Her hot tears tracked down to the heart of him, burning fire all the way down his belly. "Cade," she repeated, her voice a sweet chime on his throat.

Hearing his name spoken in her tear-thick voice broke his last thread of control. Her clear voice told him she knew him, knew it was Cade's last thread of control. Her clear voice told him she knew him, knew it was Cade Boudreau touching her, wanting her, no one else, Cade Boudreau.

He couldn't get her close enough.

Wanting her too much to go slow, he slid his hands over her legs, under the nightgown to the soft backs of her thighs, shoving back the thin cotton impatiently in his urgency to touch her bare skin, and all the time her fists held him to her.

He curled his arm around her smooth back and over her shoulder. With his other hand spread flat over her abdomen, he absorbed the tremors rippling over her, through him.

Her arms were locked around his waist, and he chinned the light material of her neckline off one shoulder, but it hung, fastened by shiny buttons. Her stomach was rippling silk against him. Cade could no more have turned her loose than he could have flown to the moon. Hampered by the constriction of her square neckline, Cade used his teeth to winkle out the eight tiny buttons.

Her gown parted and slid under her breasts. Her arms, still clasped around him, were trapped by the thin fabric.

Framed by the material, her small, moth-pale breasts fluttered in the darkness.

Cade groaned and bent to brush one tip with his tongue and felt it harden under his touch.

Blood slammed straight down. He hadn't known he could hurt so much, so long.

Like a train ramming into a mountain at full speed, pleasure hurtled him forward. "Emma Rose, you're so soft," he said, stroking up, down, wanting to touch everywhere at once, moving his hands and mouth against her.

Distantly, through the blood pounding in his head, Cade heard her say something.

"So pretty." He traced the blue veins beating in her breast with his tongue, tasting her. Under his mouth, her heart raced in echoing thunder.

Emma's knee raised, brushed against his ribs. Cade jerked. Frantically he lifted her, sliding his hands under her knees and lifting them so that he could pull her to him, closer, skin on bare skin, and still not close enough to ease the hurting in him even with her legs like a silk chain around his naked waist.

Green and primitive, the wildness of the garden was in him.

Whirling with her slight weight on his arms, he leaned against the gritty brick wall and tried to find a way to tear loose the snap of his jeans without letting go of Emma. Her arms had snaked around his neck when he turned, and her wet face was next to his as he tugged at his jeans.

With two fingers snugged between his waist and Emma's thigh, Cade popped the metal snap of his jeans. Cupping her to him, letting his hunger move unchecked through him, he took her mouth fiercely, his tongue surging and stabbing.

Wet and swollen, her soft mouth was slick and cool under the heat of his. He tasted the salt of her tears, which had never stopped their silent, unnerving slide.

Cade pulled his head back. Emma's face shone with her tears.

While his heart pounded so heavily he thought it would burst out of his chest, Cade held Emma to him as tightly as bone and muscle could grip. Taking a breath that shuddered through him, he said, "Emma Rose, I reckon this is the first time I've ever made love to someone who's there but not really." Gripping her face while her arms and legs clung to him, he said, "Where are you, Emma Rose? What makes you linger out here like a little ghost? I know it's none of my business, but I figure you're going to have to tell me about your father. You're out here because of him, aren't you?"

She nodded. Her hair grazed the underside of his chin, and Cade fought to ignore the sensations still racing from one end of him to the other, particularly the other. Passion had come off quick and fast.

"Where's your daddy, Emma Rose? Why doesn't he come home?" Cade waited with his forehead against Emma's bare, smooth breasts. "I can wait a long time. Why don't you tell me?" he coaxed. "Where's your daddy, Emma Rose?" he repeated patiently and moved his cheek to her throat.

Her convulsive swallow moved under his ear. In a child's high voice, Emma answered him, "In the cemetery, Mr. Boudreau. He won't be coming home."

Chapter 7

The sun shone in Emma's eyes Monday morning as she and Cade made their way to Francine's house. Sunglasses shaded Cade's expression as he drove in silence. His thumbs met in a triangle at the top of the steering wheel as he moved the car smoothly in and out of traffic. He appeared casual, but tension radiated from him.

He'd been just as quiet the day before. Sitting at the breakfast table with his hands folded under his chin, he'd watched Lucy and Becca closely. Emma had swallowed a few bites of the Sunday morning eggs, pancakes, sausages and grits Lucy had fixed. Lucy had said to Cade, "We all, especially Mr. Boudreau, sugar, need a hearty breakfast to start off the day." Emma tactfully refrained from telling Cade that their usual fare was toast and coffee.

Her emotions still raw from what had happened between them in the garden, she avoided Cade, and he stayed away from her like the plague. Emma felt as vulnerable as a butterfly with damp, folded wings creeping out of its cocoon. She bumped into Cade once on his way out to the yard where he spent most of Sunday hacking out kudzu and pruning bushes. He'd backed away so fast she was afraid he'd tip end over end, but he shot her a look that had seared the breath right out of her lungs.

She didn't want him watching her anymore.

That was why she'd let him drive the car today.

He saw too much. He reached that part of her she'd buried deep inside and wrenched it, shivering and naked, into the heat of his presence. Too much heat killed.

Emma had seen the Florida sun blast tiny green tomato shoots into threads in the space of hours. The farther away Cade stayed from her, the better.

She wanted to sew her mouth permanently shut every time she remembered telling Cade about her father. Family business was private. She should never have told him. He didn't need to know. She'd made a mistake. He'd keep watching, and eventually he'd corner her. He wouldn't be able to leave the missing pieces alone. He'd worry them like a dog with a bone until they fit.

Once he started digging around in the past, what would happen to that part of her that couldn't survive being dragged out into the killing sun?

"Emma, you weren't going to push me away, were you? You wouldn't have stopped me." Cade's scratchy voice shattered the silence.

Emma's leg twitched. He'd asked the last question she expected. She'd thought he'd start with questions about her father and mother. Smoothing her mint-green skirt around her, Emma forced herself to look at him.

His palm flattened her hand against her leg. "Would you?"

She would have thought he was bored except for the pressure of his hand on hers. "No." She slid her hand away, but he recaptured it, gripping it against his leg, holding it where his muscles bunched as he drove. "No, Cade, I wouldn't have stopped you." Emma watched the rows of strip malls blurring past.

"Very good, counselor. A straight answer from a lawyer." His voice was tight. "Now, just to satisfy my rude male ego and curiosity, would you mind telling me why not?" He pressed her hand hard against him. "Don't try to make me believe you were carried away by passion. I'd find that unbelievable, under the circumstances. Why were you going to let me take it all the way?''

Emma pulled her hand free and wound her fingers together. ''I don't know.'' How could she explain her passivity as she'd watched Becca? Numb, she'd wanted to feel alive. The sheer intensity of Cade's passion had burned through the deadness of her feelings.

''Into charity, counselor?'' His mouth was an angry slit. ''Don't do me any favors. I don't need charity.'' He snarled the last words.

''Would you have stopped?'' Emma returned.

''Hell, no. I'd have taken you so hard and fast in your sweet-smelling garden, Emma Rose, that it would have made your head swim. If I'd been betting, I don't think anything could have made me let you go. I don't think a gun at my head could have stopped me right then. Except you. I don't like dancing alone, beauty. When I'm making love, I want everybody at the party, not just me,'' he drawled.

''That's speaking frankly.'' Her cheeks went hot.

''Like they say, one's a lonely number.''

''Since we weren't making love, there's no problem, is there?'' Emma opened her purse and got out her sunglasses.

''Whatever you say.'' Ice clinked in his voice.

Wrapped up in the security of Cade's arms, she'd welcomed his hunger as it forced out the loneliness deep in her. How could she explain that to him when she didn't even understand it herself? ''I'm sorry if I led you on,'' she said formally. ''I'm not a tease.''

The tires thrummed on asphalt. They drove past the last of the strip malls and took the cut-off that carved through ranch land.

Cade's tension dissolved. ''Hell, Emma Rose, I know that.'' Cade tapped the steering wheel as he continued. ''I was the one with the problem, not you. Like some teenager, I wasn't thinking of anything except how hot I was. When I looked at you, *really* looked at you—'' he shot her a quick sideways glance ''—you were still weeping like there was no tomorrow. That was that. Better than standing buck naked in a cold shower, let me tell you.''

Emma remembered the other feeling that had moved through her when Cade had set her carefully on the brick wall and dried her face with his hands. His shirt had landed somewhere in the dark bushes. Loneliness rushing into her, loneliness where there'd been warmth and tenderness. "You didn't have to stop, you know. It would have been all right," Emma said quietly.

"Think so?" The corner of his mouth quirked up. "You don't know much about—dancing, beauty, do you?"

Emma shrugged. How could she answer a loaded question like that? "Enough."

"Not nearly enough if you think it's all right to make love to someone who needs comforting and not—" Cade cleared his throat. "Well, that's not my idea of a swell time. I was stone hungry for something you were in no shape to give." He took a breath. "For what it's worth, I didn't expect to get bush-whacked the way I did. Sitting there crying without making a sound, keeping everything inside, you reminded me a little of Quint—I only wanted to make you stop crying. Anyway, I thought I had everything under control." His laugh was self-mocking. "Yeah, I sure as hell did. Some self-control, huh?"

"Yes, in fact. You backed off. I didn't." Emma let the words drop like pebbles in a pond, rippling out.

"It was a near thing," Cade said, and the rasp in his low voice was husky.

Emma knew the safety Cade's arms offered was only an illusion. She couldn't surrender to it. What was the saying? About those who couldn't learn from the past being doomed to repeat it? She wouldn't repeat the past. Emma touched his shoulder. "Cade, we've both been under a lot of stress. Nothing happened the other night. Nothing's going to happen."

"Think not? A lot of something happens every time I get within two feet of you, so I wish I could be as sure as you are." Cade touched his thumb to the pulse speeding at the side of her neck. "*I* don't want anything going on between us. *You* sure don't, so I reckon everything's peachy keen, right?" He flipped the turn signal. His expression was distant as he guided the car through the intersection.

Emma still had something she needed to explain. "Cade," she began, "I'd like to tell you about my mother."

"No need to." Cade looked quickly at her. "I figure I know all I need to."

"I don't want you misunderstanding—"

This time his smile was real, bringing his firm lips up. "No chance I'll do that, beauty."

"My mother's not crazy."

"I never said she was." Cade peered through the windshield at a twisted road sign.

"You must have thought it." She knew he had. Anybody would have.

"Even I don't know what I think. How could you?"

"Some days are better. This weekend was difficult for her. She's not used to company much anymore, and changes bother her," Emma recited. "Evenings are—a strain. She expects Daddy to come walking through the door any minute, you see, and, of course, he doesn't."

"Aren't you used to it by now? The way nights are, how did you put it? A strain?" Cade did a rim shot on the wheel.

The sarcastic edge in Cade's question made Emma uncomfortable. She didn't understand what he was implying. "Lucy and I understand Mama."

"Oh, I can see that." Cade's drumming speeded up. "Y'all take real good care of her. Hell, you must have spit polished that halo around your head it's so bright, Emma Rose." Her reflection bounced at her from his mirrored sunglasses, unnerving because she couldn't tell what lay beneath his caustic tone.

"She needs us," Emma insisted. Cade couldn't begin to understand how much.

"Okay."

"We're all she has."

The dashes of the highway flashed before them in a hypnotic pattern. Just when she thought Cade wasn't going to say anything, he whipped the car onto the sandy shoulder of the road. The shoulder sloped to a drainage ditch choked with water hyacinths. Leaving the engine running, he turned to her, draping one arm across the back of the seat, letting the other rest on the steering wheel. "Just answer one question for me,

will you, Emma Rose?'' His fingers were a hairbreadth away
from her arm.

''Go ahead.'' Emma braced herself.

''When did your daddy die?'' Cade pulled off his sunglasses
and faced her. Hemmed in by the width of his torso, Emma
backed against the car door. Cade's glasses dangled from his
outstretched hand. ''Not recently, I reckon?''

''I was ten.'' Emma stared out at the purply blue hyacinths.
How could she explain the way everything had been?

Cade continued to swing his glasses. Like a metronome, they
measured out his words. ''Eighteen years is a long time to wait
for someone to come home, Emma.''

''Mama adored him. He was her whole life.''

''Where did that leave you, Emma Rose?'' Cade's glasses
brushed against her shoulder.

''What do you mean?'' Emma leaned away.

''Was your mama your daddy's whole life, too?''

''Yes.'' Emma remembered how it had been. They'd enclosed each other in a circle of their own, beautiful and glittering, touching each other all the time. No, not *all* the time. She
remembered other things, too.

''Not much room for a little girl in all that mutual adoration,'' Cade observed. ''Where did you fit in, beauty?'' He ran
the stem of his sunglasses over her shoulder.

''I loved them.'' Emma noticed a turtle at the edge of the
ditch. Maybe it would make it across the road.

''You were just a kid. Didn't you miss your daddy, too?''

''Of course I did.''

''What did you think when your mama went into her twilight world? What did you do?''

''Played make-believe with her.'' The heat was stifling her.
Surely the air-conditioning wasn't working. She touched the
vent. It was.

''Why didn't you and Lucy take Becca to a doctor?''

Shoving the bridge of her sunglasses snug against her nose,
Emma took a shallow breath. The plastic was slippery with
perspiration. She'd known he would dig. ''Mama came home
from the funeral, went to bed for a month or so, and when she
got up, she acted as though nothing had happened. Lucy called

our family doctor, who said Mama wasn't ready to face Daddy's death. Leave her alone. She wasn't crazy, he said, just coping in her own way, and she'd get better. Sometimes, during the day, she even seemed like her old self. She didn't get worse. But she didn't get better.''

"And that was that?" He traced the stem of his glasses down her neck.

"Yes."

Cade's voice was low and gentle, as if he were talking to the little girl she'd been. "But every now and then you sit all alone in your garden."

"Once in a while." She couldn't tell him any more.

"Because you miss your daddy." He was watching her, just as she'd feared, and his gentleness was taking her where she didn't want to go. "I don't reckon you're still crying for your daddy, not after eighteen years, not like that. Who do you cry for, Emma Rose?"

"Everybody." The turtle turned back to the ditch. She changed the subject. "Cade, it's too hot to sit here talking about my childhood. I'd think you'd be in a hurry to get to Francine's."

"I am, Emma, but I didn't want any mine fields lying between us when we talk to Francine. I don't want you jumping ship in the middle of things just because you were miffed with me about the other night."

She could deal with this. "I see."

"You probably don't." Cade turned to look at the highway before he pulled onto it. "We're walking a thin line. You say you believe me. Okay. I've put my trust in you. You could stick a knife between my ribs and I'd never even know it until I was bleeding on the floor."

"I'd never do that," Emma protested. She couldn't tell where Cade was looking when he turned those reflective shades her way, but she thought he was watching the pull of her blouse against her breasts.

"Yeah," he said, acknowledging her guess and turning to watch the road, "that complicates the situation. I thought that all I wanted was justice. Well, counselor, I want you, too, so the joke's on me, isn't it?"

"It's not funny," Emma said, thinking about the way her skin prickled every time he looked at her, remembering the way she'd wanted to stay in his arms in the garden. If there was a joke, it was on her, as well.

"No? I find it funny as hell." Cade's smile was mirthless. "You have to be on *my* side when I walk in to see Francine. I don't want to be worrying about falling into some pit I didn't know was there. God knows I sure don't like being jerked around by my hormones like some wet-behind-the-ears kid, but that seems to be the way of it. For Quint's sake, I have to be sure you're not going to turn on me."

"I see," Emma repeated quietly. Now she really did. He was afraid she'd try to even the score for what had happened Saturday night.

"You're my chance to get my son back, Emma, and I'll do anything I have to. Whatever you want, understand? I'll stay ten feet away from you if that's what it takes." He rubbed his hand against his jeans. "I'm sorry I let things go so far the other night. There's no future in it." Cade's face was grim. "I want my son back more than anything in the world, but I'm not going to pretend I didn't enjoy having you plastered on me like a second skin. Because I did." The words hovered between them.

Emma watched Cade's long fingers tapping the steering wheel. She understood the nervous energy coursing through him. He was a highly physical man caught in a situation where he had to stay contained. He was as uncomfortable as she was with the attraction that leapt into eager life between them whenever he touched her.

She would keep her word. She'd told him so again and again, and she thought he believed her. What he didn't believe was that she could separate what she had to do from what had blazed between them.

How could she reassure him? She'd probably be the last person to be influenced in the way he feared, but she could never explain to him why that was true. He'd have to take her on faith. Just as she'd finally accepted his innocence, taking a leap of faith in the teeth of the evidence against him. Would he be able to trust her to do the best for all of them and not betray him in the process?

"What happened between us is over, Cade. The book is closed on it."

"Think so?" One raised eyebrow expressed his skepticism.

"Of course." She wished she knew whether he meant he still wasn't sure she could put things behind her, or whether he meant he didn't think they could close the book on what had kindled between them. Emma fiddled with her dark green leather belt. She could ignore those feelings. She'd forget them once Cade was out of her life. "We both want the same thing. To straighten out whatever happened three years ago."

"As long as I can have Quint, I don't care a whole lot about the rest of it. Some, but Quint's what's important. Not all the rest of that garbage. I thought it was. I thought I wanted everyone who'd had anything to do with slamming me into that jail to suffer the way I did, but the closer we get, the more I only want to see my son." Cade started drumming on the steering wheel. He was nervous.

"There's more to it than that, Cade." Emma was beginning to feel nervous, too. "For *my* sake, I have to know the answers. Knowing the truth is important to me, too. You can trust me to deal fairly with you. I won't let personal issues influence me." She hoped she hadn't let them shape her behavior three years ago.

She'd know soon enough. Then she'd deal with whatever she learned. About Cade, Francine. About herself.

"We're here," Cade announced, parking in front of a concrete block house. A sprinkler threw streams of water from its circling arms onto grass fighting with sand for a toehold. Rainbows hung in the spray.

Emma hadn't noticed when Cade turned off the highway. Garden Grove was a subdivision developed in the fifties with narrow streets where small homes, concrete clones, lined the lots. The house in front of them was pristine and white. A pink flamingo stood one-legged in the middle of a bed of pansies.

Fumbling with the car keys, Cade rested his forehead on the steering wheel. Emma softened as she looked at him. Until this moment, she'd seen only his strength. When the keys dropped from his nerveless fingers, she reached down and scooped them up, smiling tentatively.

The man staring at her was in a deep pit with no way out.

Very gently, Emma took his clenched fist and opened it, placing the keys in his hand. She remembered the grief in his voice when he'd pounded that same hand again and again against the tree as he talked about losing Quint. As strong as Cade was, in spite of the coldness that his years in prison had encased him in, he was frightened. Emma wrapped both her hands around his much larger one. In his eyes she saw the terror that momentarily paralyzed him. For him, everything was on the line. Frightened by the thought that the nightmare would start all over for him and that he'd never again see his son, he was still unable to ask for help.

"It will be all right, Cade," Emma said, wanting to chase away the shadows in his face. "No matter what happens in the next hour, we'll survive. No matter what happens, we'll be better off than we were."

"*We?*" he said.

"Yes, *we*," Emma answered, making more than a pronoun choice. "Let's go in, Cade, and begin."

He shook himself and opened the car door. Stretching in the sun, he stuffed the keys in his jeans pocket while Emma grabbed her briefcase and stood up stiffly.

"Want to know something, counselor?" He hooked his sunglasses in his white shirt pocket and rested both open palms on the hot top of the car as he looked at the silent house with its bright orange door.

"Sure," Emma said, knowing he was still delaying the moment of confrontation, the moment, perhaps, when the truth would come out. She had a powerful hunch that whatever the truth was, getting it out wasn't going to be easy. Seeing the neat, well-kept house stirred Emma's misgivings. "Tell me something I want to know, tough man."

Her teasing brought a light to his somber face. "I never lived here."

Emma started to open her briefcase and check the address. They'd stopped at the courthouse and she'd gone in quickly, stemming the tide of questions about her early return with a hurried promise to fill everyone in later. She would, too, but she'd give her colleagues an edited version.

Cade stopped her. "No, it's the right house, but I realized as I looked at all this—" he jerked his thumb to the orderly yard "—that I never really saw this as *my* house, *my* place. It was the house Francine wanted, and I didn't care. It wasn't important to me because it was going to be temporary, so I made the down payment, kept up the mortgage and plowed all my energy into saving money. Every spare dime went for the ranch. It was going to be my future. Quint's heritage. I spent so much time out there clearing bush, working cattle, that I never put down roots here." He raked his hair. "Oh, I mowed, painted and paid the bills, but those were just chores that stole time away from where I really wanted to be." He shrugged. "Now I'm a stranger here. All those wasted years."

He laughed, but Emma heard the regret scoring the low sound. "Not wasted," she said. "Quint."

Reaching out, Cade flipped her hair free of her blouse. She shivered as his thumb lingered beneath her collar. "Yes, Quint. I hadn't forgotten. It wasn't all a waste."

Emma walked up the sidewalk, the clicking of her heels the only sound. She couldn't hear Cade behind her, but she knew he was there, close.

As she always did before speaking to a jury for the first time, she pressed her fist against her diaphragm and inhaled as deeply as she could before exhaling in a slow, controlled breath. Cade's shadow fell across her.

When she pressed the doorbell, Emma had the strangest sensation of the past rushing in at her, colliding with her present and future.

The orange door opened slowly into an air-conditioned living room. A plastic runner led from the door to a hallway, where another plastic strip crossed it.

The woman who answered the doorbell had changed during the years. Her youthful prettiness had dulled as though some-one had turned off the light. Her stiffly sprayed bright blond hair was now a natural brown, though still in the same stiff style. Though she was thin and darkly tanned, a heaviness of spirit lay over her. Her light blue eyes were lifeless. Emma knew

Francine was only thirty-one, but she looked weighted down and older than her years. To Emma, Francine looked as if someone had snapped her inner spring.

If the years had embittered Cade, Emma thought, Francine had suffered, too. If she'd lied about Cade to protect the man who'd beaten her, she'd paid her price, and it showed in her posture, in the lines around her thin mouth and in her unhappy eyes. The abuse she'd suffered had killed something in her. Maybe the man she'd protected had continued to abuse her after Cade's imprisonment, and Francine had been too spirit weary to report it.

Anger percolated in Emma. Too many women never found the courage to take a stand and say enough. They wound up accepting the blame for their injuries and pain as their courage and sense of self-worth were beaten out of them. Maybe accusing Cade had taken the last of Francine's courage, and Emma had failed her by not realizing that Francine had named the wrong man.

Acid rolled in Emma's stomach. Her notes hadn't shown negligence or misjudgment, but she still had to go through the office files with a fine-tooth comb before she could settle accounts with herself.

Emma suppressed her urge to put her arms around Francine and hug her. Instead, she stuck out her hand. "Ms. . . ." What name was she using? Chagrin had Emma gulping her words in a way she wasn't used to. "You may not remember me—"

"I remember you."

Of course she would. Emma slowed down her breathing and started over. Maybe she'd kept Cade's name because of Quint. "Ms. Boudreau—"

"Jenkins." Hesitantly, she held out her tanned hand. "Francine."

"All right." Grateful for something to do, Emma shifted her briefcase and shook Francine's hand. "Thank you for agreeing to see me. Us," Emma added as Cade switched his weight and his boot touched her shoe. She nodded toward Cade, directing Francine's attention to him.

Needlessly, though, because Francine's eyes had been flickering in Cade's direction since she'd opened the door. Now, however, she lifted her chin in acknowledgment. "Hello, Cade."

A light shone briefly in her faded eyes and died as Cade stood silent at Emma's side.

Emma wanted to kick him. Instead, she nudged his foot as she continued speaking. "I know this is difficult—"

Interrupting her, Cade spoke in a voice flat and raspy with strain. "Francine."

"You look good, Cade." Francine tugged the hem of her tan blouse.

Emma blinked. Trying again, she said. "I hope I can help smooth—"

"How's the place look?" Francine was speaking only to Cade. "I took real good care of everything." Her smile was anxious.

Emma wanted to pinch herself to make sure she hadn't gone invisible. And then Cade placed his open, warm palm right in the center of her back.

Francine's eyes followed the movement of Cade's hand, and the smile slid off her face. For a moment she looked lost and forlorn. Then she stepped back from the door. "Y'all come on in. We can't talk out here on the front stoop."

Hooking his thumb in Emma's belt, Cade followed at her heels. She was afraid if she stopped suddenly he'd walk right into her back. He shouldn't have touched her like that, not in front of Francine. He was only complicating things in a situation that needed handling like a crateful of eggs.

"Y'all want some iced tea or something?" Francine stood beside a yellow, geometric-patterned sofa covered in clear plastic.

The house was so clean and spotless Emma could almost smell the bleach.

"Yeah, I sure do want something. I want Quint." Cade ripped apart the pretense of a sociable call.

Francine's face crumpled.

"Cade, shut up," Emma whispered and shoved him onto the couch.

"That's what I want." Cade stuck his legs out, crossed his arms and stared at Emma. "Francine might as well know right up front that that's the bottom line."

Francine's face went yellow white.

Chapter 8

Francine had fled to the kitchen whispering that she'd get the iced tea.

Emma poked Cade's arm as she whispered, "Will you please let me handle this? You're ruining everything."

The plastic on the couch rustled and crackled as Cade rubbed his hands on it. "I hate this house. I can't stand being in here any longer than I have to. I can't breathe in here. I feel trapped. You've got to get me out of here as fast as you can. So how about short-circuiting the nice-nice and cut to the chase. Okay?"

"Look, Cade, you can't bulldoze your way through this. You knew that before we came here. You agreed to shut up and sit back. So do it!" Emma couldn't believe he was jeopardizing everything with his mulish behavior. "And I don't want you being nasty to Francine."

Cade's lips curled in what Emma could only think of as a blatantly nasty smile. "Okay, counselor, but I'm telling you right now, I feel about as friendly as a mean-tempered rattlesnake." Combing his hands through his hair, he left the imprints of his fingers in the heavy strands. "Look, I'm trying, but this damned place is getting to me. Can't you understand?'' He started to get to his feet. "I can't just sit here. It's like I'm back in prison. Look at it!'' He reached for her chin and made her look at the room. "Does anybody live here? Where are Quint's things? Emma Rose, you've got to get me out of here," Cade finished desperately.

"Sit down, Cade," Emma said quietly. "You can stand it. You have to. It's only for a little while, not—" she smiled softly at him, torn by sympathy for Francine and the tenderness Cade's vulnerability was stirring in her "—a life sentence."

"Oh, real funny. Turning into a comedian on me, are you, counselor?'' Cade slumped onto the couch, and the plastic rattled under him. "Damn stuff."

"Here's what we're going to do, tough guy. You're going to sit here like a meek little mouse with zippered lips. Not one squeak out of you unless I give you a sign, hear?''

Nodding, Cade glared at her.

"No more of those looks. Not at me and especially not at Francine. *We're* the intruders. I don't want you intimidating her.''

"How about you, Emma Rose, don't I intimidate you?'' He'd captured her wrist.

"You know better." Liking the way his smile moved the darkness out of his eyes, Emma let him play with her hand. "You have your moments, though." She unhooked her fingers. "Now behave yourself. Unless you're not mean enough or tough enough to sit here in this nice clean house for an hour? Even with an unlocked door?'' She challenged him with a grin.

"Can't stop, can you? Got to have the last word, don't you? Well, one of these days . . .'' he threatened.

"Sure, one of these days, pigs will fly," Emma scoffed, wistfully thinking of the way Cade had kissed her. One day would never come. A part of her wished it would.

"You never know." The sly lift of his lips let her know he'd read her mind.

"I know," she answered, not teasing. "Pigs don't fly, Cade. It'll never happen," Emma said, not talking about flying pigs at all.

Cade's booted foot slid between Emma's high heels and she colored as he tick-tocked his foot between hers.

"Probably not. I reckon it might be real interesting to see pigs fly, though," he needled as he tapped his boot against her heel. "Go sit down, counselor. I hear Francine."

Emma escaped to a brown tub chair and collapsed in a clatter of plastic and a whoosh of air, as breathless as Francine who entered with a metal tray of iced-tea glasses.

"I cut some fresh mint, for the tea." She rushed into speech.

The green sprigs sticking out of the tall glasses were carefully trimmed and perfectly placed. The three glasses could have been photographed for a food magazine. Emma thought there was something a little poignant about Francine's offering.

"Thank you, what a lovely idea," Emma said and smiled, wanting to drive out the melancholy hanging over Francine and her antiseptic house. The magazines on the coffee table were ruler-edged.

"I grow them. Herbs, mint." Francine couldn't decide where to sit. She held the tray against her stomach and settled on the edge of a black vinyl recliner, poised for flight. "Well." She laid the tray flat on her lap and put her glass on the table next to her. "You said you wanted to talk with me. You and Cade."

Emma slowly rotated the cold glass between her hands as she tried to explain. "Yes. About Quint. I appreciate your seeing us. That was gracious of you. I know this is difficult, and I discussed the points I wanted to cover with your lawyer. I asked her to sit in with you."

"I didn't want her here." Francine tightened her lips.

"I'd be more comfortable if she were here this afternoon. She needs to make sure that any questions or concerns you have are answered and protected. Francine," Emma said, leaning forward intently, "I want your interests safeguarded, too. I don't want you to feel pressured or bullied in any sense. Please, believe me. I'd be very happy to wait while you called her again and we could either wait until she gets here, or we could set up another time and place for our meeting."

Cade's resistance to the idea of waiting came at her in waves. Without even looking at him, she knew he would be scowling. All he had to do, though, was keep his impatience under wraps and his mouth buttoned.

"I don't need her to be here," Francine said doggedly. "I talked with her. So as long as I don't sign anything—" her agitation was increasing "—and I'm not going to because I'm not giving up my son. I don't have to."

"No, of course you don't. Nobody wants you to." Tension knotted Emma's forehead.

"Cade does." Francine glanced sideways at him.

"What Cade wants is to see Quint." At the edge of Emma's vision, Cade's foot swung back and forth rapidly. She prayed he'd keep quiet. "Can we talk about that? About letting Quint see his father?"

Francine flinched. "I guess so."

Tilting her head, Emma refused to look at Cade as she considered Francine. Her behavior was a fraction off center and troubling. What had she told Quint about his father? Surely she wouldn't have— Like little Fourth of July sparklers, intuition was lighting up thoughts in Emma's brain. She couldn't connect them, not yet.

"Wouldn't Quint like to see his dad? Or would it be a problem for your son?" Until now, Emma had deliberately refrained from referring to Quint in any way except by name. In particular, she'd avoided calling the boy *Cade's son*. She had no intention of letting language raise everybody's blood pressure.

"I don't know what you mean."

Emma was sure Francine did, but she'd thrown up a wall in spite of Emma's cautious approach, and Emma wasn't sure what had caused Francine to back off. "Would it upset Quint?" Emma probed carefully.

"I don't know. It could."

Francine was stacking up bricks as fast as she could, and Cade's foot was a fast-moving blur. Emma sighed. What they needed was a psychologist, not a lawyer. Nothing added up, not the house, not Francine's reactions.

Maybe Francine was only worried about Quint's reaction. "Cade doesn't want to distress Quint, just see him. That's all. He hasn't seen him in three years. I'm sure you can understand how much he's missed Quint." Emma hoped Francine would think about how she, too, would feel in the same situation. "Hasn't Quint missed his father?"

Washed-out blue eyes gleamed with tears. "Yes."

Standing up, Emma walked over to her and kneeled, touching Francine's arm. "Cade loves Quint very much, you know."

Francine's gulp was clearly audible. "I know."

"Are you afraid Cade will hurt Quint? He would never do that." A tear trickled down Francine's cheek.

Scrubbing her face with the back of her hand, Francine said lifelessly, "I know that, too. He loves Quint even more than that damned ranch."

"Would you allow Cade to talk with Quint if I stayed with them? Near them?"

Stopping the restless scraping of the tray over her knees, Francine drew her eyebrows together in thought.

Emma hoped she'd jumped the hurdle of Francine's objections. She pressed forward, trying to get more than evasiveness and hoping to clarify the nagging unease. "Are you worried that Cade will try to steal Quint away?"

Cade's foot was absolutely still. Francine dropped her head, but Emma saw her swift look at Cade.

"I won't let that happen," Emma said. Francine's reactions to Cade confused Emma. She would have understood some expression of guilt, hostility, fear. She'd even been prepared for Francine's refusal to listen. Instead, Francine had brightened in Cade's presence.

"Cade's crazy about Quint. Always was." There was weary acceptance in Francine's tired comment.

"Cade wouldn't force Quint into that kind of situation. He wouldn't do that to his son, no matter how much he loves him. That wouldn't be fair to Quint."

Francine started to stiffen up. Damn, damn, Emma wanted to bite her tongue hard enough to remind her not to be so thoughtless again. Her absolute belief in Cade's love for his son had led her into uncharacteristically rash speech. Why now?

Pressing her hand to her stomach, Emma smiled and took a breath. "Cade wouldn't want to force Quint to choose between you."

"You talk like you're awful sure. Are you?" The question was hesitant.

Emma thought gloomily that she was sure, but for the life of her, she didn't know why. Cade could not, would not, put Quint in that kind of impossible situation even though she understood the desperation that had him halfway to his feet at the moment. "Absolutely," she stated firmly, hoping saying so would make Francine believe it, too. "I'd stake my life on it. I'll give you *my* word that Cade won't disappear with Quint, Francine."

"If you think you can guarantee anything about Cade, you don't know him very well," Francine began as the back door banged open. She rose quickly, looking first at the clock in the hall and then worriedly toward the kitchen. "I guess he could talk to Quint. As long as you don't let either of them out of your sight." Her hand at her mouth, she took two small steps toward the kitchen. Clearly distraught, all her attention toward the back of the house, she said, "Y'all better go now. I'll call you. Let yourselves out."

Books banged on a counter. Footsteps clumped down the short hall.

Emma's first reaction was that Quint was going to be taller than his father. Sullen and angry, the boy slumped against the doorjamb. The same blue-black as his father's, Quint's hair was short on the sides and long in back. High tops encased his big feet. He was large for eleven, probably growing overnight and caught in preadolescent turmoil. He was awkward and ungainly, all sharp-pointed knees and scabby elbows.

He surveyed the three adults with eleven-year-old belligerence. His misery revealed itself in the truculent set of his chin and in the angry looks he threw at Cade. Quint was carrying a chip on his shoulder heavy enough to fell a grown man. Spoiling for a fight, he was looking for Cade, preferably, to knock that chip off.

Even though he was taller and heavier than Emma, she could see Quint was still just a child whose world had been torn apart through no fault of his own. Her heart broke for him.

Behind her, Cade's wide shoulders brushed against her. He'd risen so abruptly she hadn't even heard the betraying crinkle of plastic.

"Quint," Cade scraped out.

The agony in Cade's raspy voice squeezed Emma's heart.

"Quint." He stretched out a hand.

Disaster. Hoping no one noticed, Emma laid her hand on Cade's outstretched arm and stepped in front of him. "Not now. Let Francine handle it," she said and prayed he'd listen. Gripping his large wrist as tightly as she could, she held him behind her only by the strength of her will. Her muscles strained with tension.

"What are you doing home this early, Quint? You didn't skip out again, did you?" Too disturbed by the sudden appearance of Quint to step in any direction, Francine swayed from one foot to the other. "You're supposed to be at school!"

"What's *he*—" Quint thumbed toward Cade "—doing here?" Quivering with anger, the boy stepped toward his father. "You get out of here! You don't belong here no more! Get out!" His voice cracked.

"Quint! Stop this right now, you hear?" Francine's wail was ignored in the tense moment.

"I don't want him around!" Quint's thin fists doubled in front of him. All his attention was on his father. "I know what you done, and I won't let you hurt my ma again!"

"Quint, don't— Cade, I never told him—" Francine ran to Quint, who shook her off.

"Don't you ever come here again, hear? I'll beat you up if you come near my ma!" Tears mingled with dirt on Quint's contorted face. "You're nothing but an old con! You don't mean nothing to me, and I hate you!"

Holding on to Cade's arm, Emma felt the energy drain from him. She gripped his hand.

Emma risked a quick look. Stark emptiness in his eyes. She held on to him now because, in his torment, he was a man who needed the touch of another human being as badly as his child did. Emma slipped her fingers between Cade's and squeezed.

Grabbing Quint's thin, shaking shoulders, Francine held him tightly. "Why did you come home, honey? You weren't supposed to be here!"

"I heard you on the phone last night. I figured out what was going on. I knew you'd need me." Quint straightened away from Francine. "And *he's* gotta leave. Right now." He sniffed and slouched threateningly toward Cade.

Why hadn't Francine known Quint would react the way he did? Emma wondered. Surely she must have realized how deep-seated the boy's distress was. Why had she thought he would even talk to his father? How could Quint have hidden all his pent-up resentment and heartache from his mother? Or had Francine, the way grown-ups do, assumed Quint was okay just because he never talked about his father? Emma didn't know, but she remembered how secret the life of a child was.

Quint could have kept a lot of secrets from his mother.

"Are you gonna go, or do I hafta make you?" Quint pushed past Emma to Cade.

"Son," Cade said, defeat ravaging his voice.

"Don't you call me that! I'm not your son no more!"

Filled with immeasurable loss, Cade's grainy voice was the saddest sound Emma had ever heard. "You'll always be my son."

As if Cade had slapped him, Quint halted, white-faced. "No."

"Yes. Always." Cade didn't move.

"Stuff it. I wish you weren't my father, so there," Quint spit out, scrubbing his fists against his wet face. "I wish you'd never been born, that's how much I hate you!" He kept backing up, rubbing his fists into his eyes. "You're nothing but a lousy liar!" Breaking into wrenching sobs, he turned and ran.

The back door banged behind him.

"Wait!" Francine hurried after him. Over her shoulder, she looked desperately at Cade and said, "He's too upset. He shouldn't be alone."

"I'll get him," Cade said grimly. "I'm faster."

The three of them poured out the back door, Cade in the lead, and ran after the boy pedaling furiously down the road on his red ten-speed. Emma tasted her own tears and didn't know whether she was crying for Quint or for Cade. Or for herself.

Cade's long legs ate up the yards between him and his son. Running smoothly and cutting across yards, Cade narrowed the gap. Emma thought that Cade, with all that flashing speed, could catch Quint.

He could have, too, except a car speeding through an intersection barreled down on them, and Quint, throwing a defiant look over his shoulder, darted in front. The car screeched, and Cade bumped off the front fender, stopping only long enough to say something to the driver before tearing off in the direction Quint, no longer visible, had taken.

Francine gasped. "Oh, God, oh, God," she moaned and sank down on the scrubby grass.

Emma dropped beside Francine. "Where will Quint go?"

"I don't know," Francine wailed. "What am I going to do?"

"Where does Quint usually go in the neighborhood?" Emma wished she could run away, too.

"I told you, I don't know! He's been hanging around some new kids since he started junior high, and I don't know their names or where they live, or anything about them!" Francine dropped her head on her bent knees.

The neighborhood was quiet. Blank windows looked back at Emma. Nobody home. Kids at school, adults at work. Quint's terrible unhappiness ripped at her. He was only a child in a child-man's body. If anything happened to him— Unbearable.

She, Francine, Cade, they all were responsible in different ways for Quint's suffering. The harvest of the past was bitter indeed.

Jogging in their direction, Cade shook his head. When he reached them, he was breathing hard and sweat dripped down his face. A dark line of perspiration streamed down his back and under his arms. He bent over and rested his hands on his knees while he caught his breath. "I lost him after he zipped in front of that idiot." He gulped air. "Let's go to the house. We can decide what to do."

"What will Quint do?" Emma asked Francine.

"I don't know what he'll do anymore, I keep telling you! He's changed this last year."

"Come on, Francine," Cade said quietly. "He'll come back. Kid has a temper, but he's smart. He won't do anything too stupid. He's got a good head on his shoulders. He had too much to deal with, and he couldn't face it. He used to run off down the block when he was little." Cade helped Francine stand up. "Remember how hotheaded he's always been?"

The shared memory between Cade and Francine shut out Emma. Whatever Cade's sins, whatever bitterness he still might harbor, he'd changed. Quint was a bond between him and Francine. Their love for him would forever join them in some way.

Then Cade slipped his warm hand up Emma's arm. "Come on," he said, and even the hopelessness in his gray eyes didn't hide his awareness of her. "Quint will come home."

"Cade," Emma said urgently, "we can't wait too long. We'll have to call the police."

"I know. But I think we can give him a little time. Poor kid's had a lot thrown at him today." His thumb and forefinger braceleted her upper arm. "You told me we'd survive, no matter what happened. Right?"

Nodding, Emma forced back her own fears.

Black humor edged his words. "Well, have a little faith, counselor."

Back in the house that suddenly seemed emptily big without Quint, each of them staked out waiting territory. Emma wasn't comfortable walking around, so she opened her briefcase and removed files, trying to distract her thoughts from that last image of Quint's defiant look at his father.

She was more worried than she wanted either Cade or Francine to know. She knew how Quint felt, and she wasn't as sure as Cade that the boy could run off his distress and return. Keeping an eye on her watch, she decided that she would call the police if Quint didn't appear by five. If he intended to come home at all, a boy growing as fast as Quint would be there for supper.

Francine stayed in the kitchen near the phone. She made two or three phone calls before opening cupboards and the refrigerator, beginning supper preparations. She didn't ask for Emma's help, and Emma didn't volunteer.

Like a restless zoo tiger, Cade paced the house, the yard. He dragged the car keys out, asked Emma with a lifted eyebrow whether or not she wanted to go with him. She didn't. She thought the waiting would be easier for Francine with another person in the house, even if they didn't talk.

If anyone had asked her, though, she couldn't have recalled one single detail of the files she read so determinedly.

"Anything?" she asked as Cade stalked back into the house.

"Nothing." He roamed the living room, tossing the keys up and down. "There's a playground and a big dirt field a few blocks over. I scouted around, asked a couple of kids if they'd seen Quint. One smart-mouthed little squirt said he'd swap information for money. Can you believe it?" Cade rolled his eyes. "A shakedown artist at ten." The keys jangled in a nerve-shredding rhythm. "He finally admitted he hadn't seen Quint. An older kid thought Quint headed to the 7-11. I checked there. Dead end." Savagely he flung the keys up and caught them backhanded. "I'm going to get something to drink. How about you?"

Emma discovered her feet were jiggling in time with the jangling keys. She tucked her feet under her. "You go ahead."

He shoved the keys into his pocket, then pulled them out. "You want these?"

"I'm staying until we know about Quint. I don't think it's a good idea—" Emma chose her words carefully "—for me to leave."

"Yeah. I wasn't thinking. You're right."

His hands jammed in his pockets, Cade stood a moment watching her. "Francine okay?" He rocked on his heels.

"She's keeping busy. We haven't talked if that's what you mean. She's checked on me a couple of times. Cade, I know you don't want to hear this, but I like her. She's not a bad person."

"I reckon not," Cade said, rocking to a standstill. "I figured I wouldn't even want to be in the same room with her after what she did to me, but I just feel sorry for her. Crazy, huh?" He sighed and rubbed his neck. "I thought I wanted revenge, wanted Francine to feel as bad as I did, and now—hell, I can't get a handle on what I feel right now."

"So much has happened," Emma said neutrally. She wished she could ease the pain for all of them, but there was nothing she could do until Quint came home. *If* he came home. "Quint wasn't prepared to see you. You counted too much on his being the same little boy you left. He's not." That child existed only in Cade's memory. What Cade and Quint might be able to build together in the future was anybody's guess.

Smoothing the paper laid out on her briefcase, Emma thought of the pearly shell she'd left in her bedroom at home. She ached for the father and son who had once collected seashells and made up stories about them.

Even under stress, Cade's walk was easy and loose-jointed, a lazy saunter that distracted Emma. He ambled over to the window and twitched the blind, speaking with his back to her. "Quint said he hated me." Cade's mouth curled in a tired half-smile as he faced her. "Still keeping the faith, counselor?"

"Sure. How do the clichés go? Ain't over till it's over, don't give up the ship, while there's life there's hope? Did I miss any?" Emma managed a wobbly smile of her own.

"None I can think of offhand." Cade hitched an eyebrow ceilingward, clearly trying to change the mood. "Listenin' to you, a body'd think you played baseball as a kid. Here I've been thinkin' you strictly an indoor lady," he halfheartedly teased, his drawl forced.

In the kitchen, Francine dropped a dish. The shattering of glass was nerve-racking. Emma flinched, and Cade jammed his hands in his waistband, hooking his thumbs in the belt loops. He frowned.

Emma longed to erase the lines gouged around his mouth. She wanted to see one of his real, teasing smiles again. Most of all, she wanted Quint to come walking through the door with his baby macho scowl pasted all over his face and the big chip on his shoulder.

Without being able to explain how, Emma knew Cade needed comfort, but he'd never admit needing anything. She realized, too, if she so much as tried to reach out to him, he'd shrug her gesture aside. Long ago he'd stranded himself and his emotions on some island.

He needed, oh, the need showed on his harsh, stern face, but he'd never ask.

His loneliness wrung her heart.

Emma closed the file and put her briefcase aside. "Why don't you get your drink? I'll wear out the carpet while you're gone."

He didn't grin, but his eyes lightened as he watched her. He started to speak at the same moment Emma yielded to her need to smooth those lines around his set mouth and bridge his isolation. Touching his face lightly, she murmured, "I heard what he said, too, Cade, but don't give up. Quint's as tough as you are. He'll be back." Emma let her hand linger against his mouth, wishing she could wave a wand and make a fairy-tale ending for all of them.

"You're a smart lady, Emma Rose," Cade murmured as he tapped her nose. "But I know what you're doing."

"And what might that be?"

Over his shoulder, Cade tossed her a grin, but he didn't answer her.

The stillness in the air was oppressive in spite of the air-conditioning. Emma circled the living room, struck again by its sterility. Wandering down the hall to the bathroom, she couldn't help but notice Quint's bedroom facing her. Jolted by what she saw through the open door, Emma stopped.

In this room was all the life missing from the rest of the house. Football posters lined the red walls, trophies stood haphazardly on shelves. Above the bed, thrown together in an eleven-year-old's effort, an enormous blown-up maroon-and-gold football drifted lightly in the eddy of air from the vent. A football jersey was stuck crookedly with gold thumbtacks to the wall, and a dangling banner in the corner blazoned the name of Quint's school in sun-faded letters.

Along the windowsill rows of seashells marched to the edge and back.

Looking from the living room stripped of personality to Quint's room filled with color and life, Emma knew that here was the heart of the small house.

Like Cade, Francine loved her son.

Raised voices from the kitchen snapped Emma out of her thoughts. Hurrying back, she recognized the low-to-high scale of Quint's voice. Relief washed through her.

"Where have you been, young man?" Francine demanded, her voice shrill. "I've been worried sick! You know better than to disappear like that!"

"Why's he still here? I shouldn'ta come home," Quint shouted, ignoring his mother. "If he don't get out of here, I'm going to run away for real and never come home!" He shoved past Emma and ran into his bedroom, slamming the door behind him.

As he passed her, Emma saw the tear tracks down his still baby-round face. In the kitchen, Cade, head bowed and unmoving, leaned against the wall. Needing a moment to collect herself, Emma paused outside the door. She didn't know what she was going to say to Cade or Francine.

With his head still lowered Cade spoke quietly to Francine. "I never knew you hated me so much."

Emma started.

"I didn't, Cade, I swear I never told Quint why you were in jail!"

"No?" Cade wearily raised his head. "Someone did."

"Not me, Cade! People talk. He must have overheard someone, but I would never have told Quint. How could you think I'd do that?" Francine held on to the kitchen sink.

"Interesting question," Cade answered. Lifting his head, he looked at Francine for a long moment.

Not knowing whether to interrupt or not, Emma stayed at the door, unwilling voyeur to a scene from a dead marriage.

"What did I do, Fran, to make you hate me this bad? I never could figure it out." His voice grated with remorse.

"I didn't hate you, Cade."

"Was our life together that awful? I thought I was being a good husband. A good father."

"You were a wonderful father to Quint. Nobody could have been better. He idolized you."

"But not a good husband?"

"Not for me."

Acceptance rested between them.

"So terrible I made you hate me?"

Emma wanted to cover her ears as Francine answered wistfully, revealing more to Emma listening than Francine would have wished, "I don't hate you, Cade. That's not how it was."

"No? I'd sure like to know why I looked at bars for three long years. I spent a lot of time trying to understand what you'd done, and what I was going to do when I got out."

"I don't blame you. I knew you'd show up on the doorstep the first chance you could." Francine's face was screwed up with pain. "You wanted to get even with me, didn't you?"

"Yeah. I thought it'd be real nice to see you pay a little for what I'd been through. Now, I don't know. Things aren't the way I expected them to be. Quint's not the same, you're not." Cade's wide shoulders moved in weary frustration. "I'm not."

Francine's response was barely audible as she looked around the kitchen, down at her beige slacks. "You see what my life's like. If you came looking for revenge, you wasted your time. You've already got it. I hope you're satisfied."

"I can't say I feel terrific right now." Emma saw his chest move in a sigh. "I made a mess of things, didn't I?" Cade's boot scraped the floor. "I wish I could have been different, Fran, not such a lousy husband. I'm sorry."

Francine touched the sink, pulled at the edge of her blouse, sat down. She straightened the place mats on the Formica table then finally said in a thin voice, "Cade, I kept up the mortgage on the ranch. I sold the livestock, but not the land. It hasn't been worked, and it's probably in bad shape, but it's still yours. Your stuff is still there, too. The Jeep's in the shed. I packed everything and took it out there. Seemed right since that's where you spent most of your time." Jealousy sharpened her words.

"Can't you tell me why—" At the sound of footsteps pounding down the hall, Cade whirled to the door, seeing Emma and, behind her, Quint, panting and red-faced.

Once more Quint shoved Emma aside. Blinking rapidly, he held out his fists filled with seashells. "Go away. And take your old shells with you!" The boy flung them on the floor in front of Cade. "I don't want 'em. They don't mean nothing to me.

Just old garbage!'' Quint smashed his foot down on the fragile shells, hammering them into powdery bits on the immaculate kitchen floor before bolting to his room, leaving behind him a sandy white trail of shells.

Chapter 9

"Y'all go, Cade. I'll talk to Quint. He's not going to come out while you're here." Francine dragged the broom across the floor, cleaning up.

Silent and withdrawn, Cade walked out of the room, his movements stiff and painful, as if he'd aged thirty years. Like a blind man feeling his way, he held on to the wall as he plodded into the living room.

Whisking the last of the shells into a dustpan, Francine bit her lip as she said to Emma, "I don't know how Quint found out about the trial and why Cade was in jail. I didn't tell him. He must've heard it somewhere, but not from me." There was a hint of resignation in her look. "Make Cade believe I didn't turn Quint against him, will you?"

Wishing the whole situation could be swept away as easily as smashed shells, Emma said, "May I call you tomorrow?"

"After five. I don't usually get home from the hospital before then."

"If our conversation will disturb Quint, perhaps we should make other arrangements. After he overheard you talking to me the other night, he exploded. We don't want that to happen again.'' Emma stuffed the files into her briefcase. ''What do you think?'' She clicked the lock.

''If I can't talk, I'll say so. Most of the time Quint doesn't come in until supper, anyways.'' Francine dumped the shells into the lined garbage can. In a shower of bits and pieces, the shells rattled to the bottom. She rubbed her eyes. ''Quint loved those. I wish he hadn't found out why Cade was in jail. I never meant him to know.''

Through the front window Emma saw Cade sitting in her car with his head resting on the steering wheel. Quint in his bolted room, Francine in her sterile house, and Cade. And herself. All of them locked off behind walls built years ago. All of them alone. Cade had been right. So much time wasted.

Pain constricted Emma's heart. She'd always thought heartache was just an expression, but her heart did, physically, hurt as she looked around her at the emptiness.

Taking a deep breath and pressing her hand against her stomach, she willed the pain away. She would not accept that there was no way out of the muddle. They weren't going to find a solution today, but tomorrow would be different. They'd taken the first step. No pain, no gain, she thought, fighting off hopelessness.

''I'll call, then,'' Emma said when she'd finally eased the constriction in her heart and throat. She patted Francine lightly on the shoulder.

''Sure.'' Scarcely noticing, Francine stood disconsolately with the broom and dustpan clutched in her hands. ''I didn't realize Quint—'' She hunched her shoulders. ''Well, goodbye, I guess, Ms. O'Riley.''

''Emma.''

Francine was somber as she regarded her. ''Right. Emma.''

When the orange door closed behind her, Emma was breathing as hard as if she'd run a mile in her high heels. She hadn't wanted to cry in front of Francine. For a person not given to crying, Emma reflected woefully while she calmed her breathing, she'd done little else since Cade Boudreau had forced his way into her life. Like a lightning rod he'd become the focus for her long-buried emotions and brought them cracking and sizzling into the open.

He'd pitched her predictable life into turmoil.

She didn't like chaos and tumult.

Buffeted by all the turbulence, she'd never felt so alive.

"You like sitting in hot cars with rolled-up windows?" She tossed her briefcase into the back seat and sat down in front, leaving the door open. "I know you have this tough-guy image, but you don't have to prove it to me."

"What?" Cade's eyes were blank.

"Why don't you start the car, cool it off?" Emma said patiently.

"Keys?" He fumbled in his pockets.

"There." Emma pointed to the keys hanging from the steering column. "Just turn them. Works like a charm." Closing the door as he started the motor, she said on a patently false and cheery note, "Could have been worse."

"Stop it," he said. "I've seen you work this little game before, counselor."

"Really?" Emma said sweetly. "Just what do you think I'm doing?"

He scowled.

"Cat got your tongue?" Emma turned her voice saccharine.

"You're a damned annoying woman, do you know that?" he finally said, but the scowl left his face.

Relieved that she'd irritated him into the present, Emma dropped her chirpiness. "Oh, good, I was afraid I was wasting all that sweetness."

"You know, sometimes you're like a burr under a saddle, Emma Rose. You just keep itching and digging in, don't you?" Cade's eyebrows slashed together.

"I had to learn how," Emma acknowledged.

"Must've come easy." The glitter in his eyes left her unsure he was teasing.

"Don't turn too nasty, now," she scolded. "We have stuff to discuss." She drew her legs up on the seat and faced him, growing serious now that he'd left his memories and was ready to cope with the present.

"This isn't the end?" Cade breathed deeply.

"Cade, I'm not going to kid you. The situation is more iffy because of Quint's reactions, but I don't think Francine told him anything. He's heard comments, whispers. I'm sure that's how he found out about the trial. Kids always know more about what's happening in their lives than adults realize. Kids will either figure out what's going on or they'll come up with their own explanations. When a kid does that, the answer is usually distorted, and the kid is headed for serious trouble unless someone steps in and helps, because that kid will never let on he's scared stiff about what's going on in his head. He just keeps it inside where it festers. Sooner or later, the kid explodes." At Cade's sharp look, Emma realized she was revealing more than she'd intended. She finished up awkwardly. "Kids and adults do not inhabit the same world, believe me. Whatever Quint knows or thinks he knows, he picked up on his own."

"Doesn't make any difference."

"You know he wanted to hurt you by smashing the shells, don't you?" Emma said.

A bark of laughter, faint but there, under Cade's muttered, "Hell, yeah, I figured that out right away. Didn't take me long, either. Worked, too." All the sharp angles of Cade's face stood out.

Emma touched his arm. "Think about it. Quint came home even though my car was still out front. He could have waited, could have called Francine and told her he wasn't coming back until we'd gone. He knew we hadn't left."

A glow from the bright sunset momentarily chased the shadows on Cade's face. "I've never seen Quint like that. If looks could kill, I'd be lying dead on the kitchen floor. He smashed those shells like he was stomping my face."

"Weren't they important?" No matter how hard she was trying, Emma couldn't get rid of the sad pain in her heart. She knew how Quint felt, and she wanted Cade to understand what was happening inside Quint.

"Yeah." The air-conditioning droned until Cade said in his scratchy voice, "I wish he'd come swinging at my face instead."

"Don't you think Quint knew that, Cade? Don't you understand he deliberately picked those shells as the symbol of everything you two have done together? Didn't he know smashing them like that would hurt you more than anything else?"

"Think so?"

Watching the light come back to Cade's face, Emma gave him a second to digest what she'd said before hitting him with the conclusion she'd reached while standing in the hall of Francine's immaculate house. "Quint made sure you were there and that you knew how he felt," Emma insisted. "He's not afraid of you, and he's not indifferent to you. That should tell you something. Love and hate are close kin. He's very unhappy and confused, on the border of manhood but still a child."

A faint smile creased Cade's cheeks. "I love how you talk, counselor. It's a real treat. Do they have a class in doubletalk in law school?"

"Sure. B.S. 102." Emma smirked. Bringing a smile to Cade's saturnine features lifted her discouragement.

"Keep talking like that, counselor, and someone's apt to wash out your pretty mouth with soap. What would your mama think?" Cade said. "I'm ashamed of you, Emma Rose, a nice girl like you." His teasing sent the last of the shadows from his face.

"You don't work in the prosecutor's office and hang around cops without expanding your vocabulary," Emma said primly. She'd been the butt of raunchy teasing until the cops learned they couldn't shock her. "I've always considered education extremely important."

"Me, too, counselor." Cade loved Emma's naughtily pursed pink mouth. "But what do you think of hands-on teaching? Get much of that in law school?" Her blink of satisfaction eased the depression clawing him.

His pa had always insisted that if you could laugh, you weren't dead. Cade couldn't remember what had happened to the give-and-take ribbing he'd taken for granted growing up. Teasing was one more thing he and Francine had never shared.

When it came down to it, Quint was all they'd ever had in common.

"No comment?" In front of him the setting sun spilled pink and purple across the darkening sky. Emma puckered her lips again. Cade hoped she'd sass him back. He didn't want to think about Quint.

In that same prim voice, she said, "I think the teaching technique depends on the curriculum."

Cade wanted to chuckle at her pleased-with-herself grin. "Want to go back to school, beauty?" he asked, knowing good and well what she'd think he meant.

The pink of her cheeks wasn't from sun.

"You've been hanging around too many cops, Emma Rose," Cade chided. "Reckon you'd mind taking a sidetrip and going out to my ranch?" *Mine,* he thought. In spite of everything, *mine.* "I'd like to see it." He kept his voice light, not wanting Emma to know how important her answer was.

A yearning to touch the land he'd worked had grown in him with Francine's announcement. Now, with Quint's rejection, Cade needed to feel the dirt for himself, to know that something real remained for him. Knowing the ranch was still his was keeping him sane. "I want to see what it looks like after all this time. See if anything's standing."

"Terrific idea," Emma said.

"Yeah?" Cade knew a goofy grin was spreading across his face.

"Yeah," Emma said, mocking him, but her pointy chin dipped as she smiled.

"You're all dressed up, counselor," he said. Bouyed by the hope he was trying to keep under wraps, Cade gave in to his constant craving to touch Emma. Cupping her knee, he reminded her, "Nylons and heels. You sure you want to tramp around my scrubland?" *Mine,* he thought again, and let the reality move through him. *Mine.*

"Yeah," Emma said again with that teasing that stirred him like champagne bubbles fizzing against bare skin.

She was doing her best to cheer him up. Cade knew he shouldn't let himself get within a country mile of her, knew the smartest idea was to keep as far away from her as he could, knew for his peace of mind he should, but he left his hand resting on her small knee.

Her teasing had saved him.

Smiling hopefully at him, her cat face warmed the cold loneliness in his gut. Her round knee was delicate and sleek in her pale nylons. Cade circled her kneecap. The inner curve of her knee was so warm and soft he wanted to leave his hand forever on that tender place, let that warmth seep into him and melt the ice in his heart.

Instead, he gripped the steering wheel and reminded himself that touching Emma Rose only led to trouble. His palms left damp smears on the wheel as he remembered how fast passion had slammed into him, how close he'd come to oblivion in Emma's garden.

Each time he touched her, the ground crumbled under him, plunging him closer to disaster. Touching her made him hungry, and he wouldn't satisfy that hunger. Shouldn't. She'd lived all her life in her house by the river. He had nothing to offer a woman like her, and he sure couldn't complicate his life by pretending he could take her and walk away, free and clear. He didn't want any emotional ties. Emma Rose was dangerous to him.

Seeing Francine had reminded him he wasn't cut out to be a husband. As much as he loved Quint, he'd managed to screw that relationship up, too. No, Emma had no place in his life.

Cade risked a look at her. No harm in that. No danger. Above her green belt, the slippery fabric of her blouse pulled against her breasts. He'd never forget the pale gleam of them in the dark, gardenia-scented garden, or the way she'd felt wrapped around him, her skin sleeker than that glossy blouse.

His dreams had already replayed those moments, tormenting him by adding the sweet, fierce moments her tears had denied him. What ate away at him was knowing she'd been soft and yielding. She wouldn't have stopped him.

He could have slaked his thirst.

Except for the taste of her tears slipping down her cool face.

"Do you have a flashlight in the car?" Cade asked, pushing one more memory back.

"Sure," Emma said, popping open the glove compartment and hauling out a major-duty-size flashlight.

"Hell. That thing's bright enough to light up a football field." Wincing, Cade shielded his eyes. "You really believe in being prepared, don't you?"

"Always," Emma said smugly, clicking off the light. "There aren't a lot of streetlights, and when I'm out late, I like knowing I won't be in the dark. If I ever have a flat tire, I plan on flashing this—"

"Like Batman's signal?"

"It's not that bright. I thought perhaps a flashing Morse code," she concluded. "And, just in case, I have my persuader."

"What?" Cade couldn't believe Emma carried a gun around, not Emma.

Her hair swung forward and her back curved as she dug under the seat. She pulled out a short piece of iron pipe. "Here. What do you think?"

"I don't think," Cade said slowly, wondering where her persuader had been when he'd taken her from the parking lot, "that you could clunk somebody with that."

Laying it across her knees, Emma regarded the rusty pipe. "I always thought I could. I assumed I was tough enough, but you're right. I never even remembered that it was there when you surprised me. And I couldn't have hit you with this thing." She rolled the one-inch pipe thoughtfully. "Funny the things you learn about yourself under stress, isn't it?"

"Well, you said you valued education." He was damned glad she hadn't swung at him with the pipe. It would have laid his skull open. But what if it had been somebody else coming after her in the dark parking lot? "Emma, why don't you keep the pipe closer at hand? Where it's easier to remember?" Cade urged.

"As I said, I wouldn't use it anyway."

Like a bullet screaming into his brain, knowledge hit him. He didn't want Emma Rose out on any lonely highway by herself.

"Still, make sure you keep it," he said.

"Seems foolish now," Emma said and sighed regretfully. But she wedged the pipe next to the driver's seat. She peered out the front window. "How much farther? I'd like to see the ranch while there's still some light."

"We're almost there." Cade tried unsuccessfully to quell the anticipation rising in him.

A concrete gash through scrub and pine, the road ran straight and flat before them into open country. An occasional gas station rose up on the horizon and flashed behind. Cradled high in the bare branches of a dead pine tree, a southern bald eagle's nest, six feet long and made of pine needles, moss and sticks, caught Cade's attention. Circling high, floating on thermals, a red-shouldered hawk hung in the purple sky.

Cade rolled down the window. Far away and faintly on the breeze, came the high-pitched squeal of the hawk, its call of freedom. He smiled and inhaled the humid air. Emma's light touch on his arm turned him to her. "Want the window up?"

"Leave it down." She smiled at him, her face soft and her hazel eyes glowing. "You love this land, don't you?"

"More than I knew," Cade said, admitting finally what the ranch meant to him.

Turning into the narrow rut that had been the ranch entrance, Cade realized that owning the land was necessary to his soul. Only Quint meant more.

The car bumped over the gouges in the track. He'd do anything to keep this land now. He could scarcely comprehend that Francine hadn't sold it.

He'd never expected to again set foot on land he could call his own, yet here he was. *His* pine trees speared out of the scrub. *His* outbuildings were dark shadows in the distance. Emma was right. No matter what, he would survive. One way or another, he was going to scratch out some happiness.

He'd given up on that possibility, and now like the final wild blazing of the sunset, hope soared in Cade higher than an eagle.

Stopping at the frame house, Cade switched off the car engine. He stepped out of the car and let silence settle until the land began to speak to him with its rustlings and creakings, its animal sounds. A part of him knew the instant Emma came to stand beside him, and he pulled her close to him, sharing the serenity.

"It's big," Emma said in a tiny voice.

"Yeah." He grinned at her. "It is that. One hundred acres. Not the best in Florida by a long shot, but not the worst, either. I know every inch of it like the back of my hand."

"And dark," she added, stepping closer and jumping as a hooty owl screeched. "I have the flashlight," she said.

"Nope. Leave it off for now. It's not that dark, beauty, just a heavy twilight," Cade said, pulling her closer and resting against the warm car hood. "Come for a walk with me?"

"What about snakes?" Emma stood on one foot then the other. "I'm extremely biased against snakes and dark together, in the same place, at the same time. Both." She shifted again.

"Don't worry about it, beauty. I'll take care of you." Cade grinned at her.

"Easy promise. You have on boots," Emma pointed out, backing up to the car.

"You can stay in the car." Cade waited, hoping she wouldn't take him up on the offer, and not clear why he wanted her beside him.

She hesitated then sighed. "No, I'd like to see what your ranch looks like. It's just—well, you go first, okay? Make sure you do whatever you strong rugged types do to discourage wildlife." She raised her head. Her eyes were shining hazel in the last of the light.

"It doesn't matter," Cade lied. "Stay here if you'd rather."

"Not on your life," she muttered, moving close to him and looking doubtfully around her.

He linked his hands around her waist, letting his fingers linger for a moment on her narrow waist and watching the way her eyes darkened when he did. Cade decided he was a sucker for the way Emma's eyes grew big every time he touched her. He chuckled. She would hate knowing how her eyes betrayed her, so he wouldn't tell her.

"What's so funny?" she said, her breath caressing his throat.

As light as air, her breath shivered him down to his toes. "Why, nothin', Emma Rose, nothin' at all," Cade drawled and let the shivers roll on down. Emma's waist fit easily within the span of his circling fingers, and just under the edge of his palms, the delicate flare of her hips curved to his hands.

Touching Emma was like handling crystal sculpture, except Emma was warm and woman, not cold glass. Once, some college girl he was seeing had dragged him to a fancy country club wedding reception, and he hadn't been able to resist flicking the edge of a Swedish crystal goblet. That sharp, trembling ping was what he felt every time he gave in and let himself touch Emma. Ping. Down deep inside him where he had no control, some note struck, vibrating all through him.

"Let's go." He wanted Emma to see what he'd built. He took her hand and slid his fingers between hers. "You can switch on that light." He picked up a thick branch after she did. "For snakes," he said, hoping she'd think he was still kidding her.

"Right."

She didn't buy it. A city girl, but not gullible, though. Well, had to figure, hanging around cops and public defenders. She'd never have survived working with them if she'd been naive or prudish.

Cade knew he and Emma wouldn't see much, but he reckoned he'd get an idea of the work before him.

Out of breath behind him, Emma said, "How did you ever pay for this ranch in the first place, Cade? It's bigger than I expected."

"Wasn't easy." The barn didn't look too bad. The doors were on, and the roof looked solid, although it was hard to tell in the twilight. He raised Emma's arm that held the flashlight and pointed it in the direction of the barn. The roof *wasn't* solid. Emma gave him the light and he lit the way before them as he headed to one of the pump houses. "I grew up wanting to be a rancher. Seems like I was born knowing what I wanted."

"A man with a purpose. Admirable," Emma said in small puffs of speech and breathing. She stumbled, and Cade righted her.

"That's why I studied agriculture in college."

Emma was clinging to his belt and dogging his heels. He didn't want her twisting one of her elegant ankles in some burrow in the dark. He thought about offering her a piggyback ride, but he knew she'd snap his head off if he dared to suggest she couldn't keep up with him.

"Still," she said, holding tight and spacing her words so that she could catch her breath, "you had to buy this land, fill it with livestock. How did you come up with that much money?"

Cade slowed down, letting his impatience to see what had happened to his ranch take a back seat to Emma's shorter stride. She grimaced her thanks as he went on. "From the time I was twelve, I worked summers and saved my money. Finally, after college and the marines, even though Francine and I married before I finished my hitch, I had a stake. Before they died, my folks pitched in what they could, and I made the rounds of the banks until I found one that would give me a mortgage."

He stopped. The pump house had fallen down, been knocked down, whatever. Part of the tin roof was doubled up around a tree. Shining the light, Cade saw the rust spots, the dents. The shed was home to scurrying night creatures whose eyes glowed in the flashlight. Going inside the shed, Cade could see that the machinery and pipes had been smashed.

"Oh, Cade, this looks awful." Emma's words voiced what he'd avoided admitting. "Can you fix it?"

Her face was soft with sympathy, but he didn't want her seeing his failure. He remembered too strongly what the land and buildings had looked like. Swinging the flashlight inside and out, Cade beamed on anthills, large with what were probably biting red ants, huge palmetto bushes and light-colored sections of sandy soil where the grass had died out or where the sand and scrub had taken over good grazing land. He finally let the light stay on the busted pump.

"Are new pumps expensive? Maybe you could fix this one?" That unwanted sympathy flowed in her precise, soft voice, and he wanted to yell, wanted to tell her he couldn't begin to see a way to pay for a new pump, but he knew she'd just tell him to sit down and figure out another way to get a pump.

"Might be salvageable." He had no way of knowing, but she was looking at him with such confidence that he couldn't tell her it would be a cold day in hell when he ever got this pump up and working again.

"What happened?" Emma jumped again as a raccoon scooted out from under a pile of brush and took off away from the light.

"Teenagers, junkers, people looking to smash and destroy. It didn't fall down on its own," he said. Looking around at the destruction, Cade wondered if he could walk away from the ranch.

"Someone came along and did this," she admitted as she leaned against him. "But two days ago you didn't have even this much."

"You know, counselor, you could drive a person stark staring nuts with your damned optimism." Even though he wanted to throw her pity back in her face, he discovered he wasn't immune to her dogged attempts to cheer him up.

"I'm not an optimist or a pessimist," she clarified. "Practical. Possibly a realist. I don't see much sense in wasting time regretting what can't be changed."

"I see." He was letting his memories destroy the present, and as she leaned against him, he let the warmth of her small form comfort him. He'd never before let anyone in close enough to work with him or comfort him. But somehow Emma understood what he was feeling, and Cade discovered he liked having her fret over him. Emma Rose was teaching him something about himself he wasn't sure he liked learning.

Men were supposed to slug it out alone, and he always had. Until Emma Rose.

"Didn't you ever hear the story about the little engine that could?" Regret pitched her voice lower and he leaned down to hear her more clearly. Her soft, warm mouth, damp with her breath, brushed his ear.

If he turned a fraction more, her mouth would be under his. He should take her back to the car. He'd seen all he could stand of the ranch for now.

Cade straightened his shoulders, leaving behind the temptation of her soft mouth. "Emma, I figured that damned engine wasted so much time and energy getting to the top that he looked down the hill and said 'to hell with it.' I reckon that would have been the most practical thing to do, personally."

"You wouldn't." Her finger thumped his chest. "You'd barrel up that hill with steam belching out until you blew a gasket or got to the top. And you know something else?"

"Probably not, but I have a strong feeling you're going to fill me in. Fire away, beauty." In spite of the mess all around him, Cade smiled. "Emma Rose, you are determined to look on the bright side, aren't you?"

She stooped and brought up a handful of sandy earth, working it between her fingers. "Sure, your machinery's been trashed, your cattle sold, but your land hasn't been destroyed. So don't try to kid me or yourself that you could turn your back on this!" She held it to his face. Her hand was shaking. "This is you, Cade Boudreau." In the clump of sandy dirt, grass blades jutted, struggling to survive. Sand spattered onto his boots.

Opening her fist, Cade let the dirt trickle between them. Her fingers were grainy between his and the grass was slick. He rubbed her hand over his face. The dry land smell was clean, pure and mixed with the scent of Emma.

"Don't," she murmured, pulling her hand back. "I'm all dirty. What are you doing?" she asked nervously as he pressed her hand to his mouth.

"Thanking you, Emma Rose, nothin' else," Cade said in a rough low voice. As frightened as she was of the dark and snakes, she'd never hesitated. She'd reached down in the dark and grabbed a handful of his ranch without thinking twice. Reckless and rare. Cade kissed her slim fingers one by one, the small pads gritty against his mouth.

"Well, you know you wouldn't give up," she persisted in a small shaking voice.

"Let's go back to the car, Emma Rose," he said and held her sandy hand tight to him all the way to her car, where he backed her against the bumper and watched her eyes deepen and darken. His hunger for her grew like a taproot deep and powerful in him. "Can't have a first-rate lawyer coming in second best to a rattlesnake with an attitude problem," he teased gently, letting the touch of her skin vanquish his mental pictures of the ranch's deterioration. Clasping her waist once more, he swung her onto the hood and let his hands rest on the cool metal.

Settling on the car, she spread her skirt over her knees and let the flashlight drop into her lap. "Snakes don't climb, do they?"

"After tromping around in the dark, you're joking now, right?" Cade leaned closer, trying to see her face clearly.

"A little bit. But I really don't like the dark. Or snakes. And if I seriously let myself start to think about snakes crawling up the tires and bumpers, I'd scream. I would," she insisted as he began to shake his head.

"You wouldn't yell," Cade said definitely, bumping her chin with his forehead. "Not you. You might want to, but you'd tip up that stubborn little chin and keep your cool until you'd clunked the snake with your flashlight."

"Oh, sure," she scoffed. "I can see it now. I'd probably be trying to climb that pine tree over there." She gestured to the shadows.

"Nope. On the outside you'd be cool as a cucumber, but on the inside, ah, that's where Emma Rose would be screaming. She just wouldn't let anybody know, though, would she?" Cade stroked the side of her neck. That small girl in the picture haunted him. "You wear your lawyer suits and high heels and you never let anybody know you're scared, you never ask anybody for help, and you don't let anybody inside your lonely garden wall, do you, Emma Rose?"

"Think you know me, do you?" Her voice was self-conscious and distancing. She twirled the flashlight.

"If I said I did, you'd run so fast the snakes wouldn't have a chance of catching you. You ever think we're two of a kind in some ways, Emma?" He didn't wait for her answer. "Don't worry, beauty. It won't be a problem," Cade said, as she scooted away from him.

He wouldn't let this sneaky tenderness she brought out in him become a problem. He wouldn't frighten her by telling her he was coming to understand her very well. She wouldn't have a clue what he was talking about. Cade tucked the strands of hair that always seemed to blow into her eyes behind her ears. Her ears lay so neatly against her head that when he poked the hair behind them, they stuck out just enough to give Emma an endearing elfish appearance.

An elf with gold hoop earrings. Cade ran his finger inside the loop. The metal was smooth and thin. "Emma Rose, you're one tough cookie, all right."

"Darn right. Don't forget it, either," she said, making a face and sticking out her tongue. Pointy like her chin and pink as her mouth.

Cade deliberately didn't mention he was thinking about those cookies with the melting-soft filling. Emma wouldn't like that, either.

"Feel better now that you're off the ground, do you? You ever go parking when you were a teenager, beauty?"

"Sure." She cocked her head at him boldly, but her eyes were wide and innocent.

The bravado told him she hadn't—not much. And not serious parking, not by his definition and back seat experience, at least. "Okay, so I guess you're bored to death with star music, huh?" He needed to return the gift she'd given him as she'd shoved the fistful of grass and sand at him and reminded him of what was important.

Cautiously, she ventured, "What's star music? Is this some kind of practical joke?"

"Nope. This is for real. Remember watching the fireworks on the Fourth of July? And lying back on the car hood looking straight up at the sky as the colors and noise exploded overhead?"

"We never did that," Emma said.

"Listening for star music is kinda similar, except a whole lot quieter."

"Good."

"Not fond of noise and crowds, huh? What you do is, first, lie back." He took her shoulders and pressed her carefully onto the hood.

"I feel ridiculous," she announced. "This is silly, Cade. What's the point?"

"You'll see." Emma clasped her hands together over her breastbone. Her small breasts flattened into delicate curves barely there under her soft blouse. Cade unfolded beside her on the hood and nudged his arm under her head, cushioning her neck. "You can't talk," he cautioned.

"Oh, no fun." As she half rose, her hair tickled his nose. She smelled like flowers.

"Shh, Emma Rose. Watch the stars." He raised his leg and pulled off a boot, propping his stocking foot on the hood, knee bent. Then he gathered her in on his shoulder. He hadn't intended for her hair to lie across his mouth. The curl burned the corner of his lips. Cade closed his eyes. He didn't brush away the soft strand.

Emma lay against the muscled support of Cade's shoulder and looked at the early evening stars. Low on the horizon, they dotted the night. "So, where's the music?" The quiet was *too* quiet. Too intimate. She'd already spent one night under the stars with Cade Boudreau, and her world had changed because of it.

"Don't talk so much, counselor." Cade touched her lips with a long finger. "Listen to the night."

For a long time, Emma lay still and watched the slow movement of the stars. Gradually wood sounds crept in. The squeak of a night creature, flutterings in the trees and the underbrush. She forgot about snakes and her fear of the dark. She didn't think about what lay before her the next day.

Underneath her, the car hood was cool in the spring night, and down her left side the bony angle of Cade's hip jabbed her. His long body, relaxed and peaceful beside her, was a streak of warmth, making her feel safe.

And then there was a moment as Emma lay there, dizzy with the dark and the stars and Cade beside her, a moment when her soul hovered over her, blending with the night, with Cade, a moment when she would have sworn she heard the far-off music of stars, the music of past worlds coming sweet and faint into the present.

At that instant, in spite of everything that had happened, hope crept into her like stardust floating down from long-ago worlds.

Chapter 10

Emma leaned on her side to face Cade, whose arm, a solid support, was still under her shoulder. His lean face was all hollows and shadow, but his light gray eyes gleamed in the darkness. When all this was over, she would miss his scrutiny, which let her know he was aware of her, Emma O'Riley. She hummed into existence when she was near him. Even now the tension in his arm called to her. Her body answered in the heat sliding under her skin and turning her blood to wine.

Emma leaned closer, raising herself higher. What was there about Cade that made her dissatisfied, made her want to throw caution to the wind? Never in her carefully controlled life had she been tempted in the ways this tough, lonely man tempted her. Why could *Cade* spin her inside out and make her yearn to submerge herself in a swelling tide of *feeling?*

He saturated her world with color when she'd never understood it was gray.

Listening to the night hum and buzz with life, Emma believed for the first time ever that she was part of that universal blueprint—and not an outsider looking in.

Cade bridged her loneliness. She didn't know how or why, but she came alive around him. Her senses sharpened, and she craved that intensity of awareness in a way she would never have believed possible.

Needing to share with him the hope filling her, to give him hope for his future, she murmured, "Francine kept this ranch for you. I don't know why, but she did. Quint loves you. You may not believe me, but you have a good life ahead of you, Cade."

"Think so, beauty? Think the past can be forgotten?"

"Not forgotten," Emma said. "But not a ball and chain around your ankles, either."

"Funny comparison for an ex-con."

"Accurate, I think." Strobelike images of Lucy, Becca, herself flashed in the darkness. "You don't have to be a prisoner to the past." Maybe she could cut her own chains.

Cade opened one eye. "Look around you. A wasteland. It'll take me years to rebuild. Even if I can find financing, I'll have debts and mortgages coming out my ears. You said it yourself, this land is what I am. A lot of dirt and grit."

Grit was what it had taken to wrest a ranch out of scrubland all by himself, but Cade had an old-fashioned doggedness. Emma couldn't imagine the courage he had called on to survive prison. Seeing him here on his land she understood him. He was a part of this ranch in a way he'd never been anywhere else, especially not in the small, concrete house. "Cade, this land is what gives you your strength."

"Yeah, I reckon I've known that all along, but I figured I could live in two worlds. I was wrong to pull Francine both ways and let her think I could fit into her cookie-cutter life. I wasn't fair to her. I thought I knew what was best for all of us. I was wrong." His arm tightened around her and he sighed. "In prison I used to wonder how I'd screwed things up so bad when I'd only wanted to do right by her and our son."

"You built something worthwhile out here." Emma wanted to smooth the lines between his eyes.

"For Quint."

"I know." Her heart ached for Cade. Beneath his razor-honed toughness was his love for his son. "I don't believe Quint's lost to you."

"We'll see." He took a deep breath. "He's grown so tall in three years." His laugh was rueful. "He's not a little boy any more, and I miss that wide-eyed squirt. He's gone forever. This Quint and I, we're strangers to each other."

"But you're not starting at ground zero. You have shared memories to build on." Emma's heart turned over at the sadness in Cade's eyes. He'd taken a risk beyond imagining in order to get his son back, and Quint had rejected him.

"Yeah, but I don't want him hurt. I want time with him, but I don't want Quint torn in two."

Emma shifted closer. Submerging his loneliness and needs, Cade would take on his broad shoulders Quint's pain. Just as he'd submerged his desire and comforted her, letting her weep her long-suppressed childhood tears on his chest.

Cade, who had no one.

Shyly she placed her hand on Cade's cheek. Craggy bones and beard stubble were hard to the soft skin of her fingers. She outlined the scar on his eyebrow. His risk-filled life had scored his face. His life was there on his face for anyone to read if they cared to, while her scars were on the inside, her life a coded message. His skin was bristly tough, hers tender. Emma followed the ridge of his cheekbone, testing the shape and texture so unlike her own. Absorbed in her exploration, she moved her finger over the sharp blade of Cade's nose, down to his taut mouth, which softened and gave under her touch.

Gripping her wrist, Cade checked her fascinated examination. "More charity, beauty? I told you I wasn't interested." In a raspy rush, his words sandpapered her skin, but Emma heard the pride behind them.

His free arm pillowed his head and lengthened all the long muscles of his chest. His slow breathing was that of a man given over to utter relaxation, but his clenched fingers gave the lie to his casual posture.

"I don't believe you've ever taken charity in your life," Emma said. "Besides, I gave already at the office," she added, giving him a sassy look.

A muffled laugh broke through Cade's words. "We're not talking about the same thing, sweetheart."

"We might be," Emma said. She stroked the sleek shine of
Cade's hair near her captured wrist. She could barely touch the
smooth strands near his ear. "For all you know, I might have
a string of charity cases."

"Not you, Emma Rose," he said in his rusty voice, laughing gently. "Not my sleeping beauty behind her high garden
wall." He kissed her forehead. "I reckon you never even played
spin the bottle at parties when you were a kid. You probably sat
there in your nice party dress watching everybody giggle and
wished you were miles away."

He was more right than she'd admit. Those early boy-girl
parties had been purgatory. She'd never been able to joke or say
the right thing, never learned the easy give-and-take of flirt-
ing.

Cade's strong, self-possessed face hovered over her while his
cloudy gray eyes looked at her with such humor and understanding that Emma couldn't move. Down the pathways of her
mind, his seeking gaze moved, searching out her darkest secrets, accepting them.

Wrist to wrist she was fused to him, her pulse beating with his
and his becoming hers. Her breasts rose and fell with the
rhythm of his breathing until she no longer knew whether she
breathed on her own or at his will. Her breathing grew shallow
and everything in her tightened like the strings of a violin waiting for the stroke of the bow to release its imprisoned singing.

"Don't look at me," she whispered, heat gathering under her
skin. "You make me feel as though—"

"As though—what?" Cade closed the gap between their
forearms until, wrist to wrist, vein to vein, their arms met.
"Why not?" His smile was knowingly tender. "Does it make
your skin feel too tight for your body, Emma Rose?" Pendu-
lum-like, his wrist swept against hers. "What do you feel when
I look at you, touch you?"

How could she tell him? To say out loud how her blood ran
dark and thick when he touched her would be to admit— Admit what? To put into words what happened to her was to take
a step off the sandbar and fall uncaringly into the deep blue
water. She'd always turned and swum back in the green water
between shore and sandbar where the white sand underneath

her revolving arms and paddling feet showed her shadow under the glassy water.

"Tell me," he coaxed. "There's nobody here but us. What do you feel when I look at you?"

His eyes moved down her throat, and Emma trembled. Could she dare admit that he made her feel—reckless, alive? That he made her forget the lessons taught by her mother's solitary dancing? Cade made her want to dive into that darkness promised by his eyes.

"Can't say? Coward," he chided lightly. "I'll tell you, then, what you do to me." He pulled her to him, and she sprawled across him, length to length. His arms enclosed her with warmth and security. "You ever shake up a bottle of soda and thumb the mouth of the bottle? All that pressure building up a volcano, waiting to blow off the lid." He stroked the length of her back hard, with both hands, then held her with one hand cupping her neck, the other wrapped around her hips. "That's what you do to me." Moving his hand lower, he traced the curve of her fanny. "Shake me up and leave me fizzing."

Through the fabric of her skirt, her nylons, her panties, Emma's skin fizzed where he touched her. Restlessly she moved her feet. Her leg slipped between Cade's and slid along the length of his arousal. Hard against her nyloned thigh. When she drew back, he dropped both hands to her hips and pulled her tightly, shockingly to him, urging her to his heavily beating pulse.

"See what I mean, Emma? You make me feel like I'm going to explode." He pressed down on her hips and rocked slightly, bringing her closer to that heat that burned through his jeans, through her clothes, to *her*. "Do I do that to you?"

"Yes," she whispered, glancing shoreward but still leaping into the dark.

Beneath her, Cade jerked. His pelvic bones were hard against her stomach, and when she edged closer, he pushed his ankles against her instep and suddenly the part of her that ached slid against him. Emma arched her neck. Not close enough. She wanted to tell him, but the words stayed locked behind her teeth clamped on her bottom lip. A small sound escaped.

"You like that, don't you, beauty?" Cade widened his legs and, with them, hers.

Emma breathed in unsteadily. "Why do I have to say it? You must know what happens every time you touch me."

"I know what happens to me when I touch you. Everything flies out of my head." He buried his mouth in her hair and inhaled deeply. "I get drunk on the taste and smell of you, Emma Rose. See how easy the words are?" The denim on his raised knee grazed her inner thigh, and fine tremors rippled over her skin, upward.

"Not for me," she confessed as his knee slipped down again and his legs twined around her.

"Do you feel like you want to explode, Emma? Do you?" He brought her closer and higher, her breasts moving over his belt buckle to rest on his chest.

Through her blouse Emma had felt the chill of the buckle against her nipples, cold and hard against her aching breasts.

"Or have you gone off somewhere by yourself into those memories that make you cry?" He rocked once more and then cupped her neck and brought her face to his. "Give me the words, Emma, because all this sweet pain is killing me," he muttered. "Tell me," he coaxed.

Threading her fingers through Cade's heavy hair, Emma framed his face. He couldn't know what he was asking of her. She couldn't tell him what he wanted to hear. Maybe he was used to saying and hearing those wine-dark words, but she wasn't. Words were gold coins to be counted and treasured, not tossed around. "Cade, I'm here. I want to be here, with you, at this moment."

"Cautious Emma." In a half sit-up, he breathed the skin behind her ear, and Emma shivered as his mouth found one spot and lingered, tasting her. His rigid stomach muscles strained against her. "Sweet, sweet Emma. Did you know you taste like sugar candy?" He touched his tongue to the back of her ear. Then, as gently as a falling leaf, he stroked her lips and shared her taste with her. "See how sweet you are?"

The touch of his tongue speared down hot and sharp. Emma tasted only Cade.

Sliding his arms up the backs of hers, he caught her shoulders and turned her sideways, his thigh slipping between her legs and pulling her skirt tight, tight against her, so tight that everything inside her vibrated and waited.

Emma gasped. The drag of her skirt and the push of Cade's thigh spiraled through her. Her fingers strayed to the sturdy column of his neck and stayed. The vein standing out on the side of his neck drummed an urgent cadence under the sensitized skin of her fingers. She touched her lips lightly to the thrumming vein. Such power in that beating. Such power in her that she could alter its drumming with nothing more than a skim of her lips. Lost in the dark taste of Cade, deafened by the pounding of blood in her ears, she scarcely heard Cade's question.

"Why now?" Cade's words eddied past her ear with the movement of his mouth on her earlobe. Tongue, teeth, lips scraping gently until Emma's toes curled in her stockings. Down her neck his mouth slid. "What's changed, Emma?"

"Nothing. Everything." She held her breath as his mouth paused at the slope of her shoulder then bit lightly. A sigh escaped her.

"Not good enough. If this isn't charity, is it the little rich girl from the right side of the river looking for a walk on the wild side?" Anger roughed his voice, but against her neck his lips spoke of pleasure.

"Rich?" She laughed shakily. "Oh, Cade, if you only knew! Not charity, Cade, not a game. Just you." She curled her hand around his neck. "Me. And how you make me feel." Emma shuddered as his tongue flicked suddenly against her skin where he'd nipped. "You make me burn, Cade," she whispered, letting the words wing free in the searing heat of Cade's mouth against her.

The circling, hot touches of his tongue low on her neck stopped her breathing. Emma moved her palm against his chest. Buttons slid free, and she spread her hands over the hard hot skin that shivered at her touch.

"Turnabout's fair play," he said, pulling the tail of her blouse free and sliding his hands under her chemise and over her ribs. "Emma Rose, I am crazy about your underwear," he groaned as he moved his hands under her breasts. His thumbs rested on the curve of her underarms then moved across, brushing the tight buds of her breasts, which trembled and pointed at his touch.

"The only thing that's softer or silkier is you." Cade dropped his head to her breasts. "But, beauty," he breathed, and his warm damp breath wafted down the neck of her blouse, "don't you ever wear a bra?"

"Not very often," Emma said, drowning in the sensations created by his stroking, brushing fingers. "Ah." She arched her back as he tugged the peak of one breast, and all the coiled waiting inside wound tighter. "Ah," she said again and sank forward, wanting more, trying to ease the unbearable aching of her breasts against the muscled planes of his chest.

Bracing her toes against Cade's legs, Emma stretched up his torso. His palms were open and warm on her breasts as she moved, and she needed him and didn't know how to tell him. "Cade," she whispered in frustration, "Cade."

"All right, Emma," he whispered back, opening her blouse and pushing down the ribbon straps of her chemise. Taking the tip of her breast into his mouth, he scraped his teeth delicately against the straining peak, then breathed on it, the soft breath a sting of dark pleasure.

As his mouth enclosed her, Emma yielded to the convulsions corkscrewing through her, down from his hungry mouth to her restless, twisting toes and up again.

Against her breasts, he murmured, "Fizz away, Emma Rose. I won't hurt you. You're safe."

Emma scarcely heard his words, so absorbed was she by the shudders racking her. As Cade eased her on her back, holding her shoulders, she opened her eyes and saw his face, fiercely intent on her, concentrating on her as no one in her life ever had, giving her more pleasure than she'd known the world held. Cade, giving, not taking. She started to say something, but the words were blasted from her mind by Cade's knee nudging her thighs open and his hand slipping up and untangling the constricting skirt and taking its place, teaching her with its rhythmic, insistent pressure that she'd only tasted pleasure, not known it.

"Damn nylons," he grumbled as he took her mouth in a kiss that sent her tumbling into a place where pleasure became only a pale tint in the blaze of color he opened to her with the stroke of his tongue and hand.

Emma ran her hands down Cade's thighs. They were taut and shuddering under her touch, and their power was held in check. Lost and drowning in pleasure, she knew Cade was giving everything to her. "Not fair," she said and slid her seeking fingers to the waist of his jeans and under, desperately trying to find the snap and beguiled by the edge of crisp hair.

"No." Cade took her hand in his and raised her arm around his neck.

"Why not?" She sighed. She had wanted to comfort him, but she had only taken. As his hips moved against her, replicating the rhythm of his warm hand, she was aware of his hardness still straining against her. She tucked her hand into the hollow of his back, sliding her fingers under the waistband as far as she could. As the end of her finger touched the cleft of his buttocks, he jolted hard against her, and her hips lifted in response.

"Oh, God, sweetheart, don't," he groaned, lurching to a sitting position and dragging her across his lap, "I'm trying to keep the lid on, but I'm losing it." Breathing rapidly, he clipped her hands together and rested his chin on her head.

Emma rose to her knees and wound herself around him. So close now to the wildness beating through her. Cade was the source of the power sweeping mindlessly through her, and every nerve in her body was singing with life. "Cruel," she protested, "to stop now." She ran her hands frantically over his face, his arms, and curled them around his neck, shuddering against his bare chest.

"Shh," he soothed against her cheek. "I'm not going to lose control, not the way I did in the garden." In spite of the pounding of his heart, his words were steady and only a faint tremble in his arms betrayed the effort he was exerting.

Still dragged under by the riptide of sensation, Emma clung to his wide shoulders, trapped in the swelling pleasure running through her. "I want you to lose control, Cade," she murmured as liquid heat poured through her.

"No."

Drawing her fingers down his strong throat, Emma heard him swallow, and as her heart slowed, she came back into the world. Reluctantly, unwillingly, she returned from the bright spiraling world that Cade had taken her to, a place where her body sang a wild melody to his stroke.

With a wry chuckle that moved his chest against her, Cade said, "I won't lose control this time. Besides, Emma Rose, I don't have my dancing clothes with me. You're safe, sweetheart."

"Oh." Dazed, she realized they were still on the hood of her car. She touched the metal, not quite sure for a minute where reality began.

Reality had been those moments when everything in her burst free at Cade's touch. She had been safer before when she only wondered, but now, knowing, how could she abandon that secret world forever? Never plummet down that dark tunnel again?

She had been right to be afraid. Wary, she had fought the pull on her senses that Cade had exerted effortlessly from the first moment she saw him. Tonight, lost in those blazing dark moments, she hadn't thought of anything.

She, who'd always known exactly what she was doing, had surrendered all control to her impulses.

Looking at Cade, his face drawn tight, Emma knew she had made a mistake. Even with that beguiling heat draining from her, she was still drawn to him. She covered her face. Knowing, *knowing*, was worse, the confirmation of all her secret fears.

"Emma? Are you all right, beauty?" Cade brushed her hair back and she shivered, edging away. His voice low, he said, "I wouldn't have hurt you. You know that."

"Yes. I know." Overwhelmed by her tumbled, confused emotions, Emma couldn't lift her head and face him. But she had to.

Steeling herself, Emma raised her head, and tipping her chin, she looked him straight in the eye. "I don't do this—" she raised her chin higher "—kind of thing. I'm no good at—" words failing her, she struggled on "—this and that." She shook her head, unable to put her ineptitude and doubts into words and choosing to reserve that small privacy for herself.

"Oh, Emma Rose," Cade murmured, a husky laugh rippling through his words, "trust me, you're terrific at this." With two fingers he eased the straps of her chemise up over her shoulders as he concluded, "And that." He let his knuckles trail along the side of her neck.

"Let me go," she protested and wished she didn't like what he was doing.

"Nope. Not until I'm through," he said. "We need to settle a couple of things."

"Not now, please," Emma said. She needed time to herself to sort out her emotions. She had to analyze why she'd let down her guard with Cade, why she'd *chosen* to. Cade hadn't tricked her, forced her or seduced her. She had made her choice, and now she couldn't remember why.

In the tense silence between them, Cade buttoned her blouse while he kept her on his lap, not letting her withdraw even though she pushed at his chest. Finished, he stopped and held her face between his large rough hands. "Emma Rose, you're not the kind of woman a man should take on the hood of a car, or in the back seat, no matter how much he wants to." A grin curled one side of his mouth. "Not, anyway, the first time."

Emma tried to turn her face away, but Cade wouldn't let her. "Please," she muttered.

"Nope," he said, keeping her still. "Listen to me. You're a woman who deserves the best. This—" he jerked his head at the dark around them, the car, "—isn't for you. I know that. You're lawns and gardens, and I'm grit and scrub. And I'm no longer a kid who notches his bedpost. Yeah," he interrupted as she tried to speak, "I haven't wanted a woman as much as I want you since I don't know when, and sure, I got sandbagged by my hormones in the garden." He pushed her shoes onto her feet and slid off the car, swinging her down in his arms. "But I've got myself under control now. I'm not going to hurt you by taking you casually and unprotected," he said deliberately, leaving nothing to her imagination. "Got it?" he asked as he stuffed her blouse into her skirt.

Trying to match Cade's matter-of-fact tone, Emma replied,
"Got it. We don't need this kind of complication in our lives."
She edged toward the car door, wanting nothing so much as to
go home and shut the door on the sanctity of her bedroom.

Cade braced his arms on either side of her, stopping her.
"Nope, that's not quite what I meant. Sweetheart, the complication's already there. We've both realized for a while what
happens to me around you. So, no big deal. Guys have been
having that kind of problem around women since caveman
days. But now we know you're not exactly the laced-up,
starched-collar lady you thought you were." His grin bor-
dered on devilish.

Emma swallowed the retort she'd almost blurted out. She
couldn't tell him that she'd always feared what she'd just
learned about herself in his arms. In self-defense, she'd buttoned herself up. "Go on." She crossed her arms and tried to
melt into the car door. "Now what?"

Cade opened the passenger door. "Now we both know what
can happen. We're an explosion waiting to happen. Anything
can trigger it. So, we both have to be very, very careful."

"I agree." What had ever made her think she could take the
kind of risk Cade presented? She knew she couldn't. "Don't
you worry." She smiled stiffly. "I promise, you're safe with
me."

"Starching up already, beauty?" Cade rubbed his thumb
over her mouth. "Good. But I wish I could forget how you
looked, all pink and cream in the moonlight with your eyes
wide and dreamy, your hair mussed."

Defensively, Emma smoothed her hair.

"I'd give anything to have you on a big wide bed in bright
sunlight, beauty," he said, watching her intently. "It would be
something special," he murmured.

Emma's cheeks stained with heat as pictures flashed behind
her quickly closed eyes. She couldn't let him talk like this. His
words made her yearn for something she couldn't allow herself. "As you said, we aren't going to find ourselves in that
position," she said. When his grin widened, she wished she
were better at this kind of male-female jousting.

"I'll go to my grave hearing you say you wanted me to lose control, Emma Rose. But it's not going to happen." He watched as she sank into the seat. "Just do me a favor, will you, counselor?"

"What?" Wilting, Emma forced herself to sit straighter, to face whatever he was going to ask straight on.

"Don't offer me any more charity," Cade growled as he started the engine. "It's too dangerous. For both of us."

Chapter 11

Early the next day Emma drove to her office alone. From the driveway, she glimpsed Cade in the garden, grubbing out kudzu in the morning humidity. She could see progress there. Modest areas of controlled growth dotted the wilderness.

He was shirtless, and sweat shone like oil on his tanned back. When she slowed down to tell him where she was going, he turned and slicked back his dark hair. Behind his dark glasses, he leaned on the hoe and waited for her.

Emma stayed in the car and rolled down the window. She wasn't going near a bare-chested, sweat-drenched Cade. Not with him looking like the present any red-blooded woman would want to find under her Christmas tree. For a long time they stared at each other until Cade finally grinned and strolled over to her. Devil. He knew what she was thinking. They couldn't afford a repeat of the previous night. Maybe she'd turn his case over to another lawyer? She let the idea sift through her mind while she waited for Cade. She needed to solve the situation in order to answer her questions about herself. She was responsible. She would finish it, and fast, she decided as Cade leaned into the open window and her heartbeat sped up.

Emma was glad she couldn't see his eyes. Rubbing her palms on the steering wheel, she spoke carefully, controlling her tendency to rush into speech around him. "I'm going to my office. I'll start the paperwork on your petition to modify custody. I'll try to hurry it along. In order to work on your case, I promised Charlie, my boss, I'd work on a new case that came in over the weekend. I'll be gone most of the day. If you need anything, ask Lucy."

"Very efficient," Cade commented, raising his glasses. He was amused.

"I told Francine I'd call her today. I'll see what I can do about the situation with Quint." Emma recognized she was clipping off words as though giving work orders for the day to the handyman. Cade, on the other hand, was a picture of indolent composure.

"Admirable," he drawled, scrawling designs on the windshield.

Emma dropped her elbow off the window. "That's it, I think. Can I pick up anything for you? Or will you be gone?" Anxiety crept in. Maybe he should leave. She didn't want him to.

"I'm not leaving. Where, in fact, would I go?"

"You're not trapped here, you know," Emma said emphatically. He was, in fact, dependent on her for transportation, everything, at this point. She might as well be his jailer. "If you want to go anywhere, see anybody—except Quint—we can make arrangements."

"Nope. I promised your mother I'd take care of her garden. That's what I'll be doing. All day," he added as she broke in.

"Look, Cade, you're not in prison. You don't have to kill yourself on this yard. The garden's been neglected for years. It doesn't have to be transformed today."

"I made a promise," Cade said. "I'll stay. Working out here isn't about to kill me, so go on, counselor. Do what you have to do to get my son back to me. If you can." He snapped the sunglasses down on his nose and strode off.

She started to call him back and tell him that she'd planned to talk Francine into going to a special meeting of HELP, a counselling group, with her, but his rigid back changed her mind. If he wanted to stalk off, he could just wait. She'd tell him later.

In her rearview mirror as she spun off, she saw Cade stop the smooth swing of the hoe and look after her.

When she arrived at the courthouse, she understood from the averted glances that everyone knew she was handling Cade's case. She'd hoped her boss hadn't broadcast it all over, but no such luck. Her colleagues in the prosecutor's office were going to be difficult, and she didn't blame them. She didn't tell Cade, but she'd had to call in several favors to get official permission to take the dratted case. Judging from the cynical smiles and sarcastic greetings she received now, she'd have a lot of fence-mending to do when the dust settled. To her colleagues, she was a turncoat, and prosecutors didn't forgive easily. Total commitment to conviction—that was the acceptable attitude. Well, she'd been committed. Now she had to discover if she'd let her emotions interfere with justice. She didn't owe anybody an explanation. She'd paid her dues several times over, and they'd have to give her a little leeway. If they couldn't—

By the time Emma slammed the door of her office behind her, she'd worked up a temper.

Julie, her tough-as-old-gristle secretary, eleven years older than Emma, looked everywhere except straight at her, saying only, "Your messages are on your desk. Charlie said you'd be in today using your office for a civil case even though you were still on vacation. He said he okayed it." Julie took a sip from her ever-present can of cola. Over the rim of the can, her raised eyebrow was accusatory. "Hannah Westin wants to see you if you have time."

"Thanks, Julie, I'll give her a ring."

"Buddy left you a present on your desk," Julie said. "I don't think it's a love offering."

"That was fast work. What happened? Did Charlie broadcast the news on TV? Or send out a county-wide memo?" Emma couldn't believe it. "One day, and everyone knows I'm handling a civil case for Cade Boudreau? Nobody wasted any time spreading the news, Julie. Have you jumped on the bandwagon, too?'' Emma's temper boiled over. Losing Julie's support would be tough.

Julie tapped her pencil. ''Emma, I don't want to butt in—''

''Then don't, Jules, okay? I'd appreciate it if you kept your observations to yourself. What I could use is time to sort things out and a small, that's all I'm asking, Jules, just a *small* measure of faith that I know what I'm doing. Is that too much to ask?'' Emma slapped her briefcase on Julie's desk.

''Around here, kiddo? Probably. I wouldn't turn my back on anyone if I were you,'' Julie answered, crossing her long tanned legs. ''But, hey, what do I know? You get my vote, but it's not worth a hill of beans.''

''Thanks, Jules.'' Emma smiled with difficulty. ''It means a lot.'' She hadn't expected the antagonism of her colleagues to be this strong. She'd really believed they would trust her. ''Look, on second thought, how about giving Hannah a call for me? See if she can stop in before noon? I'm going to be out of here by then.''

''Sure, boss.'' Julie shot her a mischievous grin and raised her forked fingers to her forehead in the universal warding-off-of-evil gesture. She pitched her can into a large recyclables box.

''You think Charlie's going to fire me over this?'' Emma grabbed her briefcase and shook her head, laughing. ''Not Cheap Charlie. I work for the right price.''

''There's that, kiddo. Get to work. I'll fend off the sharks as long as I can.'' Julie popped the top on a fresh soda. ''Come running when the water's red under your door, will ya?''

''Sure.'' Emma wrinkled her nose and grinned. ''Right out the back door.''

The glass door of her office safely shut behind her, Emma collapsed into her chair. The square box with a gaudy red ribbon sitting in the middle of her desk was unavoidable. She pushed the ribbons off and lifted the lid cautiously. Buddy and his cohorts on the police force had been known to wrap up all kinds of things as expressions of admiration, complaint or contempt.

The yellow cupcake was enormous. Nauseatingly yellow icing piled thick on top was adding insult to injury. The guys had made their point with overkill. Stinkers.

Emma shoved the box aside. She could take the heat. You had to learn to in the state's attorney's office or you didn't survive. Sooner or later, she'd settle with Buddy. She reached for the phone and her numbers file.

During the next two hours, Emma made preliminary phone calls and did the paperwork on Cade's petition to modify custody and arranged for an investigator to interview the woman who'd been first on the scene after Francine's attack. Emma hesitated before asking the investigator to check any rumors that Francine had been seeing someone. Having met Francine, Emma was uncomfortable taking that approach, but she was determined to find out who, since it hadn't been Cade, had hurt Francine.

She made a long phone call to HELP, the shelter for abused women and their children, before she dialed Francine's number. Francine answered in monosyllables, volunteering only that Quint had gone to school, but he wouldn't talk to her. Although the conversation was difficult, Emma finally convinced her to go with her to the shelter. Emma would drive, but Francine preferred to leave from the parking lot of the hospital where she worked and return there, driving herself home afterwards. Emma understood Francine's need to have some control over the situation and agreed.

The afternoon was going to be a nightmare headache.

As Emma hung up the phone, Hannah poked her head through the door. "All clear?"

"Sure." Emma motioned her to a chair.

Hannah, a tall, no-nonsense prosecutor had appointed herself Emma's mentor the first day Emma came to work. Recently returned from Idaho where she'd been flown to testify in a murder trial, Hannah had apparently heard the office gossip. Leaning back in the chair, she folded her hands under her chin. "Big problem, Emma?"

"Nothing I can't handle," Emma returned, settling the phone into the cradle.

"You sure?"

"No," Emma said. Laughing, she added, "Right now, I'm not sure of anything, but I'm plodding along. I think I'll work everything out."

"Need any help?" As Emma shook her head, Hannah added, "If you do, ask."

"You're not deserting the sinking ship?" Emma leaned forward and pushed the cupcake toward Hannah. "Want some? It's from Cally's Bakery."

"I heard about it." Hannah ran her finger through the icing. "Lemon. Not bad. Sure, cut off a slice. Best thing to do with this baby." She licked her finger. "Buddy hasn't referred to you as the Cupcake in a long time, Emma. The boys in blue must be, to put it nicely, extremely ticked off. You know how suspicious they are. Every time one of their arrests falls apart, they complain. We don't prosecute their cases hard enough. We're too soft on the world's sleaze balls."

"I know," Emma said, nibbling at the cupcake. "Wonder if they had Cally decorate this specially? She's usually more restrained."

"They trust you. Even brag that if Mighty Mouse gets their case, they've got a sure conviction, so they're extra ticked."

"I hate that nickname." Emma mashed the cupcake with her finger, collecting crumbs and icing. Cade had almost laughed when she'd told him she had a tall personality. Telling her not to offer him any more charity. "Men," she groused.

"Make you want to run 'em over with a steamroller, sometimes, don't they? Anyway, the point is, you have a good case record, Emma. You've worked hard. The guys know it, but now they think you've let them down, that you're wussing out. They're taking it personally. You know how they are."

"Oh, yes. They made my first six months in this office hell."

"They thought you'd crumble the first time things got rough. They had you pegged for a goody two shoes until people started seeing how lethal you were in court. Then they came around. But the problem is that once they start doubting *your* commitment, the next time they have to intervene in a domestic—which we know they adore doing—they're going to wonder if you'll back them up. They want you to be so hard-nosed that a flea couldn't escape through any cracks in your case. They'll wonder why bother if you're going soft on them." Hannah shrugged. "That's the setup around here. You know it."

"I can't help what they think. If that's what they believe, that's their problem. I have enough of my own right now, and I'm doing the best I can, so tell them I said—" Emma took a breath. "Tell Buddy I said to take a flying leap, okay?" Emma wiped icing off her fingers. "I think I'll write them the sweetest ol' thank-you note for this cupcake." She grinned at Hannah.

"That's it?" Hannah stood up and stretched. "All right, Mouse. Good luck."

"Hannah, hang on a sec." Emma rubbed her neck before asking, "One quick question. Have you ever gone out to the HELP shelter?"

"Lots of times. Before you came, I handled most of the domestic violence cases, but Charlie saw that you really went to town on them, and he's been assigning them to you. I like the drug cases, personally. I purely love—" she dragged out the word with a wicked smile "—going head-to-head against those slimy creeps. They don't like facing a woman prosecutor. Makes 'em feel like nobody respects them." She left her hand on the doorknob. "What about HELP?"

"I have an appointment there today. I've never gone before." Emma brushed crumbs off her desk into the trash can. They'd never talked about Emma's reasons for taking the major caseload of domestic assault cases, and she wasn't going to begin now.

Out in the anteroom, Julie laughed and hung up her phone. Down the hall, a door slammed.

Finally, Hannah commented, "I wondered why you never went there since you were interested enough in the cases to put in so many extra hours." She paused and waited expectantly. "No comment?" She opened the door and swung it back and forth, thinking. "You may be surprised. I don't know. It won't be what you expect. Going alone?"

"No." Emma swiveled in her chair. "Thanks for stopping in, Hannah. I owe you."

"Of course you do, Mouse, but who's keeping track? Incidentally, I remember the Boudreau trial. I thought you did a good job. Interesting man, though. Very still waters and all that." Hannah flipped a farewell and shut the door behind her.

Cade was definitely still waters, and in more ways than two, Emma reflected. Waters she had no business swimming in, not without a guaranteed lifesaver. He would be no temptation if it were just the physical humming, the sense of being alive, she felt around him. Pensively she recalled the way he focused on her, as though no one else existed in the world when he looked at her. That was what she had a hard time resisting.

Emma sternly banished the image of a bare-chested Cade hacking kudzu and buried herself in catching up until it was time to meet Francine. Hurrying to her car, she almost called Francine to cancel. Maybe dragging her out to the shelter wasn't such a good idea. Maybe it would backfire. Maybe Francine would create a scene. Emma groaned. In the past few days, she'd had enough scenes to last her a lifetime.

Francine needed to see that many women were able to summon up enough courage to remove themselves and their children from abusive, dangerous situations. Abusive and dangerous went hand in hand. The women paid, sometimes with their lives, for remaining in the situation, but their children paid, too, in damaged lives, often repeating the patterns they'd learned at home, becoming abuser or victim.

Francine had to know that even though she'd lied about Cade, she didn't have to protect whoever had really attacked her. There were people and organizations she could turn to. No, visiting the shelter was a good idea.

When Emma parked her car in the hospital lot, Francine was waiting, her face grim. Emma leaned over and opened the door.

"Sorry. Am I late?" She checked her watch.

"You're early." Francine clipped her seat belt.

"I'm very grateful you agreed to come along with me. I know this won't be easy for you."

Francine glanced over quickly and opened her mouth as though she were going to say something, but then she turned away.

"We won't stay long. You'll be home before Quint."

"He's staying after school. Football tryouts for the seventh grade team. He's like his father, crazy about football. Quint said he wasn't going to go to school if I didn't let him try out for football," Francine admitted, her expression defeated.

"Oh?" Emma wondered how much she could ask Francine before being intrusive. "Does he put you on the spot like that often?"

"I can handle him," Francine said, her frown defensive. "I know what to do with my son."

"I'm sorry," Emma apologized. "Really, I didn't mean to imply you didn't. He's very handsome," she ventured.

"I know. I shouldn't brag on him, but girls call him all the time. You should see him dressed up." Francine's quick smile changed her whole face, and for a second Emma glimpsed the girl-woman who'd caught Cade's eyes. "He's real upset about this thing with Cade." Francine rolled down the window.

"Do you have any suggestions? Any way I can help?" Emma wasn't about to step over the line again.

"I don't know." Francine pursed her mouth. "I don't know what to say to him. He walks away whenever I bring up Cade's name." Francine looked as though she were going to add something, but once again she closed her mouth.

Emma almost pushed. If they'd been in court, she would have. Instead, she retreated, becoming quiet, leaving the burden of conversation on Francine. Whatever she was holding back was important. Emma's instincts were on red alert.

Before the silence became oppressive enough to make Francine talk, Emma pulled into the shell driveway of the shelter. A chain link fence surrounded the house and yard where two boys and three girls were playing. The four women in the yard with the children looked up the moment the car stopped. One of the women herded the children inside while a short chunky woman walked quickly and purposefully over to the car before Emma or Francine could get out.

Informed of the procedure on the phone, Emma waited patiently, holding out identification.

"Hey there," the woman said in a low serene voice. "You're Ms. O'Riley? Great!" Her smile was sweet, but her eyes were old with terrible knowledge. "We've been expecting you. Glad you could come. I've heard about you. You've been a real help to HELP." She shrugged as she stuck out her hand. "Sometimes the name's a little awkward, but Helping Everyone Live with Pride was the choice of the first group of women and children who voted, so we've kept the acronym. I'm Sue. No last names here."

As she shook Sue's work-worn hand, Emma revised her expectations. Sue's cheerfulness amazed her. She'd been prepared for melancholy, depression, fear, not this aggressively upbeat competence. "Thanks for letting us come."

"No problem. We call the cops on visitors unless they've been cleared, is all. They've been good about responding and have gotten here fast the few times we've called. I've already given the women inside the all-clear sign." Seeing Emma's surprise, Sue said, "We try to make sure no one looking for trouble finds us. We go overboard on security. The address is confidential, as you know, even though the contact number isn't. Our goal is to make sure the folks who come to us will feel safe and be safe while they buy time to sort out what they're going to do."

They entered the heavily reinforced side door of the shelter. Francine was quiet and stayed off to the side.

"What can we do for you, Ms. O'Riley?" Sue paused by a door with a hand-lettered Director sign.

"Basically, what I'd like, as I explained over the phone," Emma began, "is to talk to a few of the women and let them know what they can expect from my office, what kind of support they'll have in a trial situation and what they can do afterward. I know our office isn't picture-perfect, but we have a good conviction record. There's room for improvement in what happens after the abuser is released, and I'd like to make some suggestions to your people. If they have any ideas or complaints, I'll see what can be done." Emma's hands were cold. She didn't want to go inside.

"You can wander around and talk to the women. Some may not talk with you. They're still too frightened. Jumpy. You'll have enough sense, I'm sure, to give them space. We'd rather you didn't talk with the kids. If they're playing and you want to enter their game, fine, but nothing serious. When you're ready to leave, I'll check you out. Okay? Any problems with the ground rules?" Sue's friendly smile was firm. Nobody was going to mess with her shelter.

"None at all." Emma pasted a smile on her face as Sue opened the main door.

Not large, the shelter was divided into areas by plywood boards nailed together so that some places were private. Cots and bags of clothes lined these oases. There was a large community kitchen with an old gas stove and a refrigerator. Two dark-eyed boys in T-shirts, their hair spiking up all over, were drinking milk and eating peanut butter sandwiches at a Formica table. A vase of bright purple flowers adorned the table.

Neither of the boys looked at Emma or Francine. Francine sat down with them. The boys were sallow with dark circles under their eyes. They were clean and too quiet. The whole place was eerily quiet, and Emma wanted to run as fast as she could.

"How many people are you sheltering right now?" she asked as she and Sue went to the conversation area.

"Too many for our resources, but we won't turn away anyone who shows up. For some of them, it's taken more courage than anyone who hasn't been in the same boat can imagine. As of this morning, twenty women and fourteen children are in residence, but a few will give in and go back to husbands or boyfriends who promise they'll never again hit them or beat them or do whatever it was that sent these women here in the first place."

Emma said softly, "But they will. Always. No matter how many promises they make, they'll hit again." In the quiet shelter, she could hear raised voices, slaps and weeping. She touched the concrete wall and came back to the present.

"Of course they will. Unless they undergo counseling. One of the good things to come out of public awareness is that now, on a first offense, the man usually is sent to a counseling program. That's progress."

In a low voice, Emma said, "The catch is, we're talking about reported offenses. Too much goes unreported."

"Oh, sure," Sue said, and for the first time her smile wavered. "It's a hell of a situation. Women are ashamed to report they've been used as a punching bag. They buy in to the guy's line that he wouldn't have treated them like that if, gee, honey, you'd just cook better, or lose weight, or not blink at the wrong time. Whatever. They'll use any excuse to put the blame anywhere except where it belongs. On them. On their failure to deal with anger and their own inadequacies. We women keep forgiving these bastards.'' She turned away and covered her eyes for a long moment.

"For love," Emma said and felt cold to the bone. Love. The oblivion of the senses. Women willing to endure anything in the hope of being loved. Sometimes they were loved to death. Emma's hands were shaking. She searched futilely for skirt pockets, forgetting her skirt was pocketless. Finally she wound her fingers through the strap of her purse.

"Love." Sue's laugh was like a fingernail on chalk. "Somehow we have to teach each other that love doesn't mean unlimited forgiveness. We have to learn not to put up with put-downs and slap-downs in the name of love." She scowled. "God, I get so mad—these young girls, fifteen, sixteen, show up sometimes, stay a night or two and leave because they just *know* he loves them and he'll never hurt them again."

"They're young," Emma excused, knowing a painful education faced the girls.

"Oh, hell. Young, old, black, white, Hispanic, you name it. Age, education, background don't matter." Sue's voice grew vehement. "What matters is if the woman loves herself enough to know nobody has the right to slap her or her kids around. Nobody."

Emma tasted blood. She hadn't realized she'd been chewing the inside of her cheek. Startled, she looked up as Sue handed her a handkerchief.

"Here, Ms. O'Riley. Tears aren't going to help anybody here, but action will."

Emma brushed her face and her fingers came away wet with tears she hadn't known she shed.

Touching her lightly on the shoulder, Sue nodded with understanding. "Like that, is it?"

Emma couldn't answer. Not here. Not in this place with these women who'd reached down deep inside and dredged up a courage beyond imagining. If they stayed, they would save themselves. If they didn't, if they went back— "Thanks." Emma shoved her glasses up and blotted her eyes. "Listen, if you don't mind, I think I'd like to wander around by myself and visit for a while." She needed time alone.

"Sure." Sue's sturdy figure disappeared around a plywood divider, but her cheerful voice carried in the quiet as she answered a low-spoken question about clothing.

Looking over her shoulder to the kitchen, Emma saw Francine playing cat's cradle with the two boys. She was smiling and relaxed, absorbed in the solemn eyes of the children who were watching her quickly flying fingers weave intricate patterns in the string. She faltered for an instant as she glanced at Emma, then bent over the table when Emma indicated with a shake of her head that it wasn't time to go.

Although she tried to divorce herself from what she heard over and over again in the hour she stayed talking to several of the women who'd gathered in the main area, Emma couldn't. Some of the women were poor, some weren't. Some had relatives who could have offered safety but didn't want to be involved. Others, having scooped up their children and fled into the night, had no other place to go. One woman crouched in a corner, holding her infant girl, and rocked back and froth, ignoring the overtures of the other women.

Sue's cheerful pragmatism set the tone of the shelter. The women shared information necessary for surviving on their own. One middle-aged woman, with graying blond hair, an arm in a sling and a flattened nose, insisted she couldn't make it without her husband. Nobody would ever hire her. She was too old. That was what he'd told her, and she believed it. Finally, a tiny black woman with short-cropped hair leaned over and said, "Honey, don't listen to that man. He just wants you back so he can have someone to kick. You wouldn't let him kick around your pet dog the way he's been treating you, would you? Besides, honey, you'd be better off old and alone than old and whomped on." The three or four chuckles and nods told Emma their own story.

The shelter was the only safe place for these women, their last resort.

On the way to the hospital parking lot, neither Emma nor Francine talked. Emma couldn't, and Francine didn't seem to want to.

When Emma stopped in the lot, Francine got out of the car and stood for a moment with the door open. Emma waited, the shaking that had begun when she'd stepped into the shelter still running through her, until Francine said in a low, splintery voice, "You talk with Quint at his school. I'll tell him you'll be there. If you can convince him to see Cade, go ahead. But not at the house. Somewhere else. And you stay with them."

Francine shut the door and walked away, an unhappy, repressed woman with secrets Emma needed to know. All the way home in the spring afternoon, Emma thought about her own secrets while she tried to keep the car on the road.

It was almost twilight when she drove into the driveway, and she half expected to see Cade still slashing at kudzu. With the large, cleared areas around it, the house seemed more dilapidated than ever, and Emma dreaded walking through the front door. She was disoriented and apprehensive, in limbo and waiting for something unpleasant.

When she walked into the dining room, Cade, Lucy and her mother glanced up from the cards they had fanned out in their hands. Cade squinted, then he stood up abruptly. His eyes kept her upright despite the cold coming over her in waves, a glass shield dropping fast, muffling sounds.

"Hey, sugar," Lucy said.

Her mother smiled and looked at the five cards she held.

Past and present flashed and flashed and froze in a shocking still frame. Lucy, Becca and her father. No, Cade. Cade in her father's seat. Her father. The three of them looking at her with puzzled faces and silent, moving mouths.

Chapter 12

Cade slapped his cards on the table and shoved his chair back as Emma came into the room. Alarm skittered down his spine as he watched her reluctant entrance. Her soft mouth was trembling. Her eyes were an unfocused, murky hazel. What had happened to her since this morning? Cade cursed as he saw her knees buckle, and he was at her side before she crumpled to the floor. He caught her against him as her eyelids flickered and shut.

Behind him, Lucy's, "Sugar?" and Becca's plaintive, "Emma Rose?" registered distantly but, intent on Emma, he ignored them. She recovered almost instantly, but confusion and unhappiness stirred in her eyes. She stared at him with recognition for a second before awareness took over.

"Cade?" she asked, touching his cheek. Her fingers were the deep down cold of shock.

"Emma, I'm taking you upstairs," Cade said. He made his voice only for her ears, squelching his desire to snatch her up in his arms and double-time it out of the claustrophobic room.

"Sugar, come on in and say hello. We'll see about supper in a while." Lucy was tapping her cards on the table. Concern pleated her square face.

Becca ruffled her cards and fanned them, picked one and held it for a second, glancing at Cade and Emma before returning her attention to the cards. Then she placed the queen of hearts precisely on the table. Her fingernails clicked against the wood.

"Deal me out," Cade said. He stifled a vicious urge to fling the cards on the floor. "I have to talk with Emma. We'll be back," he snarled and swooped Emma forward so fast he walked her right out of her high heels. "Let's go, Emma," he muttered. "Move it."

He didn't give a damn. Something was wrong, and he was going to find out, or else.

The silence behind him lasted only until Becca said in her musical voice, "Two cards, please, Lucy."

Out of Lucy's and Becca's sight, Cade hauled Emma into his arms and took the stairs two at a time. She was a little bit of nothing in his arms, no more than a puff of air, and he could feel her hipbones against him through the folds of her skirt. Too small. Too fragile.

Curling a slender arm around his neck, she dropped her head on his chest.

She was too cold. Cade pulled her closer, warming her against him, and kicked open the door to her bedroom.

Once more she asked, "Cade? It's you?"

"Hell, yeah, beauty, who else?" he snapped. He had to get her warm first, and then, by God, he was going to skin alive whoever was responsible for the bruised, defenseless look on her white face.

Bracing her with one arm and his raised leg, Cade ripped back the spread and lay her on the bed. In a movement so quick he didn't give her time to object, he reached under her skirt and stripped off her panty hose, dropping the silky stuff on the floor where it lay, a spill of cream. He bundled the top sheet and bedspread close around her, rubbing her arms until she looked at him. As though a new picture clicked into her mind, her eyes focused on him.

"You're going to rub off all my skin if you keep that up, Cade."

"You're cold." He rubbed her legs under the spread, sneaking a hand under and checking her feet. He closed his palm around the cold arch of a foot and slipped it under his shirt against his chest, five toes icy against the heat of his skin. "What the hell happened, Emma?" He stuffed her other foot under his shirt, ignoring her protest.

"Nothing." Wrapped up tight as a papoose in the bedspread, she was all big eyes and soft mouth, her hair clinging to the pillow, and he didn't believe her for a minute.

"Bull," he said bluntly just as Lucy knocked on the door. "Don't move," Cade ordered and tucked her feet under the spread as he rose. "Don't even think about it."

If possible, her eyes got wider.

Blocking the doorway, he glared at Lucy. "What?" About time somebody checked on Emma. Hell, on this side of the river, card games seemed to be more important than Emma showing up looking like something the cat dragged in. "Cards gone dead on you?"

"I'm taking a break. Becca's waiting for me. How's Emma?" Lucy's concern was obviously real.

Cade downshifted his belligerence. Lucy wasn't to blame. If he wanted to dump blame on anybody's shoulders, he reckoned he should be shoveling it hard onto his own. After all, he'd hauled Emma, willy-nilly, into his mess. Anything happened to her, he was responsible. Nobody else. He stepped back. "In shock, but better. She hasn't said what happened. But she will," he said, turning to glower at Emma.

"How can I help?" Lucy's freckles stood out on her unsmiling face.

"I don't know." Cade didn't intend to be ignorant for much longer. "I'll let you know," he said with his hand on the door, ready to shut it.

Lucy finally let a trace of a smile sparkle in her face. "I always did admire a take-charge man." Her shrewd smile spread, gaining power, and drained Cade's immediate need to pull down the house around her ears. Or Becca's. Seeing his unwilling, answering smile, Lucy nodded. "Emma will be fine with you. I'll go see about Becca. She'll be fretting by now."

"Why doesn't she come up and look in on her daughter then?" Cade was genuinely stumped and angered by Becca's behavior. She was strange, no denying that, but, up until now, he'd thought she cared about Emma.

"Becca doesn't do real well with problems." Turning away, she added, "You should talk with Emma, if she'll let you. It's not my business to tell you about Becca's problems, but she loves Emma. In her own fashion."

Frowning, Cade gazed after Lucy. Strange way of showing love in this house. He thought about flaking paint and an untended garden. He looked at Emma's pointy cat face, still pale and stunned. Both the house and Emma needed looking after. They needed—attention.

But he wasn't the right man, Cade reminded himself as the bed dipped under his weight when he sat down.

He brushed Emma's hair off her forehead. "Hey, beauty," he said. Her skin was warming even as he touched it. He left his hand on her cheek to monitor her temperature. "Back in the right year?"

"Sure," she answered with a suggestion of her usual starchiness. Her spiky eyelashes flicked up, down, up, and she stared steadily at him. "I told you I'm fine."

"Yeah, I heard you. Hard to believe, Emma, when you look like you just walked away from a wreck. Better tell me about it. I'm not leaving this room until you do, you know," he said, putting his hand flat on her chest and restraining her as she struggled to a sitting position. Her breasts were small and soft under his hand. "Stay right where you are. You're still a chunk of ice."

"I am perfectly okay. Now get out of here and leave me alone." Her pulse trembled rapidly against the side of her neck.

"Sure you are." Cade laid two fingers against the thready beating. "Where'd you go today?" He leaned down, pinning the spread on either side of her, and bounced once. "Tell me, Emma."

She was a pint-size lump under the cover, no match for his strength and determination, and he knew it. But he wasn't going to give her any quarter. She needed help, and even if he was the wrong man at the wrong time, he was all she had. He thumped the bed once more, not gently, and waited.

"All right!" she said frantically. "I went to the office. I got a little harassment, but I expected that. I told you taking your case would annoy my office."

Watching the color fade and flush, Cade said, "That's not what you're upset about."

"I'm not upset!" she wailed, her voice rising.

"Emma," Cade said, lowering onto his elbows, "just shut up and tell me what happened, will you, sweetheart?" He sat up again and tapped her nose.

"I prepared the papers for custody change," she said.

"And?" he encouraged her, loosening the spread as the light pink stayed in her face. "Good girl. Keep going."

She shut her eyes and surrendered. "I took Francine to the HELP shelter, that's all." She turned her head on the pillow, and her hair curtained her from him.

"HELP?"

"An emergency shelter for women who need to escape husbands or lovers who are abusing them."

"Why did you go behind my back?" He leaned closer, wanting to see her face. Her too-revealing, honest eyes. Had he been wrong to trust her? Why hadn't she told him she was taking Francine there? Were they ganging up on him? Old fears nurtured in prison returned.

"I didn't, Cade. You know I wouldn't," she said and like sunlight pouring into a dark room, the truth finally hit him.

Emma would never betray him. She might not agree with him, but she would play by honorable rules. "Yeah," he said. "I'm sorry. I'm not a trusting man."

Edging closer, Cade lifted the soft puff of hair, pushing it away from her neck and smoothing it to the side, leaving the flawless white skin of her neck bare and defenseless.

"I thought going there would help Francine."

She was telling him something significant, but he didn't understand it. "Did Francine say something? About what happened?"

Under the covers, Emma rolled onto her stomach. Her muffled no didn't make anything clear to Cade.

"Come on, Emma." Easing down the spread, he placed his thumbs horizontally on the narrow line of her spine, then walked them up her tensed muscles, cupping her slim rib cage and disregarding the sweep of his fingers against the sides of her breasts.

As her muscles softened under his touch, the familiar heat rose in Cade, but he didn't stop his continuous kneading while he waited in the quiet room to hear what she would say. Under his hands, Emma's ribs expanded and contracted with her breathing, and he moved his thumbs slower and slower in synchronization, willing her to come out from behind her garden wall.

Eventually Emma spoke. "Francine said you can see Quint tomorrow if he agrees to it. I'm supposed to check with him at his school."

Distracted, Cade stopped. "Yeah?" And then he resumed his careful kneading. He knew about red herrings, too. "Think you can talk him into it?"

"I'll try," Emma said, exhaustion deadening her voice, but if she thought he was going to let her off that easily, she wasn't her usual self.

"That's good. I appreciate what you've done, Emma Rose," Cade said in a dangerously soft voice, "but I want to hear the rest of the story about the shelter."

Her muscles tightened, but he worked on the kinks, sliding her silky blouse under his thumbs and over the taut buttons of her spine until she sighed and shifted, one foot coming to rest at the edge of the bed.

The bottoms of five small toes peeped up at Cade. With thumb and little finger, he spanned toe to heel. His hand was longer than her feet.

He pulled the spread over her toes and put them safely out of sight and reach. "I'm waiting, Emma," he whispered, ignoring the current rushing strong and true and deep in his blood, not desire, not tenderness, just *something*.

Drowsy now, her words slurring, Emma said, "All those women, Cade, with their children. Their faces. The children's eyes. What they've seen. So much violence. The things those children have seen," she repeated, eyelashes fluttering and growing still against the tip of his thumb. "That's the story. But at least they're there, safe."

Clickety, clickety. Click. The tumblers fell into place, and Cade finally understood. Oh, not everything, he thought furiously as he lifted the ends of Emma's shining hair, but enough. Too much. Little girl with flyaway hair and her sunshiney-smile, gone—her childhood blown away.

Blinding anger roared through him. The room went dark, and then his vision cleared, but anger still cooked.

He remembered the smiling, handsome man in the picture hung in a place of honor in the hall.

One key piece of the puzzle was missing, but now Cade understood why Emma was so protective of her mother. He might never find out why Becca grew fretful toward evening as she waited for a husband who was never coming home again, or exactly why going to the HELP shelter had pushed Emma over an invisible edge, but, oh, yes, light was shining in the dark corners in this house.

He straightened the blue sheet around her drawn face. Emma, with her brave lawyer-lady clothes and her dark memories and no one to lean on. He stroked the silky sweep of her hair. So soft, like her.

Emma.

What was he going to do with her?

Nothing.

All he could do was stay here. For the moment.

And while Emma slept, Cade watched over her, knowing and accepting that he would never explore that strange current of tenderness and yearning running deep inside him, gouging out a new channel in his closed-off heart.

When Emma dragged herself out of bed late the next morning, she lurched into the shower, hoping the lethargy weighing her down would lift in the shower steam. Dressing, she moved in slow motion, pulling on nylons, brushing her hair and slicking on lipstick with shaky, uncertain movements.

The reflection of her washed-out face and drooping shoulders in her full-length mirror sent a flickering charge through her internal battery. She'd be no match for Quint like this.

Color, she needed color.

Pulling off the navy-and-white piped suit, Emma yanked a yellow outfit she'd only worn once off its padded hanger and threaded shiny black-and-yellow enamel earrings on her ears. She pulled a drawer open and grabbed a necklace she seldom wore and checked herself in the mirror. Against the clear yellow of the wrap-tied blouse, the large, black metal woven necklace was glittery and attention-grabbing.

Nobody would notice her washed-out face in the sheer shine of suit and necklace. In fact, all the shriekingly exuberant color pepped her up. She smiled and put on her black patent leather high heels, cinching the wide black belt with its yellow tassels around her waist. She'd lost weight.

She had to see Cade. She didn't want to see Cade. From the moment her eyelids had blearily lifted, her mind had spitefully thrown up images of Cade. Cade carrying her up the stairs, Cade staying with her. Taking care of her.

Emma paused at the head of the staircase. She didn't need Cade to take care of her. She'd always done fine on her own. The lingering memory of his large, solid presence by her side in the dark was easily forgettable. She rubbed the banister as she went downstairs. In a week she would have forgotten the sense of safety and security he'd given her.

She'd make herself forget.

Voices and coffee smells from the kitchen drew her. Emma stepped into the hall and pushed open the kitchen door.

Lucy and Cade looked up from their chicken salad. "Whooee. Lord love us, sugar, let there be light." Lucy shaded her eyes. "Come have some chicken and grapes. Your mama's not up to eatin' anything yet today." At Emma's frown, Lucy said, "She's okay. I took her some toast and coffee."

Cade watched her, and Emma couldn't stand the intensity of his gaze. Not while her internal workings were in pieces. In a few minutes she would deal with Cade. But not yet. She lowered her eyes. "Morning," she said, including both of them. "I'll get coffee and juice, Lucy."

"Nice outfit, Emma Rose," Cade said. "Cheerful."

"Thanks," Emma muttered and sipped Lucy's pitch-black coffee, welcoming the bang of caffeine. "I thought so, too."

She took a big gulp and steadied her coffee on the table as Lucy stood up.

"While your mama's sleeping, Emma, I'm going to run out to the store and pick up some chops for tonight. Y'all going to be here? If it's just Becca and me, we'll have some spaghetti I've been saving."

When Cade shrugged, leaving the decision to her, Emma said, "I don't know, Lucy. Don't plan on us, okay? If you have extra and we're back, fine. Don't worry. I'll cook if I'm here. If not, you and mama do what you want."

Thinking, Lucy paused and picked up a plate of fruit stems and leftover salad. "We can always have the chops another night. I'm going to go ahead and get them so we'll have 'em on hand." She rinsed her dishes and lined them up in the dishwasher. "See y'all later."

Not in any hurry to break the silence, Emma sipped again at her coffee. Her brain had finally decided it was alive. Sunshine through the open window was warm on her face.

Cade's fork clattered to the table. "Emma, I'm going to clean up, then I'm going out to my ranch for a while."

"What?" Emma made the mistake of looking up from the muddy coffee and into Cade's clear gray eyes. His eyes packed a jolt as strong as Lucy's caffeine-infused coffee.

"I'm going to be staying at the ranch from now on." His mouth was a thin line and his expression guarded.

"Why?" Stumbling over the word, Emma tried to untangle her numb tongue. His decision had something to do with what had happened last night. "How?"

He rose, taking his plate and cup to the sink. "I called my friend, the guy who loaned me his skiff." He glanced at her while he rinsed the dishes. "He's going to give me a ride out there while you see Quint." As she started to speak, Cade continued in an even voice, "Yeah, I heard you say you were going to set it up. You tell me where, and I'll be there."

"How?" Emma repeated stupidly, unprepared for the speed at which Cade was moving. He was making her giddy.

He closed the dishwasher and leaned against it. "My old Jeep's at the ranch. It's not worth much, but Whammer's going to help me get it running if we can."

"Whammer?" Emma looked suspiciously at her coffee.

Grinning, Cade folded his arms. "Whammer's an ex-football player. He hasn't been Nathan Bedford Forrest Robert E. Lee Jones since he was twelve pounds. His daddy is an unreconstructed Southern history buff," Cade explained when Emma rubbed her forehead.

As Emma moodily stuck her spoon in the black coffee and stirred, she contemplated the idea of an infant burdened with that kind of tribute to history. "Whammer," she said. "It's an improvement, I think."

Staying on the other side of the kitchen from her, Cade went on. "I'll come back for a few more mornings and work until I beat your mama's garden into submission, so whoever you hire after I'm gone—" he scuffed his boot on the floor "—can keep it under control." His look was hard and direct. "I want my own things around me."

She hadn't wanted him here in the first place. So why did she feel forsaken at the thought of Cade's leaving? She needed more coffee. Coffee grounds and a tablespoon of coffee clumped in the bottom of her cup. Well.

"It's for the best, Emma." His boot tapped the floor.

Staring at his boots, Emma nodded her head. "Yes." She didn't want him to go. She swallowed. "Definitely. You have to start getting your life in order."

"So do you." His arms were folded across his wide chest and his boot kept up its steady tap, tap, tapping. "I've messed up your life enough."

"Oh, well," Emma said, and lowered her coffee cup to the table. Coffee grounds mixed with dark liquid spilled onto the table as she set the cup down unevenly.

In front of her, Cade's wide, large hands sloshed a dishrag over the puddle and wiped everything clean. "Where do you want me to meet you? How about the park we passed yesterday? Close to the house?"

Nodding, Emma touched a grain of coffee Cade had missed. "All right. It will be easier on Quint that way. Francine wanted me to stay while you talk with him, but I won't intrude." Emma looked up finally.

Hunched over the table, Cade was at eye level. "I know you won't. I'll be there, waiting." His knuckles were white. "Emma, please." He stood up. "Convince him. I just want to talk with him. It's been so long. I—" He flung the dishrag into the sink. "Please."

"I'll do my best, Cade. Can you be there by four?"

Nodding, his back to her, Cade straightened out the dish-rag. "I'll be there. Don't worry."

"I hope Quint will be, too." Emma pressed her cool fingers to her throbbing temples. Well, she should have expected a headache. She saw Cade check himself at the back door, flipping the latch up and down, but then he went outside. She would convince Quint to see his father if it killed her.

Emma went upstairs. There was something she had to take with her.

The noise from the sixth grade classroom blasted Emma's ears. When the bell rang, a steady stream of kids trickled into the hall, which was rapidly filling with students hurrying to waiting yellow buses. She couldn't believe the variety of shapes and sizes of the kids. Difficult to tell in some cases which were students and which teachers.

She pulled the door of Room 211 open and stepped into sixth grade science, Quint's last class. She spotted Quint, a head taller than the other boys clustered around two wooden cages. No, Emma decided, looking more closely, two girls had their hands over the sides of one cage. Chicken-wire tops with latches leaned against the floor cupboards.

Smiling at one of the girls, Quint had such a look of Cade that Emma caught her breath. Tiny, blond and shy, the girl peeped at Quint through bangs gone amok with mousse and spray. Quint's hands were cupped protectively around whatever he was showing the diminutive blonde.

Quint's dark hair stuck up in a cowlick in back. Emma wanted to slick it down so that the wide-eyed girl-woman wouldn't reject him.

Instead, she stepped into the room. Quint, of course, saw her first. His head snapped up, and surliness spread across his face. The girl looked up, too, and smiled bashfully at Emma. The girl returned her attention to whatever Quint was holding and asked him a question. Quint's answer was a shrug.

Quint might think he was tough, but he *was* only eleven, and Emma knew more about what was going on in his mind than he could guess. She had an edge. And she didn't have to act cool in front of an eleven-year-old blonde.

As the other kids in the room realized she was there, they glanced at Quint, expecting him to take the lead. Their excited chatter diminished.

Thinking Quint needed some sense of control over his life, Emma decided to let Quint make the first move. When he clumped over to her, shoelaces flying on unlaced high tops and his hands still protecting whatever he held, she restrained her smile. Aggressive, expecting trouble, he'd even walked like Cade.

"Yeah? Whatcha want?" Up close, he was wary. Unhappiness oozed from him. Quint's whole life was falling apart around his ears, and he didn't have a clue how to fix it. He'd learned his threatening stance from movies, Emma decided, not from Cade.

Turning so that the whole room couldn't hear her, Emma said, "Your mom said I could talk to you. May I?"

"Maybe. But you ain't got nothin' to say worth hearing." He shook hair out of his yes. "Nothin' *I* want to hear."

"Probably not. I thought you might be fair enough to let me say what I came to, though."

He scowled. "I'm fair."

"I'm not surprised." Emma stepped back, hoping he would follow.

"What do you mean?" The scowl deepened, but curiosity was there, too.

"I've found your father to be a fair man. You're like him in many ways." Emma jammed her hands in the pockets of her bright yellow skirt and curled her fingers around her talisman.

Quint glared. "No, I'm not," he said low enough so that none of the other students would hear. His whisper was miserably frantic. He glowered. Then, as though struck by an idea, said, "You want to see what we're doing first?"

"If you want to show me." Emma prepared herself. No chance Quint was being hospitable, so he probably had a sneaky trick in mind. She'd let him have his revenge. He needed to come out on top, at least in front of his friends, and she needed to get him to see Cade. "I was never very good in science. I didn't like to dissect the worms."

His grin was pure boy. "Here." He thrust the small creature in her face.

Emma blinked. She was glad she wore glasses. Dark, beady eyes blinked up at her, and the pointed nose twitched, whiskers vibrating. Tiny paws scrabbled at Quint's fingers, while a long, scaly tail looped around Quint's arm. "Careful, you're scaring her. Him."

"Really?" Dismayed, Quint looked at the lab rat. "Yeah, she's new." He stroked the shiny fur. "That was dumb of me." He set her on his shoulder where the beady eyes watched Emma curiously.

Emma patted the quivering nose. "You're very good with her."

Pride shone in Quint's eyes. "I like animals."

"What are you going to do with her?" Emma shoved her hand in her pocket and surreptitiously wiped her fingers.

"We're finishing a unit on nutrition. This is Chocolate. Over there's Sugar," Quint said, pointing to a red-eyed white rat running up and down a girl's arm. "She's kinda hyper."

Assuming Quint meant the rat and not the giggling girl, Emma asked, "Have you been feeding all of them different things?"

"Oh, yeah," Quint said, pulling Chocolate away from his hair. "We're being real careful, though. We keep track, but if any of 'em start looking sick, we change their diet. That's what happened to Cinnamon. She bit Katie and got in a fight with Sugar, so we've been giving her broccoli and apples and stuff." Quint made a face. "It's supposed to be good for her."

"What will happen to all of the, uh, rats after you're finished with your unit?" Emma couldn't have touched Chocolate's tail, but the bright-eyed intelligence in the animal's face was appealing.

Beaming, Quint said, "We get to have a lottery for 'em! I'm gonna see if Ma will let me put in for Chocolate. She's real nice." He scratched Chocolate between the ears.

She couldn't imagine Chocolate in Francine's house, but since Francine had apparently centered her life around Quint, Emma wouldn't bet against Chocolate's finding a home with Quint. "Good luck, but could we talk in the hall? About the reason I'm here?" Emma tilted her head and patted Chocolate's nose a last time.

Not quite ready to give in to curiosity and abandon the attention of the six kids in the room, Quint scratched Chocolate again and wound the tail around his finger. Chocolate sat quietly in Quint's palm and rubbed her quivering nose with her paws. "Lemme put Chocolate in her cage. I don't want anybody being rough with her. She's real smart. She already knows her name. I taught her," Quint bragged, meandering to the cage and talking to the blond girl for a moment before carefully placing Chocolate in the cage and rejoining Emma.

Without Chocolate as a distraction, Quint seemed at a loss for words, his hostility, for the moment, diffused. Emma dived in. "Your dad wants to talk with you."

"I don't want to talk to him," Quint insisted, not looking at her. "Not after what he done to Ma."

Taking a risk, Emma asked, "Did your mom tell you your dad had done something bad to her?" How could a child his age understand any of what had happened?

Not lifting his eyes from the tiled hall, Quint said, "Nah. I heard it. And he was in prison, so it musta been true." He glowered. "I hate him."

But it wasn't hate Emma heard in the young boy's voice, not hate under the pain and bluster. Reaching into her pocket, she closed her fingers around the smooth shell she'd remembered at the last moment to bring. Holding it out flat, she extended it to Quint. "Your dad told me the story of how he used to carry you into the water and keep you from being afraid of sharks."

Between them, the shell shone in the fluorescent school light. Emma's hand trembled as she saw Quint's shoulders slump and grief shape his face. If he'd been younger, she'd have taken him in her arms and let him cry out his misery.

But Quint wasn't going to cry on anybody's shoulders.

"You sent him to jail! Why are you sticking up for him now?" Quint accused, his mouth quivering.

"Why don't you ask your dad," Emma said very gently, "and see if he can answer your questions? I'll wait downstairs for ten minutes in my car."

Quint turned to the classroom then whirled on his heels and faced Emma. "I can't!" Misery warred with confusion in his pubescent voice.

Rocking the shell with a finger, Emma looked straight at Quint, not letting him see her fear that he would reject her plea. "Please come, Quint. Your dad loves you more than anything in the world. If you believe anything, believe that." She touched his arm. "I'll wait. Ten minutes."

Walking down the long hall of the junior high without Quint was one of the longest walks Emma had ever taken.

She didn't look back.

Chapter 13

From a block away, Emma saw Cade leaning against an oak tree in the park. He was tossing a football up and down, rolling the ball in his grip and spiraling it high into the spring air, catching it with absentminded ease. His long, smoothly muscled thighs braced and flexed with his movements, and his maroon-and-gold Florida State T-shirt moved loosely over the flow of his shoulders as he tossed the ball. Over and over he spun the brown oval into the blue sky.

Until he heard the car. Cade turned, the wind lifting his dark hair, and saw the empty seat next to Emma. The ball bounced on the ground beside him. He cracked his hands together and bent to pick up the ball. He straightened slowly and stiffly and looked at Emma bleakly.

He had worn the same expression the night he had taken her from the rain-veiled courthouse lot.

Parking on the sandy strip next to the park, Emma turned off the key and turned to Quint, slumped down on his tailbone in the passenger seat. By the time he had strolled out of the school building twenty minutes after Emma's deadline with no apologies or explanation, she was in the throes of a full-blown headache. She'd stayed, irrationally hoping Quint would come.

And he had. Sort of.

Retreating behind his earlier surliness, slouching down and saying nothing.

When Quint had opened the car door, the relief had been so great that Emma's headache had burst loose, stabbing into her brain and holding on. Light hurt her eyes, and she wanted to shut them and go to sleep until the pain passed.

"Go ahead, Quint. I'll wait here in the car," she said as he remained in the car.

The look he threw her was pure panic. "He better not say anything bad about Ma."

"I promise you, he won't," Emma said, trying to smile through the shafting pain. "Go on. Your dad's waiting. You have things to say to each other."

With his don't-mess-with-me-walk, Quint sauntered over to Cade. Emma grimaced. Even baby males had to strut their stuff. All that testosterone. Endearing, but exhausting. She left the windows rolled down and laid her throbbing head on the seat, wishing she could shut her eyes against the splintering light and the drama unfolding in front of her.

Quint approached Cade and the boy's father chucked the ball to him. Quint caught it one-handed, in an echo of his father's skill. Like Cade, he tossed it up and down and then, as hard as he could, corkscrewed it to his father.

Cade saw the ball coming hard enough to knock off his head and hauled it in, looking at Emma. Her hair lay in a dark sweep against the car seat. How had she persuaded Quint to show up? The kid looked as though he'd sooner eat poison. "Nice throw. You have a good arm."

Quint slouched, his hands deep in his pockets, not giving an inch. "So?"

Too many changes in the lost years, Cade thought. He wasn't ready for this kid who was more than ready to go one-on-one with him. Cade didn't know how to approach him. "You like football, huh? This is one of mine from college. Want it?" He lofted the ball toward Quint.

The ball bounced off the boy's chest as he left his hands jammed in his pockets and scowled at Cade. "I didn't come here to jaw about football. Ma said I had to listen, so say what you gotta so I can go to my friend's.'' Quint kicked the ball over to Cade.

"All right." Cade squatted and twirled the ball on its pointed end. "I want to straighten things out between us."

"Fat chance." Quint sneered. "After all you done? No way!"

"What did I do, Quint? Spit it out. If you're so tough, tell me what I did." Frustrated, Cade issued the challenge. He might as well be blunt. They weren't getting anywhere.

"You beat up my ma!" The words ripped out of Quint's mouth, and he looked as though he'd like to reel them in. "And you went to jail because you were bad." He'd said close to the same thing the other day.

He'd never get through to Quint. "I went to jail. I never hurt your mom. Or any other woman," Cade said. "You know I wouldn't."

Quint's hands stayed in his pockets, but he took a quick step toward Cade. "Oh, yeah, and I'm supposed to believe you? Just like that? Baloney. Why would I believe you?" he said, insult in every line of his face and body.

"Because I'm your father," Cade said quietly, looking at his furious son. "Because I've never lied to you."

"You're lying. They wouldn'ta sent you to prison if you wasn't guilty! If you didn't do anything, why'd you let 'em send you, huh? If you was innocent, are you saying Ma lied? 'Cause she wouldn't, would she? Can't answer that so easy, I bet!" Quint was snarling in anger and hurt, moving back and forth.

"Quint, listen to me. Think. *Have* I ever lied to you? Ever? Think!" Cade was motionless, afraid any movement would send Quint running off. He wanted to beg his son to think about all the times they'd spent together. There were so many things he wanted to tell Quint, and he didn't know how.

Raging and stumbling in front of him, Quint poured out his hurt in a furious spate. "I don't care! You never loved me or Ma! You wouldn'ta gone off if you did. You'da fought harder. I know you would've, but you went off and left us!"

Whether he was talking about prison or the divorce, Cade didn't know. It didn't matter. What was important was the pain tearing apart his son. Cade stood and gripped Quint's shoulders, forcing him to be still. "Listen to me," Cade repeated, "I'm telling you the truth. I don't know how your mom was hurt. I wasn't the one who filed for divorce. Now think, son!"

"I told you already, don't call me that," Quint shrieked, throwing off Cade's hands. "You ran away!"

Cade wrestled him still. "I never did, Quint! Why would I? I didn't want to go to prison! I didn't want to lose you. I did everything I knew how to keep you because I love you!"

In his confining grip, Cade felt Quint go still.

In a strained, high voice, the boy said, "No. You don't love me. Or Ma. You never did, or nothing would have made you leave."

"What can I say to make you understand?" Cade wouldn't turn his son loose no matter how hard he was squirming. "How can you talk like this? You're my *son,* Quint. Everything I've done has been for you."

Jerking away, Quint said in a suddenly bleak and surprisingly adult voice, "I heard you and Ma arguing about stuff, about the ranch and all. I heard her crying and saying how you never loved her, how you wouldn'ta married her except for me."

Cade's hands were shaking. What could he say? Quint was too young to understand how things had been. "Quint," Cade said desperately, feeling everything slide between his fingers, "whatever is, was, between your mom and me, that has nothing to do with *you.*" Helpless, Cade stared at his son, looking deep into the eyes so much like his own, willing Quint to believe.

Ignoring him, Quint rushed on. "Ma loves me. She needs me, and you don't. She don't have nobody but me, and me and her don't want you around, so you're just gonna have to forget you ever had a son, hear? We're better off without you."

The finality in Quint's words struck Cade in the heart. Quint meant what he said. Grief and heartache stared at Cade from his son's eyes. The torment in Quint's face was more than Cade could stand.

He removed his grip from his son's broadening shoulders. Relief spread over Quint's face.

"I could never forget you're my son." Cade swallowed the hard knot in his throat as he watched Quint's eyes fill and overflow.

"Might as well, 'cause I'm going to forget you were my dad, hear?" Quint said, tears dripping down. His fists came out of his pockets and a gleam flashed in one tight fist as Quint rubbed his nose, but then he hurried on, "'Cause we don't need you."

With one quick kick as he walked off, Quint whomped the football in a beautiful, arching pattern. It spun high into the sky and down the length of the playground.

Watching the oval tumble end over end in the clear deep blue, Cade felt a pain so intense he couldn't breathe, as though something in his chest had fragmented and shattered in a million pieces. He tried to call Quint, but he couldn't get the words past the lump growing huge in his throat.

Not need him? Not need Quint?

"Quint!" Cade's shout was a whisper blowing toward his vanishing son. Taking a step, Cade tried to run after Quint, but his muscles, for the first time in his life, failed him. Heavy and dead with grief, his legs trembled and wouldn't move.

And Quint was gone.

Cade looked around at the sunshine lying peacefully on the green playground, the shadows lengthening under the monkey bars.

Not need his son?

Soft fingers curled into his empty ones. Emma. Not looking at her, Cade gripped her hand tightly. "He doesn't want anything to do with me."

"I heard." Her hand stayed in his, warm and small, holding him to reality.

"Everything? How I don't love him or need him?"

"Yes."

"Funny, huh?" Cade couldn't look away from the empty sky and its bright, cheerful sun. "All those years in prison, planning what we'd do once I got out and fixed everything. And now he hates me. Funny." He took a breath, drawing it past the sharp splinters in his chest. "No cheer-Cade-up speech?" He stared at the sky until his eyes ached.

"No. I don't have any more speeches, Cade." She leaned against him. "So sorry."

"I have to see Francine," Cade said suddenly, knowing with a clarity he'd rarely experienced what he had to do. "I need a ride. Whammer dropped me off here. Can you take me there and then out to the ranch? Maybe you'd better be with me. As a witness. As my lawyer. Whatever." The words exhausted him, and he glanced at Emma in her sunshine-yellow dress. Her lashes were damp.

"Of course. Are you sure?"

"I've done everything I can. There's nothing left." Resting his chin on her glossy hair, Cade swallowed his tears, the hot ache in his chest growing and growing.

When Francine opened the door to his knock, she smiled tentatively. "Come in." She glanced at Emma, who'd followed Cade up the walk.

Shaking his head carefully, every move an effort, Cade said, "No, Francine, I just came by—" he swallowed and took a deep breath so he could push the rest of what he had to say out while he still could "—to tell you I talked with Quint."

Her frown was worried. "What did he say? What are you going to do now?"

"I'm letting the custody order stand. I won't petition for joint custody."

"What?" Her hands flew to her mouth too late to stop the moan. "Why?" Agitated, she turned to Emma. "Did you tell him to do this?"

"It's Cade's decision."

"Cade, I—"

"Don't worry, Francine. I won't bother you." He wanted to be angry with her, but the old anger had gone. Nothing was left except emptiness. And Emma beside him. He focused on that while he explained. "Quint— I can't tear Quint apart like this. He's— I'm hurting him. I never wanted that."

A butterfly landed on Francine's shoulder. Dimly Cade remembered a story he'd read about a guy making a trip to the past. Cautioned to stay on the path, he'd ignored the warning, of course, crushing a butterfly in one careless step. When he returned to his own time, the universe had changed. The butterfly effect. Every action had a result.

His story. He should never have tried to go back. Trying to get his life the way he wanted, he'd done enough damage. Time to get back on the path, leave things alone. The butterfly winged off into sunshine. The past was just faded pictures in an album at the ranch.

"Cade, wait a while, will you?" Francine was upset. "This isn't right. I thought we were getting everything straightened out. Where's Quint?"

"He'll be coming along. He's okay—not the way he was the other day. Not going off half-cocked. He's thought about what he wants. He—he said you needed him." Cade swallowed.

Francine was terribly still. "I do," she whispered. "He's all I have."

Behind him, Emma moved.

"I reckon you're the one with the perfect revenge, Fran. The last laugh's on me. If you ever wanted to get even with me for all my failures, you have." Cade forced a laugh. "You said I wasn't a very good husband—"

"You would have been if you'd needed me."

"That's what Quint said. That I don't need anybody." Cade rubbed his head. He'd failed Quint, too.

"You didn't *need* me, Cade. I was just this person with a label, *wife*. You never shared yourself, never cared what I was thinking. You were never *there* for me! I wasn't important to you. I knew I wasn't, and it was destroying me. Our marriage had no *core* to it, nothing except we both loved Quint. If you had loved me the way I—" She wiped her eyes. "That was all I ever wanted from you."

"Doesn't matter anymore, Fran." Cade smiled in spite of the effort it took. He'd never loved her. She was right about that, but he had made love to her, made a child with her, formed a life. Now it was gone, all of it. Still, he honored their failed attempt. "All in the past. We were wrong for each other, nobody's fault. You were right. I was a piss-poor husband, and it turns out I wasn't as good a father as I thought."

On his ribs, Cade felt the warm imprint of Emma's palm, steady and connecting.

"But you were, you are! I'll talk to Quint," Francine said.

"Don't. He's made his decision. I have to respect it. If I forced it into court, a judge would want to know Quint's feelings anyway, and I can't put my son through more hell." Cade let the warmth of Emma's hand center him. He focused on the five spots where her fingers pressed, on the warm circle of her open palm. "I'll write. If he wants to answer—" Cade stopped. "Why didn't he ever answer my other letters, Francine? Did you give them to him?"

"I didn't want to, but I did," she answered, looking at the white step. "I wanted him to forget you, but he didn't. That hurt me. I don't know why he didn't write you. Maybe he thought he would hurt me more if he wrote," she said, folding her arms defensively.

"I reckon that's it," Cade said and spun on his heel. "Anything else that needs working out, let me know."

"Where will you be?" Leaning forward, she stretched out her hand.

"At the ranch, Fran. Where else?" Cade stumbled as he stepped off the stoop.

"I didn't want it like this, Cade," she said. "I swear it."

He couldn't make sense of what she was saying, not with the howling grief smashing his control. He had to get in the car. Get away. He fumbled in his pockets for Emma's car keys. Had to leave. Fast.

Yellow flashed in his peripheral vision, and Emma touched his arm, saying, "I'll call Francine next week and tie up loose ends. Until then, don't rush things."

"Sure." Where in hell had he put the keys this time? Cade tore at his pockets.

"Cade, here," Emma said.

He held on to the car keys she extended, the metal warmed by her touch. Breathing shallowly through the splinters stabbing his chest, he said, "I never expected I'd fail. I expected I could force my life back the way it was. Make my life over." He pulled the keys toward him, bringing Emma closer.

Her chin was tilted, her eyes soft. "If anyone failed, I did. I'm the one who failed, from the beginning."

"What are you talking about?"

She released the keys. "Me. My failures. I should have picked up the clues that Francine was protecting someone. If you want to blame anyone, blame me." She straightened, and as she did, her yellow suit flowed over her small curves, sliding and shining in the sun.

"Thanks, counselor. Mighty decent of you," Cade said, somehow angered by her willingness to shoulder the blame of his past. His failures with Francine, which had brought his world crashing down. "That ground was tilled a long time ago. Don't be so damned eager to take credit for the weeds, okay? I made my mistakes all by myself. You were dragged into this. *I* dragged you into it. Remember?" He cupped her elbow. "I want to get away from this place before Quint comes back."

As Emma climbed into the car, yellow skirt flicking over her legs, she insisted, "I was in charge. It was my call. *I* blew it."

"There's enough blame to go around, so don't think you have to rescue me. I don't *need*—" he stressed the word bitterly "—rescuing, especially by someone half my size." He leaned toward her. "I can handle it." He rubbed his chest and half expected to see blood. "I can handle what's happening," he repeated.

"That's what it comes down to, isn't it? You can do it all by yourself. You didn't *need* my help when you took me to the island. I *owed* it. You won't accept comfort from anyone because you don't *need* it. Was Quint right, after all? What *do* you need, Cade Boudreau?"

Pushing on the accelerator, Cade tried to speed away from all his mistakes, but Emma wouldn't let him. She might not realize it, but she was pure steel under her delicate skin.

"Can't you answer?" Like a gadfly, she stung, distracting him from the pain cracking him apart.

"You fight dirty, counselor." Her barbed words pushed him to the edge of control.

"I've learned to," Emma said. "Take no enemies and scorch the earth behind you."

"That's one of the reasons you had to win the case against me." He could attack, too.

"One of them," she agreed, calm as a mirror-flat bayou but with the same trace of darkness lying underneath. "You haven't answered my question."

They drove the rest of the way in a tense silence. When they reached the ranch Cade switched off the engine and got out, heading for the house. He couldn't recall the drive, what streets or turns he'd taken. He'd driven on automatic.

Emma followed him to the porch. She said, "After storing up all that anger and bitterness in prison, wanting revenge against all of us who sent you there, hating us, what now?" Push, push, offering her own brand of charity. "Come on, Cade, what do *you* need?" Her small hand lay in a slash of sunlight on his arm, and her tip-tilted face was half sunlit, half shadowed, and distressed.

She'd pushed too far. Cade's control snapped.

Grabbing her shoulders, feeling the slide of sunshine under his fingers, he crowded her against the screen door and moved right up against her, pushing his knee between her legs. "What I *need* right now is something basic, counselor. *You,* under me, on top of me, all around me." He bared his teeth, everything slamming into him at once and smashing his defenses. Spearing his fingers in her hair, he lifted her clean off her toes and took her mouth with all the fierce loneliness and grief roaring through him and taking him into a darkness where nothing mattered except Emma's tender mouth growing soft and full and hot under his, surrendering.

His need was brutal, primitive, a thundering rush in his blood he couldn't stop. But she could. And didn't.

"Oh, Cade, I'm so sorry, about everything," she murmured against his mouth. Water in the desert, her voice poured over him.

Pinning her against the door with his mouth and body, he ran his hands urgently under her straight skirt, shoving it up and over her sleek thighs, his thumbs coming to rest in the center of her lacy pants, his palms gripping her hard around her hips, pulling them against his pelvis while he opened her mouth wide under his, sinking, sinking into her softness. Emma made a tiny sound, and shudders ran through him, sending him past thought and into a place where he'd never been, a place where desperation drove him.

Over and over his rough thumbs rasped against the juncture of her thighs while he kissed her deeper and deeper, his mouth tasting her, consuming her, his gnawing hunger unsatisfied. Boneless, she melted into him with a whimper, her mouth urgent, too, as she swept a line of kisses up his throat and under his chin.

Groaning, he wrapped one of her legs around his hip and opened his hand over her, pressing hard and cupping, the heel of his hand a relentless stroke against nylon and lace. Her head dropped back and her eyes closed. Her silky hair haloed around her. Cade let her slide down until her toes touched the wooden planks of the porch again and her weight rode his hand. Her metal necklace scratched his forehead, and he shoved it over her shoulders. Yanking her blouse free of the wide black belt with one quick pull, he lowered his head impatiently to the tip of her breast straining against yellow silk and kissed her there, his tongue wetting the thin silk and drawing it tight against the small peak.

Emma shivered, and her sigh fluttered over his ear like the touch of a butterfly.

Cade dropped to his knees and pulled Emma's legs open around his hips. Rising with her clasped in one arm, he wrenched the screen door open with his free hand. Burying his face in her sweet-smelling hair, he heard the bang of the slamming door as a muted rip in a space where the only important sounds were her breathing and his, rasping, mingling.

The edge of his belt snagged against her panty hose, and the susurrus of its shredding was a quiet counterpoint to Emma's tiny moan as he followed the rip with his finger, edging under nylon and panties to the soft small center of her. Where he touched, her skin shivered and rippled.

His heart was thundering under his ribs.

Blind and immersed in Emma, Cade found the way somehow to the bedroom he'd cleaned that afternoon. His elbow bumped on the narrow doorway and he ducked his head. His shins whacked against the steel bed frame. Bracing a knee on the sheeted mattress, he followed Emma down to the sun-whitened bed.

Her whisper came from kissed-red lips. "Is this casual, Cade?"

Brushing her hair from her face, Cade said in a voice rough with urgency, "Whatever it is, Emma Rose, I swear to you, it's not casual. Never that." He kissed the edge of her mouth, scraping her lower lip with his teeth. "Not casual," he muttered. "On my soul, I swear it."

"Thank you," she breathed into his mouth as she looked for a long time into his face. "I needed to know." She shut her eyes and slid her arm around his neck.

Cade took her other hand and placed it against his heart, letting her hear the storm inside him, telling her without words that what they were about to do was important to him, that *she*, Emma Rose O'Riley, was important.

Pulling open the waist ties of her blouse, he spread the edges against the sheet. Her chemise straps looped over both arms, and the lemon-yellow fabric clung wetly to the peaks of her breasts. Cade pulled the shiny dampness against her, outlining her sweet curves. Sliding down, he dragged the chemise with him, kissing the indentation of her belly button, dipping his tongue into the tiny oval until fabric clung there, too, and slowly, so slowly that it was torture to him, he rolled her chemise down, over the yellow-tasseled black leather belt, past her hips, and dropped it on the floor.

Bunched around her hips, her tight yellow skirt draped the tops of her legs, and her metal necklace, intricately woven and shiny black, lay across her pale skin near the top of her pink-tipped breasts. A trail of pink flushed and trailed his hand as it swept from her belt to her throat. With the betraying color running over Emma's skin, a barbaric pleasure beat in Cade, and he reached under her elegant silky skirt. With a twist of his wrist, he ripped off the rest of her nylons and kissed the soft skin above her knees.

Emma turned, shifted, brought her knees together, but Cade ran his hands up the backs of her thighs and down her throat, over her breasts and stomach, again and again, as color ebbed and flowed in the satin cream of her skin. The lace at the bottom of her panties was white and flimsy to his rough hands, checking the flow of his hands over her softness.

Impatient, aching, Cade thrust his thumb under the edge and jerked. The tearing sound brought Emma's eyes, hazel and dazed, to him. When she raised an arm to shield her face, Cade took it and anchored it beside her head. "Let me see you, Emma," he urged, swimming in their depths. With one hand he clipped her wrists together and lowered himself over her, brushing against her bare breasts and capturing her twisting feet with his.

"I'm embarrassed," she murmured, turning her face away.

"You won't be," Cade promised and lifted the feathery yellow tassel of her belt to her breast, brushing the raveled ends against the taut pink until she shuddered. "Look at me, Emma," Cade coaxed, brushing the velvety tassel over her skin until she opened her eyes again. "Is it embarrassment you're feeling?" he asked and touched the tip of her breast again with the tassel.

"No." Innocence and desire stirred and shifted in the deepening green eyes as he stroked the tassel over her, everywhere, until he could no longer endure the subtle twisting and shifting of her slight body under his and substituted his lips for the tassel, turning her wrists loose as he let hands and mouth move over her and savor the tremors running wild and hot under her skin, losing himself in the taste and touch of her until dark prison dreams and bright spring sun merged into one scorching, consuming darkness where there was only Emma, burning and leaping into the flames with him.

Emma had been lost from the moment he had stumbled off the porch with the look of a man sentenced to a living death. Too much pain for all of them, and the only power she had was the anodyne of her body to give him forgetfulness for a short while. She meant to give, wanted to erase the sharp lines of pain from his hard-edged face, but somewhere in the fierceness, she lost herself in the driving urgency he turned on her, and wanted, wanted.

Her body understood the silent language of his, translating the terrible hunger of his strong male body into the cry of need he couldn't utter, and as she slid his belt out of the loops and lowered the zipper of his jeans, her body answered his, feminine to masculine, need calling to need wordlessly.

His belt slithered out of the loops and to the floor. The metallic snick of his lowered zipper merged with Cade's harsh breathing, her murmurings, as he kicked out of his jeans and his legs settled between hers, holding her ready for him. Emma clenched his hands or he clenched hers, she no longer knew, but there was an instant when he hesitated above her, looking straight into her soul, and his gray eyes, hot and filled with her, were free of pain.

"Emma?" He groaned, hesitating one second longer, asking her the age-old question. His chest was shuddering under her fingers and she ran her palms over his long, muscled back, flanks, letting her hands speak for her, wanting him more than she'd ever wanted anything in her life.

"It's a safe time," she whispered, knowing it was the age-old answer to his question, knowing, too, there was no such time.

"Sure?" Cade took her mouth under his and, sweeping his warm hand down her stomach, pressed a spot where all her yearning focused and she opened to him, flowering in a springtime she'd never dreamed possible.

"Yes," Emma said deliberately, choosing. With a sigh, she closed her eyes, lifted her legs around his thighs and took him home, holding him tight to her as his hard length entered and stroked in a spiraling rhythm that tightened in her until pleasure overrode the small instant of pain and she cried out, dying with the pleasure he was giving her. His mouth closed over hers and swallowed her soft moans while again and again he thrust into her until with one final, deep surge, he hung, shuddering at the edge, and plunged over.

With every stroke and touch he took her to a place she never wanted to leave.

Sheets tangled around them as Cade swept her with him into a private space where everything frozen in her vaporized in the heat of his body on hers, everything empty in her filled with Cade taking her past the boundaries of skin and body to that place where his guttural urgings in her ear stirred dark, rich places in her blood, to that place where her soul merged with his in homecoming.

And all the time, he spoke to her with his beautiful body in a winding, coiling, sinuous language of loneliness and need, of yearnings and fulfillment.

Around them the spring afternoon was silent and hushed, sunlight suspending them in honeyed amber.

Chapter 14

Emma never knew when afternoon merged into night or night into morning.

Once, with the moon low on the horizon through the uncurtained window, Cade turned to her. "I made a mistake, Emma. I swore I'd leave you alone, but I couldn't. I wanted your sweetness, and I took. Too fast, too rough. Let me make it right. Let me show you how good it can be for you. Please."

"Shh," she said, spreading her hands over his smooth chest and trailing her lips down his ribs over his scar, trying to show him wordlessly how right it had been. She was where she wanted to be, in Cade's arms, spinning in darkness among the stars, and she never wanted to return. "Shh," she repeated, kissing the slope of his abdomen.

Then he turned her and began touching her with his callused hands, every slow stroke light and teasing, tormenting. Fever burned in her with each hot touch of Cade's mouth and hands, yet he pinned her under him with his hips, his fingers gripping her wrists and keeping her from caressing the hard smoothness of his skin until she twisted and shuddered, every quivering nerve in her body strung out to the dark universe whirling in space, needing, needing.

With exquisite slow care, he entered her, withdrew, advanced, winding her tighter and tighter until music sang in her blood.

"Emma, I don't deserve you or this night, but I'd live in hell if I lied and said I regret one minute of this." Cade groaned softly, kissing the tip of her breast with a delicate flick of his tongue. He took her hand and placed it between them, letting her feel the way their bodies joined, and he shuddered at her light, skimming touch. Emma arched and dissolved, all liquid, feminine sea to his male lightning, creating the world anew in one shining moment of joy like nothing she'd ever known.

But it was more than their bodies, she wanted to tell him, and couldn't as he moved deeply inside her, shaking suddenly with the shudders running from her to him to her in an unending circuit, and she was flung into brilliant, dazzling dark.

Emma woke to a noisy spring morning and reality. Cade lay sleeping beside her with sunlight bathing his back. Looking at the bronzed, long muscles of his back, the faint red streaks her short nails had left in his skin, she was grateful he was asleep. Panic curled her into a fetal position as she remembered what they had done together.

Wanting to ease his grief, she had been mindless, her skin slipping away until they reached a point when she no longer knew or cared where she ended and Cade began, a point where they merged and were one. Curling tighter, she stifled a moan.

She'd thought she could set limits to what she felt, but she'd been as vulnerable as she'd always feared. Knowingly she'd taken the risk, but she hadn't wanted that terrifying loss of self. Already she craved—what? *Cade.* She craved *him.* Surrendering to that craving would chain her in all the ways she'd feared. She needed her boundaries. She needed her separateness. She didn't want to be vulnerable to him. She wouldn't let him be that important to her.

Scrambling to a sitting position, Emma pulled the sheet around her. She couldn't face Cade. She would have to leave before he woke up because she'd never be able to make him understand.

When she slid her feet quietly to the floor, Cade's broad, rough palm against her bare belly stopped her. She bent her head and clutched the sheet tightly to her as her body answered his touch. Too late. She'd never had a chance.

Coming completely awake as Emma's softness slipped away from him, Cade growled, "Where are you going?" Her hair swung forward over the white column of her neck. He couldn't resist the dusting of fine hairs down her curved spine and traced them to the dimples on her fanny. Her answering quiver fed the wakening hunger in him and he hooked his hand over her shoulder, snaking his fingers under the edge of the sheet.

Softness, her breast filling his palm, the peak swelling as he stroked, and he was pulling her onto him, sliding his fingers through her rumpled hair, and he remembered. "Emma, I was careless."

She wouldn't look at him. "I told you it was a safe time. Please, let me go," she choked out and moved slightly.

"Not yet," Cade said, as all the things he'd ignored last night swooped in on him. Quint. The sympathy in Emma's face. Her tightness and the slight resistance he'd barely noticed. He swore. "Emma Rose." He smoothed her mussed hair. "Are you okay?"

"Yes," she muttered, moving away from him. "I have to go home."

He didn't blame her. Driven by his prison dreams of her and the fact of her softness under him, he had been too rough. He'd thought he could be around her and still keep from taking her. He'd been wrong. Softhearted, she'd offered him charity once too often, not understanding the nature of his hunger for her, and he'd taken her.

Would again. He hadn't guessed she would be this important to him.

Holding her waist, Cade knew he had to shove her away to save her. He'd promised himself he wouldn't touch her. He'd failed. He'd promised her he wouldn't be careless. He had been. Oh, sure, she'd said it was safe, but *he'd* made the promise. And broken it. One more failure in a long column.

If Emma Rose stayed around with her big-eyed sweetness and tender heart, he'd keep taking and taking, and he had nothing to give her. From the right side of the river, she was the wrong woman for someone like him with nothing but a broken-down

Jeep, a wasteland of a ranch and a son and ex-wife who hated him.

A failure at attaining his life's goals, a failure in his marriage. He'd loused up his relationship with his son. He would only bring Emma heartache. He'd taken enough of her generosity and tenderness.

His tough luck that he wanted more.

Cade ran his finger up Emma's china-white skin. Satin and cool.

"Don't," she said, shrugging off his finger and inching off the bed, dragging the sheet behind her.

Watching her profile, Cade already knew loss. She believed she was so tough, but because she was a sucker for lost causes and loyal to a fault, she'd keep trying to rescue him. He, because it seemed he couldn't resist her, would let her. He would use her again and still not be satisfied. If she was in reaching range, he'd grab. He'd kiss her until her eyes blurred and she quit pushing him away.

Now that it was too late, Cade knew how badly he'd fooled himself.

"Cade, you're on the sheet," Emma whispered desperately, tugging and glancing quickly at him from under her spiky lashes.

He held on to the edge. "So I am." If she hated him, she wouldn't look at him with those big eyes that turned dark with emotion. If she despised him, she'd keep up her guard and she'd be safe from him.

For her sake, he'd turn her sympathy to hate. Cade reckoned he ought to be good at that.

Tangled by his touch, her hair framed her face in cloudy disarray. He wanted to run his hands over it one more time. He didn't. In spite of everything that had happened, he had that much sense left.

"Well, counselor," Cade drawled, "that was quite a night." Letting the sheet fall, he stretched his hands behind his head as he lay on his back and studied her. Her uncertain glance was salt water in a raw wound. "You really know how to comfort a man. I reckon I owe you thanks. The world sure looks better

this morning," he said, looking out the open window at desolation. With effort, Cade smiled.

He hadn't realized being a bastard hurt so much.

She flinched. "Don't do this," she whispered. "You know
it wasn't like that."

"Counselor, I'll tell you a secret. It was almost as good as my
dreams." He stretched and cracked his joints in apparent satisfaction. "I don't know what a romp between the sheets is like
for you folks in the white-columned houses, but last night was
worth the wait. Reckon we can do this again soon?" Cade sat
up, letting the sheet fall to his waist, searching her face.

She ducked her head away and drew a ragged breath. She
looked as though he'd knocked the wind out of her. "Well,
maybe not," he conceded, scratching his bare chest, "but, listen, I haven't forgotten I promised Becca I'd clean up the garden. I'll try and get over in the mornings, okay?" Cade stood
up, throwing aside the sheet and smiling for all he was worth.
She had to hate him. He hated himself.

"Why are you saying these things?" she whispered.

"Oh, counselor," he drawled, making his voice careless and
light and not able to look at her, "you know how men are. We
love the chase, but afterward, well, variety's the spice of life."
He smiled and made himself meet her eyes steadily. Even on the
football field, he'd never hurt anyone as viciously as he was
crushing Emma. Every knife he slung her way cut him, too. He
had to finish as quickly and cleanly as he could. For her sake.

Her chin lifted, and her spine straightened as though he'd run
a steel rod from top to bottom. "Yes. I understand." Her voice
was chilly and controlled, but he knew her now, and he heard
the soul-deep pain. He wanted to tell her it was all a lie.

Cade walked to the window and gripped the windowsill in a
death grip. The greedy part of him that said he should let her
stay yammered in his ear.

He *wanted* her to stay.

Behind him, sheets rustled and Emma's feet made soft
sounds on the floor. When he turned, naked, leaning against
the sill, arms crossed over his chest, she was barefooted and in
her sunshine-yellow blouse. Her slim thighs disappeared into
the skirt she dragged over them. Her blouse hung askew at her

waist. Cade didn't rebutton the covered waist buttons thrust into the wrong holes.

He didn't dare touch her.

Emma shoved her blouse into the waistband of her skirt. She deserved an award for number-one fool of the year, of any year. Believing in Cade, she'd taken a risk when she should have been smarter. She was smart enough to know being smart didn't save you when emotions were involved. The women at the shelter, her own mother, had all proved that. She'd been guilty of bad judgment on several counts. She'd always trusted her intuition about people, but when desire was involved, apparently her intuition wasn't worth much.

Cade's amused reaction to the night they'd spent together undermined her trust in herself. Inside, where she'd never let it show, she was bleeding.

Scooping up the bits and pieces of her clothes from the floor, Emma raked her fingers through her hair and faced Cade.

Leaning negligently against the sill with his face in shadow, he'd been watching her the whole time she collected her clothes.

He bent and caught her ripped nylons with his forefinger and extended them to her. "Want these? Or shall I keep them?" His smile was wide. He rubbed the nylon between his fingers. "Very nice, counselor."

Emma flushed but took the scrap of material, stuffing it in her skirt pocket. "Last night was nothing to you, was it?" she said. No matter how much it hurt, she wanted to make him spell it out. She'd believed she was special to him. No more pretending. She continued, "Whatever happened was all in my mind, wasn't it?" It was time she faced things and dealt with them regardless of the pain the truth brought.

She'd done enough hiding. Survival depended on facing fears, not pretending they didn't exist or that they weren't valid. In her head, she'd accepted that, but the visit to the shelter had carved that truth in her heart.

"Oh, it was something, all right," Cade said in his scratchy voice, not moving a muscle, his smile never wavering. From the top of his carelessly swept back black hair to his crossed ankles, he was as comfortable in his nakedness as an animal in its skin. The light streaming through the window outlined him with radiance. Undressed, he appeared more at ease than she, clothed. His body had moved over hers in unforgettable, private ways and now, dismissing what they'd shared, he flaunted it.

In one blaze of anger, Emma hated Cade for that easy acceptance of his nakedness.

"Quint was right, you know," she said slowly, "you don't need anybody, do you?"

His face darkened as he straightened. Abruptly abandoning his casual post, he stalked her. "Good recovery, counselor, but leave Quint out of this."

"He knew the truth. That's why you couldn't answer me last night. Because Quint was right. I thought I understood you, but I don't! It was all a game to you." Wounded and angry, Emma searched the room for anything she'd forgotten. She wanted to leave nothing behind.

"I know I don't need a smart little lawyer from the right side of the river tagging after me trying to fix up my life, hanging around and clearing up my disasters just because we spent a night or two in bed. You're good, counselor—" his raspy chuckle scraped her raw "—but your price is too high."

The blood drained from Emma's head. "Don't worry. You're the last person I'd *hang* around. I don't belong here," she snapped.

"Well, then, let me give you a souvenir of your walk on the wild side," Cade said in that infuriating drawl as he ripped the sheet off the bed and tossed it to her. "Keep it, and let it remind you to stay on the right side of the river next time you're curious. Keep your charity for the folks who need it. I don't."

Swaying, Emma let the sheet fall at her feet. There was a tension in Cade she couldn't explain, but her humiliation was too great for her to analyze the sense of wrongness plucking at her. "I made a mistake," she said. "I believed in you." She paused. "I'll finish what I started. I won't leave any loose ends concerning Quint, but I don't want to see you again," Emma whispered through trembling lips and headed blindly for the door. She wanted out of Cade's house as fast as possible before she threw up.

"Emma!"

She turned. "What is it, Cade? You want applause?" She clapped her hands slowly. "My experience is limited, granted, but I'd give you an A. Maybe an A plus for effort?" Emma stood so straight that the spot between her shoulder blades ached.

"Don't," Cade muttered and walked toward her. Dusky red streaked his harsh cheekbones.

"Not give credit where it's due? For whatever satisfaction it gives you, and I hope it's some," Emma said, speaking slowly and clearly, pride writing her script, "I'll never, even if I live to be ninety and have a hundred lovers, forget last night. I won't let you destroy what I felt." She glanced at the sheet on the floor. "Even if it didn't mean anything to you, it did to me. I was such a fool I thought I was falling in love with you."

Willing herself not to cry, Emma walked out the screen door and to her car. When she was halfway there, she heard the door open, but she kept walking. The door slammed with a crash that rang in her ears.

Before she went home, she stopped in a filling station bathroom to wash her swollen eyes, put on makeup and tuck in her blouse. Her hands shook in a constant tremble as she brushed the snarls out of her hair. She couldn't think about what had happened yet, but she would. Emma leaned over the sink for a second as she remembered the other risk she'd taken during the night. Her mother's daughter after all. Her tears fell into the stained porcelain sink.

She'd been a fool.

The next day, sitting at her office desk after a sleepless night, Emma tried to decide whether or not to withdraw Cade's custody petition. She rested her forehead on her hands. In mind and body she was sore and exhausted, her brain mush. She'd slipped in without anyone seeing her, and she planned to leave the same way. She still had, technically, two more vacation days, and she had no energy to fend off any snide comments.

The memory of Cade's body on hers lingered so powerfully that every time the fabric of her clothes brushed against her skin, she remembered Cade, Cade touching her, stroking her until she couldn't breathe without him. Cade, imprinted on her.

Suddenly Julie knocked on the door and opened it simultaneously. "Boss, someone to see you."

Emma lifted her heavy head and looked straight into Francine's eyes, staring for two ticks of the clock before recognizing her. Emma straightened in her chair and reached for a pencil. She could tell that Francine had made a decision.

"Can I talk with you?" Francine sat on the couch and carefully crossed her legs. Calm, she looked years younger. Emma realized with considerable surprise that Francine wore makeup.

"Sure," Emma said cautiously. "How's Quint?"

"Confused." Francine uncrossed her legs and leaned forward. "He knows I'm here and why. I've told him everything. But he's not the main reason I'm here." She worried her lips for a moment. "I came to correct what I told you before. In court." She rubbed her hand once on the couch arm.

"Before you say anything, Francine, I have to caution you. You swore to your testimony. Changing it now could result in your being charged with perjury. Do you understand what I'm saying?" Emma willed Francine the courage to keep going.

Francine took a long breath and expelled it on a sigh. "I understand. I knew it wouldn't be easy."

"I'd like to have my secretary take notes. Okay?" Emma was light-headed. Now she was going to learn where she'd taken a wrong turning three years ago.

"Sure." Francine leaned back and waited until Julie came through the door with a notepad.

Motioning Julie to a seat, Emma went to the couch and sat down next to Francine. "I'll help you. I promise," Emma said, knowing what courage Francine had needed to walk into the courthouse. "Go ahead."

"It was all wrong," Francine began, looking at Emma. "I was scared."

"I know," Emma encouraged her. "Anybody would have been."

"No!" Francine said sharply. "You don't understand."

Julie's pencil moved rapidly over the pad. Emma decided to let Francine find her own way to the difficult truth. Francine began again, speaking slowly but going faster as the story unfolded.

"Cade was always busy at the ranch. I was lonesome. Just me and Quint. He was all I had, but I was jealous. He only wanted to be with Cade, and Cade wasn't ever at home. Quint and him, out at the ranch, me home by myself. I was bored and jealous."

Emma frowned.

"One night—" Francine took a shaky breath. "We were staying for the week at a friend's beach cottage. Cade hadn't come to the beach, of course, but he decided to come that night."

Julie looked quickly at Emma and kept writing.

Francine bent forward, hiding her face. The room grew quiet. Julie caught up with Francine. Emma waited, wishing she'd thought to have Julie transfer all phone calls. Trying not to distract Francine, Emma reached for the phone, but Julie, out of Francine's sight, read Emma's mind and leaned over, switching off the phone.

"I didn't know he was coming to the cottage. I hadn't seen him all week. I was trying to make up my mind about the divorce. I'd told him I wanted one, but I didn't, not really. I just wanted him to—want me." The last words were barely audible. "It didn't make any difference. He still went his way, taking Quint usually, but I'd insisted Quint was to stay with me at the cottage. You have to understand—I hadn't been drinking!" Francine became agitated. "It just happened!"

Taking Francine's hands, Emma spoke softly. "I know you weren't drinking. Go on."

"I fell asleep on the couch, watching TV. I thought I heard something. I didn't like staying by myself!"

Emma tried to sort out what she was hearing. She'd been sure Francine had expected a man to come to the cottage. Had a burglar burst in? No, Francine would have said so.

"I don't, either," Emma said, pouring and handing Francine a glass of water.

Stirring the ice in the water with a finger, Francine continued in a flat voice. "I got up. I was groggy." She inhaled and slipped her hands around the glass. "I hadn't been sleeping well. I was upset. About the divorce, wanting it, not wanting it, wanting Cade to be the kind of husband I thought he should be. I wanted him to be satisfied with our house—it was nice!—and go out dancing with me on Friday nights, that kind of thing.'' She trailed off and sipped water, her hands clasping the glass loosely. "I almost wish Cade were here so I wouldn't have to explain this again.''

"I don't think that's a good idea," Emma said. Cade was the last person she wanted in her office. She didn't need any more reminders of Cade's ability to turn her into quivering jelly. Francine's revelations would be impossible to deal with if Cade were there. Emma hadn't sorted out Francine's feelings about him, much less her own.

"You want me to hurry up, don't you?'' Francine looked sharply at Emma. "I wish I could. I wish I didn't have to be here.''

"Tell the story your own way. We have all the time you need," Emma said, suppressing the urge to hurry Francine. Francine's intuition was right on the money, but they would go slowly.

"I got up and went to the head of the stairs. They were steep and went straight down from the kitchen door to the concrete at the bottom. I was wearing those rubber thongs. There was always so much sand inside!''

Emma held her breath. There had been no thongs in any of the pictures she had seen. Only Francine, barefooted and beaten.

Francine was gasping in shallow, rapid breaths. And then she went absolutely still, her eyes staring at Emma. "I fell," she whispered. "I fell," and her voice rose, each repetition stronger and surer. "I fell.''

Julie's pencil clattered to the floor. "Sorry, boss," she muttered, picking it up quickly.

Emma blinked. Francine *fell?* That was the classic battered victim's lie protecting the abuser. Emma protested, "Why are you lying about this now?''

"It's the truth." Francine's eyes were clear.

"Look." Emma leaned toward her urgently. "If you're afraid of whoever did that to you, I *promise* you, we'll put him in jail, even if you perjured yourself. We won't abandon you!"

"I lied before. No one hurt me. I fell. That's what happened."

"Why did you lie, then? Why didn't you change your testimony earlier?" Emma was furious. After all she'd done to make sure domestic violence cases weren't sloughed off or excused with worn-out and dangerous rationales, now, to have Francine pull this. Francine couldn't be telling the truth. It didn't add up.

"I fell." Francine grew stronger and more serene by the second, as though absolved. "The neighbor heard me scream and tumble off the railings. When she came over, Cade was standing at the bottom of the steps with Quint's bat. I didn't trip on the bat. I just fell."

Emma's headache, which had begun at Quint's school and lain skulking in her brain for the past two days, bloomed anew with a vengeance. "Why did you let the trial go on?" she asked dully.

"Because I was angry with Cade and jealous of him and Quint. Because I was scared and lonely and hurt. Everything went so fast, and once I lied, I didn't know how to stop it. I couldn't think straight, and then it was all over and Cade was in jail. Can't you understand that I panicked and didn't know what to do?"

Stunned, her head throbbing, Emma leaned against the back of the couch. It had all been so simple, but she hadn't caught on. Francine had cleaned and cleaned her house, scouring her house in an unceasing effort to scour her conscience. She'd punished herself. "Yes," Emma said, dragging the words out. "Tell me, Francine, do *you* understand exactly what your lie did?"

"I know," Francine said. "I've lived in my own prison while Cade was in his. I perjured myself."

"No! It's more than what *your* life was like because of your lie or what will now happen to you! Didn't you *see* the faces of those women at the shelter? Do you have even the remotest idea how much courage it took for them to walk out of their lives

and go there? Can you comprehend what their lives were like
before they made that phone call to the crisis hotline?''

"I'm sorry," Francine said, her voice catching. "I'm sorry."

"That doesn't help!" Anger overrode Emma's usual caution and her very real concern for Francine's predicament. "Do
you know how hard a lot of us have worked in order to make
sure that a battered woman has a chance to get her case to
court? Police hate to intervene in domestic situations. It's the
old, old assumption. A man has the right to do what he wants
to with his woman."

Tears welled in Francine eyes. "I was scared."

"I know you were. That, as much as anything, convinced me
you'd been abused. But, Francine—" Emma stood up, shaking with outrage "—those women at the shelter lived every day
in terror until they escaped. There are women who never find
the courage to make the first move. They live with fear until
their spirit is killed. Or they are. Until their children learn that,
hey, when you're mad, you beat up somebody, preferably
somebody smaller and weaker. Or you let them beat up on you
and you pretend it never happened because maybe it was your
fault after all, and you deserved the black eye. Or they become
afraid to love anyone." Emma walked to the window and
looked down at the parking lot. She could hear Francine
weeping, but she couldn't muster comfort at the moment.

"I didn't mean for Cade to go to prison. I thought people
would believe him," Francine said, weeping.

Turning and facing Francine, Emma felt the whole founda-
tion of her life shaking. "You're still missing the point. It's not
a question of Cade. It's what will happen the next time a domestic battery case comes to my office. I'm afraid your lie will
always be in the back of my mind, making me wonder if other
women are lying as you did. I can't afford that cynicism."

Francine bowed her head and covered her face. "I didn't
mean for all this to happen."

"But it will. You can't begin to comprehend how much more
difficult you've made my job."

Francine's weeping rose and fell in the room. Emma was exhausted. Julie got up and came back with a box of tissues.
"Here," she said, offering one to Francine.

She couldn't sustain her anger. She didn't even know who to be angry with. Herself? Francine? Becca, maybe. Emma sighed. "Do you understand why I'm upset?" she asked.

"I made a bad mistake, and I'm trying the best I know how to fix it. I'm not the same person I was back then." She leaned forward. "You have to believe me." Her face shone with conviction. "I need your help. I don't have anyone else I can ask."

"What has changed now after three years? What made you decide, finally, to fix things?" Emma had never thought of the possibility that Francine had simply fallen. Her testimony, the witness, the investigator's report, had all supported the idea that Francine had been attacked, and Emma had prosecuted for all she was worth.

"Seeing Cade again, not being able to deal with Quint any longer. Maybe I'm tired of living a lie. I'm just tired of trying to keep everything hidden."

Emma stared.

"When Cade said he wasn't going to try for joint custody because it was tearing Quint up, I realized I couldn't keep waiting around for things to work out on their own. Unless I admitted what had happened, nothing was going to get better. I had to come clean. You have to help me."

Gazing unseeing at Francine's determined, tearful face, Emma saw her own mother's face, beautiful, dreamy and bruised, saw her mother's careful posture and winces on some mornings, heard her mother's elegant voice with its musical lies, all the lovely lies that had ruled Emma's childhood.

At least Francine had the courage to face her lie. She loved Quint enough to step out of the shadows.

Becca never had.

Chapter 15

Cade sloshed his cold coffee down the drain. Afternoon shadows striped the ground outside the window, while inside, warm sunlight puddled on the counters and floor. He didn't see the yellow light of the waning day, only the shimmer of Emma's skirt as she walked away from him. For the past two days, no matter how hard he worked, he'd carried her with him. Her wounded face wouldn't leave him. Pride smashed, humiliated, she'd walked out of his house with her back straight and her chin up.

Naked, playing his part, he'd sauntered after her to the screen door. He should have known there would be no backward glances, but letting her march steadily away had almost brought him to his knees.

She'd never again look at him from under her spiky lashes and gently tease him. Her soft hair and silky skin would never move like water across his aching body and cool his thirst. He'd never have Emma Rose soft and sweet and giving in his arms again. Not until she was walking away forever did he understand what he was losing.

Cade had opened his mouth to call her back, had taken a step out the door.

Instead, he'd slammed the door after her, every low, rotten obscenity he'd ever learned spewing forth in a steady stream as he paced until with one final, especially vile word, he slammed his fist through the wooden panel of the door. His knuckles were still swollen and scraped, maybe broken.

Even today, running cold water over his hand, Cade didn't care. Nothing mattered without Emma around, not even the ranch.

He'd spent yesterday working on the Jeep and making the house livable. Today he'd made the rounds of banks and utility offices. He'd gone to the county agricultural office to see if running cattle on a shoestring operation was possible in the current market, and if not, what other options were open to him.

And as each day passed, hard, cold emptiness settled and stayed in his gut, taking up permanent residence, an everpresent, aching lump in his soul.

Watching the sun fire red before diving into the horizon, Cade was lonelier than he'd ever been in his life.

When Emma had opened her arms to him and sighed, her sweet-smelling breath entering him as he entered her, he'd felt as though he'd come home for good. He'd wanted to stay deep in her, immersed in her. Everything had seemed possible while he lay joined with her.

But night spun too fast into morning, and reality and honor intruded with their burdens. Cade wrapped the dishrag around his sore hand. He'd done what he had to do.

He'd made sure she wouldn't come back.

Cade walked heavily across the floor to the bathroom, stripping his clothes and dropping them on the floor. When the phone stopped him, he picked it up, expecting the loans officer.

Emma's voice ran through him and shivered against the cold ache inside him.

Cade sank onto the edge of the bed. Her voice in his ear, her fragrance still on the sheet remaining on his bed. Emma. He cleared his thick throat. "Yeah?"

"Francine came to my office this afternoon."

"Yeah?" He wanted her beside him with her face bracketed between his palms, her mouth full and pink under his, her fragrance filling him. Cade curled his fingers tightly into the phone cord, tracing the vinyl coiling around them, the smooth plastic no substitute for Emma's skin.

"There are a number of legal problems, but she made a revised statement clearing you."

Exaltation should have filled him. "That's good," Cade said and meant it, but there was still that emptiness deep in him— down where it counted in a man. "Thanks." He cleared his throat again while silence stretched and hummed between them along the wires. *Emma, forget what I said. Come home to me.* He leaned against the brass headboard. *Come go with me again to the star-spangled darkness and warm me, warm me. I want you here, next to me. I'm empty without you.* "What now?"

"Francine will have to go before the grand jury. She may or may not be indicted for perjury. I hope not. You'll have to testify before the jury, too. I'll recommend a lawyer for you." Suspended at the other end of the phone line, Emma tried not to think of Cade as she'd last seen him, tried and failed as his image, magnificently naked and smiling, lingered with the last of the sunlight in her office. *I miss you, Cade. I don't understand what happened.*

"Who attacked her?" Cade wanted the man in jail or somewhere he couldn't beat up anyone else. *Emma Rose, you're everywhere I look. Here, right now, on the sheet next to me I see you, smell you, want you.* Vinyl slipped between his fingers.

"No one. You'll have to talk with her. It's complicated. She was angry with you and wanted her own revenge. She got caught up in her lie until she was too scared to tell the truth." Emma watched the sun flare brilliantly into the darkening sky. *Cade, I can't stop thinking about you, and I want to. I don't want to be a prisoner of memories the way my mother is. I don't want to be half-alive in limbo.* "My secretary needs your signature on some papers. I don't need to see you."

No? But I want to see you, Emma Rose. I want to see you soft and pale and blurry-eyed in this bed. One more time. "When do you want me to come in?" Cade closed his eyes and rested the phone on his bare stomach. Against him, the phone seemed warm. Emma was in the room with him, whispering in his ear.

"Whenever it's convenient for you. I withdrew the petition to modify custody." Emma drew her fingers over the lamp. Jarred loose, a moth fell to the desk. Dead. Flew too close to the light. "I've started arrangements for an appeal to the governor for clemency. If it does as I expect, your name will eventually be cleared. That's important." Emma's throat ached with all the things she wanted to ask Cade and wouldn't, so she clung to the phone and its distant link to him. *Why were you so cruel, Cade? I still don't understand. What happened between night and morning to make you act as if what we'd shared was nothing?* Emma paused. There was nothing else to discuss. They had finished the business begun on a rain-filled spring night. "Good luck, Cade," she said in a small voice and hung up.

The receiver buzzed in Cade's ear for a long time before he carefully replaced it on the cradle, letting the phone stay on his belly. His empty hand stretched palm down where Emma had curled next to him. Darkness swooped into the room while he lay on the bed with his head thrown back, and ached, *ached,* for Emma.

For three weeks Emma lived in a world drained of color. Every night when she came home, the pruned bushes, raked flower beds and piles of leaves and debris were visible reminders of Cade's presence. But she never saw him.

Becca was Becca, and Lucy kept her comments to herself, once saying, "Cade Boudreau does more for jeans than any ad I ever saw. It's a treat to watch that man workin' in the yard. Makes my whole day. Man makes me hum."

Emma knew what Lucy meant.

Easing back into work like a child learning to walk all over, Emma found that, at first, she was slower, less positive in her decisions, not trusting her instincts. Her professional self-confidence raised its bloodied head a little with each successful case. Buddy, Julie, Charlie and the boys in blue gradually came around. Worried they'd treat her like an outsider, Emma had been overcautious. Time, however, rubbed off the edges of their annoyance, and she knew she'd been forgiven the day Buddy slapped a hunk of French cheese on her desk. The stuffed mouse taped to the top of the wedge stayed on her bookcase, a reminder of how narrow a line she walked in her profession.

When she had a moment, she found herself obsessively drawn to the records of Cade's case. In the typed words there should be an explanation of why her instincts and judgment had failed her. Emma blamed herself. If she'd been wiser, smarter—something!—she could have kept Francine from trapping herself in a net of lies. Poring over the papers, Emma told herself there had to be a shred of evidence somewhere that she could have caught. She read until her eyes and head ached and found nothing, but still she opened the folders.

Sometimes she wondered if agonizing over the folders was her way of answering her body's cry for Cade. She realized one night that it was her soul's cry for him that remained unanswered. When Cade had looked at her, he had made her feel as though there were no one else in the world. He had teased her, made her laugh and stormed the walls of her loneliness, entering into her solitary world and filling it with him.

She was only half a person without him, and that terrified her.

Her nights were unending. Digital numbers flashed the hours and she counted them, waiting for exhaustion so that she wouldn't think about Cade. She told herself that if she just knew why he'd been so brutal after their night together, she'd be free of him.

She knew she lied.

One day she came home and the yard work was finished. It would turn to jungle without care, but for the moment, filled with flowers and shrubs Cade had wrestled out of the wildness, the garden was lovely with promise.

She missed Cade.

Unable to sleep, Emma had gone barefooted just before dawn out to the freshly spaded flower plot and plunged her fingers deep into the moist earth Cade had worked. Cool and damp, with tender green plants shooting up to the light, the dirt crumbled easily between her fingers. Her hands filled with the

rich earth ready to bloom, Emma listened to the wind sough-
ing in the oak tree and passing through the gardenia bushes,
lifting the small rose leaves. She listened and heard the sound
of life passing her by.

Walking to her room in a daze, she began to wonder if she,
like her mother, was slipping, uncaring, over some line.

Days drifted into weeks. Loneliness sharpened, deepened,
and Emma wondered how she'd endure the rest of her life with
this gnawing emptiness in her.

And then Francine called.

"Quint's out of control," she said, weeping. "He's been
running away from home, skipping school, and getting into
fights. He won't mind me at all. I had to tell him I'd lied, and
now he storms around and won't talk to me. The school told me
he was disrupting his classes." Away from the mouthpiece, she
blew her nose.

Emma wanted to weep herself for the angry, unhappy child.
She understood him, but there was nothing she could do. "Did
the school suggest counseling?"

"That's why I'm calling. We've been going, but things aren't
improving. The counselor believes Quint has to confront all of
us. That he's not going to get better until he does."

"What?" Emma swiveled to the window.

"He wants a session with everyone involved. Will you
come?"

No! "Why me?" Emma stood up.

"Quint blames you, too. He's so angry, I can't handle him.
I thought everything would be good after I told the truth, but
these last weeks with Quint have been awful. I don't know what
to do anymore."

I can't face Cade. "When?" Emma looked over to the
stuffed mouse. She'd failed Francine once before. Not again.
"I'll be there." Heat rushed over Emma. The tingling of her
nerve endings alarmed her. She would have to see Cade.

Sitting inside the counselor's office, Emma didn't see how
she could help. Hostility rolled toward her from Quint, who sat
on a couch close to the counselor. Francine sat next to him, but

Quint's shoulders and legs were turned away from her, an
inescapable message of rejection. He wouldn't look at Cade.

Nor did Emma after one unavoidable glance. Haggard, tired
and somber, he sat with his legs stretched out toward Quint. He
had the look of a man stretched on the rack.

When Emma walked into the room, Cade's head whipped
toward her. In the instant she looked at him with her eyes
wounded and confused, his heart did a drumroll and the world
fell out from under him. As she glanced quickly away, Cade
knew she was remembering his last words to her.

He'd done a good job. He'd meant to. So why did he wish he
could turn back the clock? More than anything, he wanted to
go to her and tell her he hadn't forgotten one second of that
night, that he'd relived every moment until he thought he was
going crazy.

He wanted to gather her in his arms and ease the unhappiness clouding her face. Wanted to take her with him to that
place they'd created in darkness.

Judging from his reaction to her, he'd still have to force her
away. He couldn't trust himself around her. How had she bur-
rowed under his skin until he wasn't free of her? Night and day
he thought of her, dreamed of her, wanted her.

Sitting across from him, though, were the proofs of his failure as a husband and father.

Cade listened and hoped as Tom Janes, the round, red-faced
counselor, a cheerful man in his sixties, skillfully led Quint into
talk. Maybe, Cade thought, maybe, and didn't know what he
hoped for.

Sullen and monosyllabic, Quint swung his foot back and
forth, kicking the edge of the counselor's desk.

"Quint," Janes said, his voice surprisingly sharp and star-
tling after its gentleness, "instead of whomping the hell out of
my desk, why don't you tell us what you're really angry
about?"

"All right!" Quint sat up. "Why shouldn't I be mad?
They're all liars, that's what!"

"You were lied to. Correct."

"I know it!" For the first time Quint looked at Cade.

Cade would have spoken, but the counselor motioned him silent.

"What are you going to do about all these lies?" Janes cracked his knuckles.

"Me?" Quint's mouth fell open and he glared at the counselor. "What do you mean? *They* did it all."

"Let me see if I have this right." Janes scratched his balding head. "Your mother lied to you, correct?"

"About him." Quint pointed to Cade.

Janes handed Quint a piece of gum, man to man, ignoring the other adults. "That was a big lie. What do you want her to do now?"

"Huh?" Quint said through a wad of gum.

"Well, what happens next? I mean, you're pretty ticked off and miserable. You don't want to go through the rest of your life like this. You've got stuff out there that's more interesting, I'd think. So what are your plans? What do you want your mom to do?" Janes unwrapped a bull's-eye candy and popped it into his mouth, chewing while Quint, dumbfounded, watched him.

"I dunno," Quint finally said.

"What about Emma?" Janes continued. "For weeks now, you and I have talked about all of this, and I've asked Emma, Cade and your mom to come in today so that you could spell out exactly what you want from each of them, so let's get on with it. The show's yours, and Emma's on stage."

Quint looked at Emma and scowled in spite of cheeks puffed out with gum. "It's all her fault," he said. "She sent *him* to jail."

Cade started to speak and sat back at Janes's fractional nod. Why would Quint think any of what happened was Emma's fault? Looking at her, Cade noticed the dark circles making her eyes even bigger.

"That was her job."

Still watching Emma, Cade saw her sit straighter, as though struck by what Janes had said.

"Yeah, but—"

"What?"

"I dunno." Quint subsided. "*She* changed everything." His foot began its erratic swinging but missed the edge of the desk.

Janes let Quint sit for a while, then said gently, "Wouldn't things have changed anyway, Quint?"

The boy's head dropped to the couch arm.

"Weren't things already changing?"

"Yes! They were going to get a divorce! I heard 'em!" Quint lifted his head, tears gushing down his cheeks, and Cade wanted to go to him. "*He* didn't love her. My mom said so, I heard her. I heard them!"

"Why are you angry with your father?"

Quint's gulping sobs were the only sound in the room. He brought his knees to the sofa and huddled with his arms around them.

Cade remembered Emma, forlorn and weeping, sitting the same way, and his heart twisted with pain.

"Come on, man, you want something from all of them. They've lied to you—"

"He left me!" Quint's shriek went right through Cade, and he stood up.

"When?" Janes was relentless, and Cade wanted to stop him, tell him to leave his son alone, he'd suffered enough. "Answer me, Quint. When did your father leave?"

"I loved him, and he went away." Quint's voice was that of a very young boy, his sobs shaking him. "He would have stayed if he'd loved me."

"How, Quint?"

"I dunno," the boy cried, weeping out the pain he'd held in for years. "He just would've."

"Your father's here now, Quint. What do you want from him?" Water dripping on a stone, Janes's steady voice kept on.

"I want him to stay with me. I want him to love me! I want everything the way it used to be! And it's never gonna be like that again," the boy wailed. Francine touched his shoulder and then dropped her hand, letting him release the anger and tears he'd held back as long as he could.

Cade couldn't stand Quint's ragged weeping. He knelt and held Quint with all the love that had swept through him the first time he'd held the skinny, squalling infant waving his balled-up fist at him. "I love you, Quint. I always have. I can't stand to see you hurting like this. I'm not going to leave you ever again." Over his son's shaking shoulders, Cade looked straight at Emma. In that quiet moment, Cade recognized fully what he'd lost when he'd sent her away. Looking into her wounded eyes, holding his son in his arms, he felt completed somehow. *Emma, I never meant what I said. I was cruel because I was too dumb to know what else to do. I wanted to protect you, that's all, but I look at you and want the impossible.*

Emma slipped out of the room. She stuffed her fist into her mouth to hold back the tears. Cade and Quint had a chance now. They might work out their problems because Francine had had enough courage to face the past. And change it.

Pushing open the bathroom door, Emma kept one fist against her mouth while deep, noisy sobs shuddered through her. Her shoulder blades shoved against the cold tile wall, she let the rending sobs tear through her.

The door banged against the wall.

"What the hell's wrong, Emma?" Cade strode in, walking right up to her past the stalls, not even glancing at them.

She tried to turn, to hide, but he pulled her into his arms and against his strong, steadily drumming heart. She couldn't take her fist out of her mouth, or the force of her pent-up grief would have shaken her apart, but Cade took her hand and held it against him, and the wrenching anguish she'd hidden burst free.

"Why aren't you with Quint?" she sobbed while Cade picked her up and set her on the counter.

"Easy," Cade said, grabbing a wad of brown paper towels and blotting her face, holding her all the while. "Janes kept him a while longer. Francine's waiting for him. I saw your face when you left. Emma, tell me what's wrong," he ordered as he dabbed her cheeks with the rough brown paper. "Is it because Quint blamed you? Are you blaming yourself because of the way you prosecuted my case?"

"Don't you get it, Cade?" She grabbed his shirt. "I wanted you to be guilty! I didn't want you to be innocent!"

"I figured that out, Emma Rose."

"What do you mean?" Emma couldn't stop her noisy weeping and buried her face in Cade's shirt.

"Your reaction that night you came back from your visit to the shelter. Your dad and Becca. He abused her, right?" Cade slowed and looked at her. "You've spent most of your grown-up life getting even with him. My case was one more tick in the plus column, one more chance to revenge your mother, that's all."

"It was personal." Through her tears, she went on. "That's what I can't forgive. I let it become personal."

"All right. You hated your father and what he'd done to your mother. I would have felt the same way. You'd have prosecuted anybody as hard as you could. You hated him."

Emma beat against Cade's hard chest. "Yes! I hated him! And I loved him! That's what I can't forgive myself for. In spite of everything he did, I loved him." Her sobs were wild. She had to make Cade understand what had happened, and her guilt.

Cade held her tightly. She was so pale he could see the veins in her temples beating blue under her translucent skin. He touched his lips to the fragile blue line. Her mouth trembled. Her eyes were drowned in tears, and he wanted to erase from her mind whatever scenes from the past she was seeing. She needed him, and he couldn't turn her away, even if he should.

"I was on the stairs waiting for him to come home. I liked to do that. Sometimes he'd throw me over his shoulder and carry me up to bed. Other times, he'd talk to me. About being a lawyer, about the courthouse." She smiled and rubbed her pink nose. "If I begged hard enough on Saturdays, he'd take me with him sometimes and let me sit over in a corner while he worked. I became a lawyer because I loved him. Because I hated him."

"Emma Rose," Cade murmured, stroking her hair, "what happened?" He jammed his heel against the leaky faucet dripping monotonously into the sink. He wasn't turning Emma loose.

She turned her face away from him, but he wouldn't let her. He needed to see her. "Daddy was late, but I was half asleep when he came in. I started to come down. Mama was already there and he started—he grabbed her!"

Emma jerked as though Cade had grabbed her. He hadn't. Red-hot anger at her father scalded him, but he cradled Emma on his chest, his booted foot propped on the counter next to her.

"He was like a stranger, not my daddy anymore. I was so scared!" Emma seized the paper towels from him and stuffed the brown wad in her mouth, stifling her sobs.

"Tell me, Emma Rose. You have to." Cade pulled the paper away from her and held her close and tight. He understood more clearly why she sometimes huddled in the dark garden and wept silently. But this harrowing grief was different, long buried, like Quint's anger, and needing release.

Lost in what she was seeing, Emma still knew Cade held her securely. "I followed them. He shoved her into his study. He slapped her again and again, swearing, telling her he'd seen her smiling at somebody—I don't know who!—and then he hit her, hard! She fell to the floor, her lavender dress floating around her. She had blood on her mouth and it smeared on her pretty dress. All those streaks on the purple." She covered her ears. "Sometimes I still hear mama's whispers and see my daddy's face. Red with anger and then sorrowful as blood dripped from my mother's nose. I made a sound and covered my mouth. They looked out into the hall and saw me, but nobody said anything. I hid all night in my closet."

No one had come....

The next day, Becca had said, "You had such a silly nightmare last night, darlin'. Are you better?" Her mother had smiled at Emma. "I expect I woke you up with my clumsiness, bumping into that old door." She lifted her coffee cup and drank.

Emma had begun to notice the number of times her mother was clumsy, began to hear the raised voices and hide in her room, but she still went to the courthouse when her father offered to take her. She remembered that. She always went....

"No wonder you hated him," Cade said, his voice harsh.

"I loved him," Emma gasped. "He was my daddy and I hated him and I loved him, just like my mother. I didn't do anything to stop him."

"Ah, sweetheart." Cade stroked her neck. "Too much for you to bear by yourself."

Warm on her neck, Cade's touch soaked into her. Emma let it radiate through her. "You still don't understand," she whispered. "When I saw you for the first time, I felt as though someone had sent me hurtling into space. I was horrified. I couldn't believe you were guilty and that I could be attracted to you. I told myself I was weak. That's why I said I failed and let it become personal. I *had* to win. You *had* to be found guilty. I wouldn't be weak and vulnerable like Becca." She straightened. "But I am. Just like her."

"No."

"I let you turn what we'd done into something cheap and ugly and didn't do anything."

"You left." Cade cupped her elbows and massaged them.

Emma looked at him and knew that she'd come as close to heaven as she was going to, and he'd slammed the door in her face. "So I did. And look where I am now." She glanced at his arms around her. "I'm my mother's daughter, all right."

He freed her, but stayed where he was.

"Go away, Cade. I can't take any more. You have your ranch, your son's talking to you. Leave me alone. I'm begging you. I'm at the end of my rope," Emma said tiredly and dropped her head into her hands. "Just go away. Please. I can't go through hell again. I need peace. Go away."

The door closed behind him.

Emma sat for a long time. She'd never told anyone her family's secret. They'd all pretended they were the perfect family while underneath the secret rotted, and Becca's clumsiness became a kind of strange family joke with Becca smiling at her awkwardness. Becca, so exquisitely graceful, couldn't stay away from doors, it seemed.

Driving to her home where the lights shone in a false welcome behind the peeling columns, Emma knew she had to make an attempt to find out why Becca had gone along with the pretense, why she never admitted, even to Emma, who'd been there, what happened, why she'd left Emma alone in her confusion. She'd never talked to her mother, Lucy or her daddy about what she'd seen. She should have.

Letting herself in with the key, Emma went to the garden. Becca lay on her chaise longue in the twilight. "Hello, darlin'," she murmured drowsily. "Is it that time already?"

Sitting beside her, Emma took her hand gently. "Mama, I want to ask you something." She held her mother's gaze. "I need to know."

"Well, darlin', don't be so serious. You'll get frown lines." Her mother smiled, and her fingers twitched in Emma's grasp.

"Mama, why did you pretend daddy didn't beat you? Why did you let me think what I saw that night was only a bad dream?"

Growing agitated, Becca tried to draw her hand back. "Emma Rose, don't be naughty. Your daddy never laid a hand on me in his life! Why would you say such a thing?" Her eyes were deep, deep green and troubled.

For a moment, Emma saw a flash of comprehension and fear. "Mama, I've lived so long with what I saw, what I knew, and we pretended nothing happened! Why didn't you stop him? Why did we pretend?" Sadness moved in Emma.

Becca smiled. "Nothin' happened, darlin'. What a strange idea." Her hands scrabbled on the chaise.

"Mama, you know I love you. Why can't we talk about this?" Emma gripped her mother's hands. "You don't know what all this secrecy and pretending has done to me! I've been so alone, Mama, never knowing what was real, what wasn't. Why did you lie to me?" Emma brought her mother's twitching fingers to her own tear-damp cheek. "I loved all of you so much, Mama, why couldn't you love me enough to be honest with me?"

For a moment Becca's eyes shone, and Emma hoped. But the light went out, and Becca said, "I love you, darlin', you know that. You're just being silly."

Emma rubbed her wet cheeks against her mother's beautiful hands. "I love you, Mama," she whispered, and let the past sift through her fingers with her tears.

"Sugar." Lucy came out wiping her hands on a dish rag and took Emma into the kitchen. "Leave your mama alone."

"I was always on the outside, Lucy, watching the three of you, feeling left out and never understanding what was wrong with me. The three of you were a closed circle, and I had no one."

"Emma, I'd change things if I could. I didn't know until later that you'd seen anything, and I guess I thought what wasn't talked about was best forgotten. I was wrong, sugar." Lucy touched Emma's arm awkwardly. "But Becca did the best she could. We were ashamed, so we covered up for Andrew. The more we excused his little irritabilities, the worse they grew. Your mama loved Andrew so much that she blamed herself every time he lost control. He was her whole world, sugar, and he destroyed her. So let her have her illusions. She's happy now, waiting for him to come home. He'll never beat her again, and the past is whatever she wants it to be. It's too late for her to change."

"What about you, Lucy? Did you love him, too?"

Lucy shrugged. "He was charmin' when he wanted to be. We dated before he met your mama, but once he saw her, there was no one else for either of them. Your mama asked me to come live with them because Andrew was better with people around. She needed someone to be with her, and I was family." Lucy sighed. "Come in and have supper, sugar. It's just a sad old story from the past, best forgotten."

"I want to go out for a few minutes, Lucy. I'll be in after a while." Emma wandered to the flower bed. Already, without Cade's diligence, the kudzu was creeping back. Lucy was right. It was just a sad old story, but the saddest part, Emma thought as she knelt on the grass and dug weeds from between the flowers, was that none of them had understood that it didn't have to be that way.

You couldn't change the past, but you could learn from it. Weeding steadily into the night, working the life-rich dirt, Emma thought about herself, the way she was. She thought, too, about the look in Cade's eyes as his gaze trapped hers in the counselor's office. She thought for a long, long time about that morning at his ranch.

And, finally, she remembered the way Cade had held her in the bathroom, not giving a damn who walked in, just cradling her while she poured out her grief.

A pile of weeds surrounded Emma and the smell of the earth, of life, filled her. Thoughtfully, she wiped her face, smearing dirt from her ungloved fingers across her cheek.

Chapter 16

Sweat streamed down Cade's back and soaked his bandanna. He wrung it out and soaked it under the pump before tying it around his forehead again. He circled the huge, gaping hole in front of the shed and went inside to cart out more trash.

He worked, but there was no joy in what he did anymore.

He worked because it filled his days. He worked until he could drag himself to the house and collapse into oblivion. Sometimes he sat through the night, drinking, waiting for unconsciousness to wipe Emma's face from his mind. But she was always there, in his mind, in his dreams, in his heart. So he worked. There was nothing else he could do.

Long before he saw the car, he heard it. Leaning the shovel against the shed, he walked outside. Emma's car rolled to a stop in front of his house. The door opened, and long, long, blue-jeaned legs swung out. Out in the pasture, Cade groaned as Emma sauntered toward him, daintily sidestepping holes.

An enormous rosebush rested in the crook of her arms.

Under her wide-brimmed cowgirl hat, her eyes anxiously searched the ground. Rattlesnakes. Cade grinned and rubbed his neck. When she came closer, the expression on her face wiped off his grin and had him stumbling backward toward the shed.

"Hey, tough guy," she drawled, "you can run, but you can't hide."

"Who the hell painted you into those britches, Emma Rose?" Cade loved the little twitch of her fanny as she sashayed in front of him.

"Like them?" Her grin was pure mischief and her eyes sparkled. Or maybe it was the sun glinting off her belt buckle blinding him. "I needed some new clothes. And shoes." She stuck out a booted foot.

"Boots?" Cade reckoned he was back in one of his dreams, those dreams he'd had since she'd lain with him in his brass bed through the night. Those dreams always ended with a smiling Emma walking to him through a pasture filled with cattle. He didn't have any trouble figuring out the meaning.

"They have high heels." She shrugged. "Here," she said, shoving the rosebush at him.

"What's this?" Cade shifted the plant from hand to hand before placing it carefully on the ground between them. He wished it were a tall hedge so he couldn't see her. No, he didn't, he thought, as he drank in the sweetness of her before him.

"A housewarming present, Cade Boudreau, that's what." Her smile was anxious, but then she got that teasing look in her eyes. Tilting up her hat with her forefinger, she hitched her thumbs in her belt. "Well, cowboy, I've come for a showdown." Her hands were trembling, and he figured she wasn't quite as sassy-sure as she looked, but he took another step backward. Her grin widened. She stepped up to him and poked his bare chest, wet with sweat and pump water. "Scared, Cade?" she taunted.

"Damned right I am," he growled and took another step away from her. She was playing with fire and didn't know it, that was all.

"Smart man," she murmured, staying where she was. "You know, I got to thinking."

"Always a sign of trouble," Cade muttered, shoving his hands under the pump and sluicing water over them and his chest. He needed cooling off.

"Don't you want to know about what?" she teased, fanning herself with her hat.

"I don't think I do," he returned, straying to the shade under the shed roof. What he wanted was to sweep her up in his arms and take off at a dead run across the pasture and throw her across his bed and shuck her out of those greased-on jeans. "Go on home, Emma."

"I will. After I've had my say." She became serious. Her chin tilted at him. "I think we have some unfinished business."

"Not likely."

"Cade Boudreau, you are a lot of things but you're a terrible actor." She'd dropped her drawl and her low, sweet voice was the one that haunted his nights and days.

He frowned. "What do you mean?"

"Oh, that really swell performance you gave the other morning." She looked at the ground and scuffed it with the point of her new boots.

Cade bet her toes were hurting. "Don't know what you mean."

"Liar." She smiled softly, throwing his line back at him. "You made love to me that night, Cade."

"Well, hell—" he bluffed.

"No—" she stopped him with a touch of her cool finger on his lips "—don't. *We* made love to each other. At the time I knew what I was doing and feeling, but the next morning I was too scared and confused to think. I panicked. You know why, now."

Nodding, Cade felt her finger slide to his chin and stay there. She couldn't know what she was doing now, that was for sure. A red flag to a bull was nothing compared with what was happening inside him with each careless touch she gave him.

"So I panicked and you went all noble on me."

Cade shrugged. "I don't know what you're talking about."

"Sure you do, tough guy," she teased, letting her finger drift down his chest and stop at his belt. "Nice buckle," she said and flicked the end of his belt.

"Come on, Emma, stop it." Cade took one more backward step, and bumped against the shed wall.

"No, I don't think so. I'm not through with you yet." She flipped his belt end back and forth slowly. "Somewhere in your code of honor, you decided you had to save me from myself. That's insulting, you know."

"Emma," Cade began, "I was wrong to say all those things. I should have said so sooner. If you've come for an apology, you've got it."

"An apology's not what I'm after, Cade Boudreau. I'm after your heart and soul, that's what."

Cade blinked. He was sun-struck. Emma couldn't be saying what he thought he heard. "Excuse me?" He shook his head.

"I've done a lot of thinking, Cade, about my family, me, you, and I've learned something. I always believed I had to be careful not to make the same mistake my mother did, loving a man so much I'd lose myself in him completely and let him treat me any way he wanted. I'm not like that, you know." Her face was pensive and sweet as she stared at him. "I'm strong. I didn't know that before. All along, I've tried to do the right thing. Even when the guys in my office hassled me, I didn't cave in, not when I thought I was right."

"Emma, stop." Cade knew where she was going, and he couldn't let her.

"See what I mean?" she said and smiled at him, her pink lips curving lightheartedly. "You and I both know I'm going to finish what I've come to say."

Shutting his eyes, Cade tried to shut out Emma and couldn't.

"I love you, you know," she said casually, and Cade snapped to attention. "No, don't interrupt," she cautioned. "I spent a long time figuring it out. Since it's the first time I've ever felt like this, I suppose it's natural I didn't recognize it."

She was turning pink, bravado leaking away, but he wasn't going to help her throw herself away on him.

"I never thought I would love anyone the way I do you," she said. "It's a gift I never expected, even if you don't feel the same way."

"I don't, Emma. This is a mistake," Cade forced out.

"Is it?" Her face clouded. "Maybe, but I have to risk it. That's another thing I've learned. Life doesn't have any safety nets. You can stay on the ground, or you can take a risk and fly. I don't want to stay on the ground any longer, Cade.''

Her smile was soft and tremulous, and Cade turned away. He had to, or he'd kiss her. "Go back to your own kind, Emma. I told you you don't belong here. There's nothing here for you."

Emma almost gave up. Her courage wasn't as strong as she thought. The man wasn't giving an inch. Maybe he didn't realize it, but he loved her. He'd shown it with every touch, with every tender giving of his body to hers. "Okay, Cade, have it your way," she said. "But if there's nothing here for me, I'll go on living."

"Good. You should," he grated out.

"And I'll haunt you," Emma said. "You'll see me in town with my children—oh, yes, I'm going to have children—and you'll know they could have been yours. You'll see me with my husband—even if I don't love him the way I love you, I'm going to make him happy if I can—and you'll know you're the one I wanted. *You're* the man I wanted walking through my door at night and parking his boots under my bed."

"Emma, don't." A groan escaped Cade, and Emma dared to hope. "Life doesn't have happy endings. I can't let you throw yourself away on an old rawhide like me. I don't know when I'll see my son, and I'm not sure I can make a living out here. I don't have anything to give you."

"Nothing to give me?" Emma whispered. "Everything I want, that's all. You, Cade, your passion, your tenderness. The way you make me feel as though there's no one else in the world when I'm around. *That's* what you give me."

"I don't want you here," he insisted.

"Don't you, Cade? Can you look me in the eyes and say that?" Emma stepped so close to him she could feel the heat rising from his strong body. Taking his face in her hands, she held his gray gaze and took the biggest risk of her life. "Tell me you don't love me, Cade. I'm giving you the chance of a lifetime. Choose, tough guy. Me, or the emptiness we both feel when we're apart."

His eyes told her everything he wouldn't say.

Finally he looked at the ground. "I don't want you here."

Emma sagged. She'd risked everything and lost. "Okay. Stay here and be an old swamp creature, all alone and bitter, if you want to, but I'm tired of being half alive. If I can't have the life I want, I'll settle for what I *can* have. I want children and a family and someone who loves me. I'm not going to live in twilight like my mother, so when you're out here by yourself, Cade Boudreau, think about what you threw away." She turned to go.

Watching her walk away with her spine straight and her shoulders squared, courage in every inch of her, Cade couldn't breathe. He'd let her go before, and he was going to have to do it one more time. She'd offered him everything he wanted. *She* was everything he wanted, needed. Stunned, Cade reeled. He *needed* her. Without her, his life was nothing. He *needed* Emma, or that cold emptiness inside him would spread until he was all emptiness.

"Hey, cowgirl!"

Almost at her car, Emma heard him. Rooted, she couldn't turn around. The sound of scratching in the ground brought her around. Cade had a long stick in his hand, and he was scratching a line in the sand.

"What's that?" Emma asked carefully, her heart beating like a tom-tom.

"Think hard, Emma Rose, because you won't get another chance." Cade frowned.

Emma couldn't breathe. The look on Cade's face sucked all the air out of her lungs and had her trembling in her boots. He was looking at her as though he'd swallow her up, as if there were no one else in the world but the two of them.

"Sweetheart, take one itty-bitty step over that line in your new boots, and I swear to God, I'll never let you go as long as I've got a breath in my body. You'll never be free of me. You'll be stuck with me forever, hear?"

Emma couldn't move. She watched the play of expressions over the hard planes of Cade's face and saw life blaze into color around her. Joy rushed into her and she swayed while the love and tenderness warming Cade's gray eyes promised, promised everything she'd ever longed for.

But it was the uncertainty that freed her from her spell.

She took a running jump and leaped across the line into Cade's arms. "Shh, cowboy, you talk too much."

Twirling her in his arms, Cade kissed her face and tasted her tears. He heard her whisper over and over in his ear, "I love you, I love you, I love you, Cade Boudreau."

And when he stretched next to her on his sunwarmed sheets and unsnapped the metal studs of her new blouse and slid down the zipper of her new blue jeans, Cade touched every inch of her soft skin, murmuring over and over in a song of love, "I need you, Emma Rose." Poised over her in the bright sunlight, no shadows in the small room, he framed her face as he entered her, holding her gaze all the way as he took her home with him. "I love you, Emma Rose," he whispered.

And he did, all through the afternoon and night.

Epilogue

Summer brought the smell of roses through the open window.

On the sill behind the couch, five seashells were lined up, a shark's eye placed in the middle. Quint *hadn't* left it at the school that spring day.

Emma filled in another word in the crossword puzzle. Cade and Quint huddled on the floor next to her with a chessboard between them. Cade grabbed her ankle. Quint poked his bishop into a square and waited with his tongue puffing out his cheek for Cade's capitulation. When Cade lifted both hands, Quint war-whooped, "I won! I beatcha, Dad, fair and square! Awright, I won!" He danced around the room.

They were waiting for Francine to pick up Quint. She'd been working at the women's shelter one afternoon a week, her way, she explained, of making up for what she'd done. On those days Quint came to the ranch. Quint had been worried that Francine would be tried for perjury, but Cade had testified for her, and the grand jury did not indict her.

When he'd decided to testify on Francine's behalf, Cade had explained to Emma, "Revenge's a two-edged sword, sweetheart. She's Quint's mother. I couldn't stand seeing her go to jail, and it would destroy Quint. Besides, what would be the point?'' Then he'd kissed Emma hard, his hands roaming leisurely over her, and she'd wiggled encouragingly. "Besides, I've got my revenge," he smiled wickedly.

"What's that, cowboy?" she's sassed, stroking his ribs.

"You in blue jeans and boots, cowgirl." He'd tickled her until they fell, laughing, on the bed. The headboard had shaken and knocked against the wall for a long time that afternoon....

Now, outside, a horn beeped.

Going to the door, Cade squeezed Quint's shoulders. "Bring the football next time, okay?"

Emma watched Cade's arm stay on Quint's broadening shoulders, saw the love for his son in the lingering touch.

"Yeah," Quint said in his deep voice. He looked at Emma, grinned impudently, then patted the slight swell of her belly, crooning to it, "So long, munchkin, see ya next week. Don't let the old folks give you grief." He tapped her tummy again, saying to Emma, "Don't forget to drink your milk. And eat your broccoli." Then he ran outside to the waiting car.

Holding the door open to wave goodbye, Emma saw the small movement of Francine's hand. As she and Quint drove away, a rooster tail of summer dust rose behind the car.

Cade pulled Emma to him, one hand resting on her belly. He twined the other in her hair. "C'mere, Emma Rose." Heat kindled between them, a slow, steady heat. He smiled.

"Devil. It's broad daylight." She laughed, lifting against him, feeling the bump of objection from the baby in her womb.

"I know." He grinned, lifting her. "I love to see you in my bed in the sunlight, sweetheart."

"Even now?" she asked hesitantly.

He spread his hand over her abdomen, and Emma was warmed to her toes. "Especially now, Emma Rose. You've given me my life back. I need you so much I can't stand it sometimes, and I want to throw down my stuff and come running across the ranch to find you and love you." He kissed her hard and fiercely. "I couldn't live without you." He unbuttoned her blouse and unsnapped her jeans. "Oh, good. Green.

You do have the prettiest underwear, sweetheart. I dream about it."

"Sex fiend," she murmured against his seeking mouth.

"Damn right," he said, bumping his elbow on the door. "Let me take you home, Emma," he whispered against her ear.

She shivered and kissed his neck. "Oh, yes, Cade. Please."

*   *   *   *   *

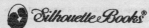

MILLION DOLLAR JACKPOT
SWEEPSTAKES RULES & REGULATIONS
NO PURCHASE NECESSARY TO ENTER OR RECEIVE A PRIZE

1. Alternate means of entry: Print your name and address on a 3″ ×5″ piece of plain paper and send to the appropriate address below.

In the U.S.	In Canada
MILLION DOLLAR JACKPOT	MILLION DOLLAR JACKPOT
P.O. Box 1867	P.O. Box 609
3010 Walden Avenue	Fort Erie, Ontario
Buffalo, NY 14269-1867	L2A 5X3

2. To enter the Sweepstakes and join the Reader Service, affix the Four Free Books and Free Gifts sticker along with both of your other Sweepstakes stickers to the Sweepstakes Entry Form. If you do not wish to take advantage of our Reader Service, but wish to enter the Sweepstakes only, do not affix the Four Free Books and Free Gifts sticker; affix only the Sweepstakes stickers to the Sweepstakes Entry Form. Incomplete and/or inaccurate entries are ineligible for that section or sections of prizes. Torstar Corp. and its affiliates are not responsible for mutilated or unreadable entries or inadvertent printing errors. Mechanically reproduced entries are null and void.

3. Whether you take advantage of this offer or not, on or about April 30, 1992, at the offices of D.L. Blair, Inc., Blair, NE, your sweepstakes numbers will be compared against the list of winning numbers generated at random by the computer. However, prizes will only be awarded to individuals who have entered the Sweepstakes. In the event that all prizes are not claimed, a random drawing will be held from all qualified entries received from March 30, 1990 to March 31, 1992, to award all unclaimed prizes. All cash prizes (Grand to Sixth) will be mailed to winners and are payable by check in U.S. funds. Seventh prize will be shipped to winners via third-class mail. These prizes are in addition to any free, surprise or mystery gifts that might be offered. Versions of this Sweepstakes with different prizes of approximate equal value may appear at retail outlets or in other mailings by Torstar Corp. and its affiliates.

4. PRIZES: (1) *Grand Prize $1,000,000.00 Annuity; (1) First Prize $25,000.00; (1) Second Prize $10,000.00; (5) Third Prize $5,000.00; (10) Fourth Prize $1,000.00; (100) Fifth Prize $250.00; (2,500) Sixth Prize $10.00; (6,000) **Seventh Prize $12.95 ARV.

   *This presentation offers a Grand Prize of a $1,000,000.00 annuity. Winner will receive $33,333.33 a year for 30 years without interest totalling $1,000,000.00.

   **Seventh Prize: A fully illustrated hardcover book, published by Torstar Corp. Approximate Retail Value of the book is $12.95.

   Entrants may cancel the Reader Service at any time without cost or obligation (see details in Center Insert Card).

5. Extra Bonus! This presentation offers an Extra Bonus Prize valued at $33,000.00 to be awarded in a random drawing from all qualified entries received by March 31, 1992. No purchase necessary to enter or receive a prize. To qualify, see instructions in Center Insert Card. Winner will have the choice of any of the merchandise offered or a $33,000.00 check payable in U.S. funds. All other published rules and regulations apply.

6. This Sweepstakes is being conducted under the supervision of D.L. Blair, Inc. By entering the Sweepstakes, each entrant accepts and agrees to be bound by these rules and the decisions of the judges, which shall be final and binding. Odds of winning the random drawing are dependent upon the number of entries received. Taxes, if any, are the sole responsibility of the winners. Prizes are nontransferable. All entries must be received at the address on the detachable Business Reply Card and must be postmarked no later than 12:00 MIDNIGHT on March 31, 1992. The drawing for all unclaimed Sweepstakes prizes and for the Extra Bonus Prize will take place on May 30, 1992, at 12:00 NOON at the offices of D.L. Blair, Inc., Blair, NE.

7. This offer is open to residents of the U.S., United Kingdom, France and Canada, 18 years or older, except employees and immediate family members of Torstar Corp., its affiliates, subsidiaries and all other agencies, entities and persons connected with the use, marketing or conduct of this Sweepstakes. All Federal, State, Provincial, Municipal and local laws apply. Void wherever prohibited or restricted by law. Any litigation within the Province of Quebec respecting the conduct and awarding of a prize in this publicity contest must be submitted to the Régie des Loteries et Courses du Québec.

8. Winners will be notified by mail and may be required to execute an affidavit of eligibility and release, which must be returned within 14 days after notification or an alternate winner may be selected. Canadian winners will be required to correctly answer an arithmetical, skill-testing question administered by mail, which must be returned within a limited time. Winners consent to the use of their name, photograph and/or likeness for advertising and publicity in conjunction with this and similar promotions without additional compensation.

9. For a list of our major prize winners, send a stamped, self-addressed envelope to: MILLION DOLLAR WINNERS LIST, P.O. Box 4510, Blair, NE 68009. Winners Lists will be supplied after the May 30, 1992 drawing date.

Offer limited to one per household.

LTY-S791

SILHOUETTE·INTIMATE·MOMENTS®

IT'S TIME TO MEET
THE MARSHALLS!

In 1986, bestselling author Kristin James wrote A VERY SPECIAL FAVOR for the Silhouette Intimate Moments line. Hero Adam Marshall quickly became a reader favorite, and ever since then, readers have been asking for the stories of his two brothers, Tag and James. At last your prayers have been answered!

In August, look for THE LETTER OF THE LAW (IM #393), James Marshall's story. If you missed youngest brother Tag's story, SALT OF THE EARTH (IM #385), you can order it by following the directions below. And, as our very special favor to you, we'll be reprinting A VERY SPECIAL FAVOR this September. Look for it in special displays wherever you buy books.

Order your copy by sending your name, address, zip or postal code, along with a check or money order for $3.25 (please do not send cash), plus 75¢ postage and handling ($1.00 in Canada), payable to Silhouette Reader Service to:

In the U.S.	In Canada
3010 Walden Ave.	P.O. Box 609
P.O. Box 1396	Fort Erie, Ontario
Buffalo, NY 14269-1396	L2A 5X3

Please specify book title with your order.
Canadian residents add applicable federal and provincial taxes.   MARSH-2

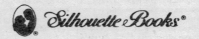